Collier's *Junior* Classics

Series Editor
Margaret E. Martignoni

A B C GO!

A completely new selection of outstanding children's stories and poems compiled for enrichment reading by a distinguished editorial board of children's librarians.

Series Editor
MARGARET E. MARTIGNONI
Former Superintendent
Work with Children
Brooklyn Public Library

Editor-in-Chief
DR. LOUIS SHORES
Dean, Library School
Florida State University

Managing Editor
HARRY R. SNOWDEN, JR.

Volume Editor
ROSEMARY E. LIVSEY
Coordinator, Children's Services
Los Angeles Public Library

Collier's *Junior* Classics Series

THE CROWELL-COLLIER PUBLISHING COMPANY • NEW YORK

A, B, C: GO!

Copyright © 1962 by The Crowell-Collier Publishing Company
Library of Congress Catalog Card Number 61-17993
Printed in the United States of America
Twenty-eighth Printing

Introduction

Collier's Junior Classics Series

We are children only once, and then only for a few brief years. But these are the most impressionable years of a lifetime. Never again will the world and everything in it be so eternally new, so filled with wonder. Never again will physical, mental, spiritual growth be so natural and unavoidable. During these years, habits become ingrained, tastes are developed, personality takes form. The child's whole being is geared toward learning. He instinctively reaches out for truth and, having no prejudices, seizes upon that which is good, just, beautiful. For these reasons, a child deserves what Walter de la Mare has called "only the rarest kind or best."

What do we mean by "best" in a book for children? Best books reflect universal truths with clarity and artistry. Such books reveal that man is essentially good and that life is infinitely worth living. They do not deny the existence of evil, but rather emphasize man's thrilling struggle against evil through faith, courage, and perseverance. They awaken the young reader's imagination, call forth his laughter as well as his tears, help him to understand and to love his fellow man. The reading of such books constitutes a rich heritage of experience which is every child's birthright.

The librarian-editors of *Collier's Junior Classics* have combed the best children's books of the past and present to assemble in a single series a sampling of the finest literature for boys and girls. High standards have been maintained for the art work also, which in most instances has been taken from the original book. No attempt has been made to cover all fields of knowledge or to include factual material for its own sake. The emphasis here is on good literature, chiefly fiction and biography, folk lore and legend, and some poetry. Special attention is given to the American scene and American democratic ideals, but many selections cover other cultures, geographical areas, and historical periods.

The purpose of *Collier's Junior Classics* is to introduce boys and girls to some of the best books ever written for children, to stimulate young readers to seek for themselves the books from which the selections have been drawn as well as other good books of similar appeal, and to encourage children to become discriminating, thoughtful, life-time readers. Author, title, and publisher are given at the foot of the page on which each selection opens. This enables readers to ask for the complete book at a library or bookstore. When necessary, brief introductions set the scene for the selection, while follow-up recommendations, complete with publishers' names, appear at the end of most stories.

Collier's Junior Classics is a series of ten individually indexed volumes. A, B, C: GO! has been lovingly compiled for the youngest, and consists of nursery rhymes, favorite folk tales, best-loved poems, and stories for reading aloud. Four volumes have been assembled for the intermediate group: ONCE UPON A TIME, a wonderous collection of fables, world folk tales, and modern fairy tales; MAGIC IN THE AIR, selections from great masterpieces of fantasy; JUST AROUND THE CORNER, excerpts from warm-hearted stories of other lands; and IN YOUR OWN BACKYARD, selections from stirring books about our own country. Four additional volumes cater to the interests of more mature boys and girls: GIFTS FROM THE PAST, memorable selections from world classics; LEGENDS OF LONG AGO, selections from great myths, epics, and American tall tales; ROADS TO GREATNESS, excerpts from biographies of some of the greatest men and women of the world; and CALL OF ADVENTURE, selections from action and suspense stories of today and yesterday. Finally, and most unusual of all, is the volume entitled HARVEST OF HOLIDAYS, a feast of stories, poems, documents, and factual material about twenty-two American national and religious holidays. Although perhaps of greatest interest to the intermediate group, HARVEST OF HOLIDAYS will intrigue and delight all ages.

The tables of contents for the ten volumes read like an all-time Who's Who of distinguished writers. A brief mention of only a few of these authors would include such names as Lewis Carroll, Kenneth Grahame, Charles Dickens, Mark Twain, Louisa May Alcott, Pearl Buck, Laura Ingalls Wilder, Eleanor Estes, Genevieve Foster, Robert Louis Stevenson, Robert McCloskey, Valenti Angelo, Carl Sandburg, A. A. Milne, Eleanor Farjeon, Elizabeth Enright, and Margaret Wise Brown. Among the illustrators, many of whom are also authors, are to be found the Petershams, the d'Aulaires, Wanda Gág, Louis Slobodkin, Helen Sewell, Lois Lenski, Roger Duvoisin, Maurice Sendak, Kurt Wiese, Marguerite de Angeli, Steele Savage, Howard Pyle, Lynd Ward, James Daugherty, Arthur Rackham, Fritz Kredel, and Gustave Dore.

Collier's Junior Classics is intended primarily for the home, although libraries will find the series valuable for browsing as well as for introducing children to many different books. Because each book is an individual volume, complete with its own index, it can be shelved where the librarian believes it will be most useful to the children.

No pains have been spared to make the individual volumes a series of stepping stones to all that is best in the magic world of children's books.

Margaret E. Martignoni
SERIES EDITOR

Contents

Nursery Rhymes

Favorite Folk Tales

Best-Loved Poems

THIS HAPPY DAY

TALL PEOPLE, SHORT PEOPLE

GOOD NIGHT! GOOD NIGHT!

Stories for Fun

A, B, C: GO!

Childhood is a wonderful whirl of newness. Words are new, sounds are new, rainbows are new. So are dogs, mud pies, rubber balls, and friends. Life is an endless series of wide-eyed adventures, filled with a succession of curious "why's."

In this world where everything is new, where each day brings a fresh discovery, the land of books is the most exciting discovery of all. Between the covers of books lies an enchanted wonderland of words and pictures—a world that delights with the familiar, sparkles with the fantastic.

A, B, C: GO! is a passport to this enchanted land where the magic of imagination reigns supreme, where time and distance know no bounds. Here, young visitors will meet Old King Cole and Jack Sprat. They will go to the ball with Cinderella and visit Red Riding Hood's grandmother. They will tour the poetic countryside—talking with barbers and ice-cream men, and frolicking with fairies in storied glens. They will dance with Kiki, ride to the fair with Little Pear, and cry when Suzanna loses her toys.

They will visit the *Five Chinese Brothers* at the other end of the world, stop off in ancient times to see *The Funny Thing*, and join *Peter Churchmouse* on his crusade for recognition. They will love and laugh and learn—all at the same time. For these are the happy hours, the joyous childhood days, when all of life is a wonderful game and all the world is new.

ROSEMARY E. LIVSEY
Coordinator, Children's Services,
Los Angeles Public Library

xv

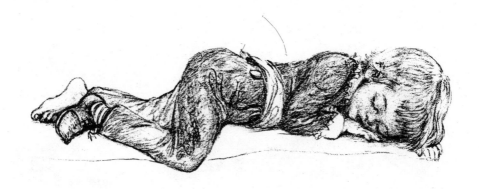

NURSERY RHYMES

Ring-a-ring o' roses,
A pocket full of posies,
A-tishoo! A-tishoo!
We all fall down.

Georgie Porgie, pudding and pie,
Kissed the girls and made them cry;
When the boys came out to play,
Georgie Porgie ran away.

Hey diddle diddle,
The cat and the fiddle,
The cow jumped over the moon.
The little dog laughed
To see such sport,
And the dish ran away with the spoon.

Old Mother Hubbard,
Went to the cupboard,
  To get her poor dog a bone;
But when she got there,
The cupboard was bare,
  And so the poor dog had none.

She went to the baker's
  To buy him some bread,
But when she came back
  The poor dog was dead.

She went to the joiner's
  To buy him a coffin,
But when she came back
  The poor dog was laughing.

She took a clean dish
  To get him some tripe,
But when she came back
  He was smoking a pipe.

She went to the fishmonger's
  To buy him some fish,
But when she came back
  He was licking the dish.

She went to the alehouse
  To get him some beer,
But when she came back
  The dog sat in a chair.

She went to the tavern
  For white wine and red,
But when she came back
  The dog stood on his head.

She went to the hatter's
   To buy him a hat,
But when she came back
   He was feeding the cat.

She went to the barber's
   To buy him a wig,
But when she came back
   He was dancing a jig.

She went to the fruiterer's
   To buy him some fruit,
But when she came back
   He was playing the flute.

She went to the tailor's
   To buy him a coat,
But when she came back
   He was riding a goat.

She went to the cobbler's
   To buy him some shoes,
But when she came back
   He was reading the news.

ILLUSTRATION BY MARGUERITE DE ANGELI

Baa, baa, black sheep,
  Have you any wool?
Yes, sir, yes, sir,
  Three bags full:
One for my master,
  One for my dame,
One for the little boy
  That lives down the lane!

ILLUSTRATIONS BY TASHA TUDOR

There was an old woman who lived in a shoe,
She had so many children she didn't know what to do;
She gave them some broth without any bread;
She whipped them all soundly and put them to bed.

A diller, a dollar,
A ten o'clock scholar,
What makes you come so soon?
You used to come at ten o'clock,
But now you come at noon.

Jack be nimble,
Jack be quick,
Jack jump over
The candle stick.

Mistress Mary, quite contrary,
How does your garden grow?
With silver bells and cockle shells,
And pretty maids all
                in
                a
                row.

Little Bo-peep has lost her sheep,
  And doesn't know where to find them;
Leave them alone, and they'll come home,
  Wagging their tails behind them.

Little Bo-peep fell fast asleep,
  And dreamt she heard them bleating;
But when she awoke, she found it a joke,
  For they were still all fleeting.

Then up she took her little crook,
  Determined for to find them;
She found them indeed, but it made her heart bleed,
  For they'd left their tails behind them.

It happened one day, as Bo-peep did stray
  Into a meadow hard by,
There she espied their tails side by side,
  All hung on a tree to dry.

She heaved a sigh, and wiped her eye,
  And ran o'er hill and dale-o,
And tried what she could, as a shepherdess should,
  To tack to each sheep its tail-o.

Jack and Jill went up the hill,
    To fetch a pail of water;
Jack fell down, and broke his crown,
    And Jill came tumbling after.

Then up Jack got and home did trot
    As fast as he could caper,
And went to bed to mend his head
    With vinegar and brown paper.

Hushaby, baby, thy cradle is green;
Father's a nobleman, mother's a queen;
Sister's a lady, and wears a gold ring;
Brother's a drummer, and drums for the king.

Little Tommy Tucker,
    Sang for his supper:
What shall he eat?
    White bread and butter.

How shall he cut it
    Without e'er a knife?
How shall he marry
    Without e'er a wife?

ILLUSTRATION BY TASHA TUDOR

Sing a song of sixpence,
    A pocket full of rye;
Four and twenty blackbirds
    Baked in a pie.

When the pie was opened,
    The birds began to sing;
Wasn't that a dainty dish
    To set before the king?

The king was in his counting-house,
    Counting out his money;
The queen was in the parlour,
    Eating bread and honey.

The maid was in the garden
    Hanging out the clothes,
When down came a blackbird
    And nicked off her nose.

I had a little nut tree,
 Nothing would it bear
 But a silver nutmeg
 And a golden pear;
The King of Spain's daughter
 Came to visit me,
 And all on account
 Of my little nut tree.

ILLUSTRATIONS BY TASHA TUDOR

See-saw, Margery Daw,
Jack shall have a new master;
He must have but a penny a day,
Because he can't work any faster.

Three little kittens they lost their mittens,
  And they began to cry,
"Oh, mother dear, we sadly fear
  Our mittens we have lost!"
"What! lost your mittens, you naughty kittens!
  Then you shall have no pie."
    "Meeow, meeow, meeow."

Three little kittens they found their mittens,
  And they began to cry,
"Oh, mother dear, see here, see here,
  Our mittens we have found."
"What! found your mittens, you good little kittens!
  Then you shall have some pie."
    "Purr, purr, purr."

ILLUSTRATION BY MARGUERITE DE ANGELI

Hickory, dickory, dock,
The mouse ran up the clock.
The clock struck one,
The mouse ran d
$$o$$
$$w$$
$$n$$

Hickory
Dickory
Dock.

ILLUSTRATION BY TASHA TUDOR

ILLUSTRATION BY TASHA TUDOR

Old King Cole
Was a merry old soul,
And a merry old soul was he;
He called for his pipe,
And he called for his bowl,
And he called for his fiddlers three.

Ding, dong, bell,
Pussy's in the well.
Who put her in?
Little Johnny Green.
Who pulled her out?
Little Tommy Stout.
What a naughty boy was that
To try to drown poor pussy cat,
Who never did him any harm,
And killed the mice in his father's barn.

ILLUSTRATION BY
MARGUERITE DE ANGELI

Little Jack Horner
Sat in the corner,
    Eating a Christmas pie;
He put in his thumb,
And pulled out a plum,
    And said, What a good boy am I!

Pussy cat, pussy cat,
    Where have you been?
I've been to London to visit the queen.
Pussy cat, pussy cat,
    What did you there?
I frightened a little mouse under a chair.

15

Simple Simon met a pieman
  Going to the fair;
Says Simple Simon to the pieman,
  "Let me taste your ware."

Says the pieman to Simple Simon,
  "Show me first your penny;"
Says Simple Simon to the pieman,
  "Indeed, I have not any."

Simple Simon went to look
  If plums grew on a thistle;
He pricked his fingers on a thorn,
  Which made poor Simon whistle.

Simple Simon went a-fishing
  For to catch a whale;
All the water he had got,
  Was in his mother's pail.

He went for water in a sieve
  But soon it all fell through;
And now poor Simple Simon
  Bids you all adieu.

There was an old woman tossed up in a basket
  Nineteen times as high as the moon;
Where she was going I couldn't but ask it,
  For in her hand she carried a broom.

"Old woman, old woman, old woman," quoth I,
  "O whither, O whither, O whither, so high?"
"To brush the cobwebs off the sky!"
  "Shall I go with thee?" "Ay, by-and-by."

The Queen of Hearts
She made some tarts,
All on a summer's day;
The Knave of Hearts
He stole the tarts,
And took them clean away.

The King of Hearts
Called for the tarts,
And beat the knave full sore;
The Knave of Hearts
Brought back the tarts,
And vowed he'd steal no more.

Little Miss Muffet
Sat on a tuffet,
Eating her curds and whey
There came a big spider,
And sat down beside her
And frightened Miss Muffet away.

This is the house that Jack built.

This is the malt
That lay in the house that Jack built.

This is the rat,
That ate the malt
That lay in the house that Jack built.

This is the cat,
That killed the rat,
That ate the malt
That lay in the house that Jack built.

ILLUSTRATIONS BY RANDOLPH CALDECOTT

This is the dog,
That worried the cat,
That killed the rat,
That ate the malt
That lay in the house that Jack built.

This is the cow with the crumpled horn,
That tossed the dog,
That worried the cat,
That killed the rat,
That ate the malt
That lay in the house that Jack built.

This is the maiden all forlorn,
That milked the cow with the crumpled horn,
That tossed the dog,
That worried the cat,
That killed the rat,
That ate the malt
That lay in the house that Jack built.

This is the man all tattered and torn,
That kissed the maiden all forlorn,
That milked the cow with the crumpled horn,
That tossed the dog,
That worried the cat,
That killed the rat,
That ate the malt
That lay in the house that Jack built.

This is the priest all shaven and shorn,
That married the man all tattered and torn,
That kissed the maiden all forlorn,
That milked the cow with the crumpled horn,
That tossed the dog,
That worried the cat,
That killed the rat,
That ate the malt
That lay in the house that Jack built.

This is the cock that crowed in the morn,
That waked the priest all shaven and shorn,
That married the man all tattered and torn,
That kissed the maiden all forlorn,
That milked the cow with the crumpled horn,
That tossed the dog,
That worried the cat,
That killed the rat,
That ate the malt
That lay in the house that Jack built.

This is the farmer sowing his corn,
That kept the cock that crowed in the morn,
That waked the priest all shaven and shorn,
That married the man all tattered and torn,
That kissed the maiden all forlorn,
That milked the cow with the crumpled horn,
That tossed the dog,
That worried the cat,
That killed the rat,
That ate the malt
That lay in the house that Jack built.

ILLUSTRATION BY TASHA TUDOR

One, two,
Buckle my shoe;
Three, four,
Shut the door;
Five, six,
Pick up sticks;
Seven, eight,
Lay them straight;
Nine, ten,
A big fat hen;
Eleven, twelve,
Dig and delve;
Thirteen, fourteen,
Maids a-courting;
Fifteen, sixteen,
Maids in the kitchen;
Seventeen, eighteen,
Maids in waiting;
Nineteen, twenty,
My plate's empty.

Polly put the kettle on,
Polly put the kettle on,
Polly put the kettle on,
　We'll all have tea.

Sukey take it off again,
Sukey take it off again,
Sukey take it off again,
　They've all gone away.

ILLUSTRATION BY MARGUERITE DE ANGELI

There was a crooked man,
　And he walked a crooked mile,
He found a crooked sixpence against a crooked stile;
He bought a crooked cat,
　Which caught a crooked mouse,
And they all lived together in a little crooked house.

ILLUSTRATION BY TASHA TUDOR

Pease porridge hot,
Pease porridge cold,
Pease porridge in the pot
Nine days old.

Some like it hot,
Some like it cold,
Some like it in the pot
Nine days old.

Jack Sprat could eat no fat,
His wife could eat no lean,
And so betwixt them both, you see,
They licked the platter clean.

To market, to market, to buy a fat pig,
Home again, home again, jiggety-jig;

To market, to market, to buy a fat hog,
Home again, home again, jiggety-jog.

There was an old woman
Lived under a hill,
And if she's not gone
She lives there still.

     Bye, baby bunting,
     Daddy's gone a-hunting,
     To get a little rabbit's skin,
     To wrap his baby bunting in.

          Cock-a-doodle-doo!
          My dame has lost her shoe,
          My master's lost his fiddlestick,
          And knows not what to do.

          Cock-a-doodle-doo!
          What is my dame to do?
          Till master finds his fiddlestick,
          She'll dance without her shoe.

What are little boys made of?
What are little boys made of?
  "Snips and snails, and puppy-dogs' tails;
  And that's what little boys are made of."

     What are little girls made of?
     What are little girls made of?
       "Sugar and spice, and all that's nice;
       And that's what little girls are made of."

Goosey, goosey, gander,
Whither shall I wander?
Upstairs and downstairs
And in my lady's chamber.
There I met an old man
Who would not say his prayers.
I took him by the left leg
And threw him down the s
t
a
i
r
s
.

Curly locks, curly locks,
    Wilt thou be mine?
Thou shalt not wash dishes
    Nor yet feed the swine,
But sit on a cushion
    And sew a fine seam,
And feed upon strawberries,
    Sugar and cream.

Ride a cock-horse to Banbury Cross,
To see a fine lady upon a white horse;
Rings on her fingers and bells on her toes,
And she shall have music wherever she goes.

ILLUSTRATION BY TASHA TUDOR

Humpty Dumpty sat on a wall,
Humpty Dumpty had a great fall.
All the king's horses,
And all the king's men,
Couldn't put Humpty together again.

The north wind doth blow,
And we shall have snow,
And what will poor robin do then?
Poor thing!
He'll sit in a barn,
And keep himself warm,
And hide his head under his wing.
Poor thing!

ILLUSTRATION BY TASHA TUDOR

Hickety, pickety, my black hen,
She lays eggs for gentlemen;
Sometimes nine and sometimes ten,
Hickety, pickety, my black hen.

Rock-a-bye, baby, on the tree top!
When the wind blows the cradle will rock,
When the bough breaks the cradle will fall,
And down will come baby, cradle and all.

Peter, Peter, pumpkin eater,
Had a wife and couldn't keep her;
He put her in a pumpkin shell
And there he kept her very well.

ILLUSTRATION BY MARGUERITE DE ANGELI

A frog he would a-wooing go,
  Heigh ho! says Rowley,
Whether his mother would let him or no.
  With a rowley, powley, gammon and spinach,
  Heigh ho! says Anthony Rowley.

So off he set with his opera hat,
  Heigh ho! says Rowley,
And on the road he met with a rat.
  With a rowley, powley, gammon and spinach,
  Heigh ho! says Anthony Rowley.

"Pray, Mister Rat, will you go with me?"
  Heigh ho! says Rowley,
"Pretty Miss Mousey for to see?"
  With a rowley, powley, gammon and spinach,
  Heigh ho! says Anthony Rowley.

They came to the door of Mousey's hall,
  Heigh ho! says Rowley,
They gave a loud knock, and they gave a loud call.
  With a rowley, powley, gammon and spinach,
  Heigh ho! says Anthony Rowley.

ILLUSTRATIONS BY RANDOLPH CALDECOTT

"Pray, Miss Mouse, are you within?"
  Heigh ho! says Rowley,
"Oh yes, kind sirs, I'm sitting to spin."
  With a rowley, powley, gammon and spinach,
  Heigh ho! says Anthony Rowley.

"Pray, Miss Mouse, will you give us some beer?"
  Heigh ho! says Rowley,
"For Froggy and I are fond of good cheer."
  With a rowley, powley, gammon and spinach,
  Heigh ho! says Anthony Rowley.

"Pray, Mr. Frog, will you give us a song?"
  Heigh ho! says Rowley,
"Let it be something that's not very long."
  With a rowley, powley, gammon and spinach,
  Heigh ho! says Anthony Rowley.

"Indeed, Miss Mouse," replied Mr. Frog,
  Heigh ho! says Rowley,
"A cold has made me as hoarse as a dog."
  With a rowley, powley, gammon and spinach,
  Heigh ho! says Anthony Rowley.

"Since you have a cold, Mr. Frog," Mousey said,
  Heigh ho! says Rowley,
"I'll sing you a song that I have just made."
  With a rowley, powley, gammon and spinach,
  Heigh ho! says Anthony Rowley.

But while they were all a-merry-making,
  Heigh ho! says Rowley,
A cat and her kittens came tumbling in.
  With a rowley, powley, gammon and spinach,
  Heigh ho, says Anthony Rowley.

The cat she seized the rat by the crown,
  Heigh ho! says Rowley,
The kittens they pulled the little mouse down.
  With a rowley, powley, gammon and spinach,
  Heigh ho! says Anthony Rowley.

This put Mr. Frog in a terrible fright,
  Heigh ho! says Rowley,
He took up his hat and he wished them good-night.
  With a rowley, powley, gammon and spinach,
  Heigh ho! says Anthony Rowley.

But as Froggy was crossing over a brook,
  Heigh ho! says Rowley,
A lily-white duck came and gobbled him up.
  With a rowley, powley, gammon and spinach,
  Heigh ho! says Anthony Rowley.

So there was an end of one, two, three,
  Heigh ho! says Rowley,
The rat, the mouse, and the little frog-ee.
  With a rowley, powley, gammon and spinach,
  Heigh ho! says Anthony Rowley.

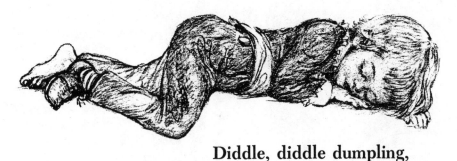

Diddle, diddle dumpling,
    my son John.
Went to bed with his breeches on,
One shoe off, and one shoe on,
Diddle, diddle dumpling,
    my son John.

ILLUSTRATION BY MARGUERITE DE ANGELI

Tom, Tom, the piper's son,
Stole a pig and away he run!
The pig was eat, and Tom was beat,
And Tom ran crying down the street.

ILLUSTRATION BY TASHA TUDOR

Illustration by Marguerite de Angeli

Little Boy Blue,
   Come blow your horn,
The sheep's in the meadow,
   The cow's in the corn;
Where is the boy
   Who looks after the sheep?
He's under the haystack,
   Fast asleep.
Will you wake him?
   No, not I,
For if I do,
   He's sure to cry.

FAVORITE FOLK TALES

Henny Penny

RETOLD BY VERONICA HUTCHINSON

Illustrations by Estelle Hollingworth

ONE day Henny Penny was picking up corn in the farmyard, when an acorn fell out of a tree and struck her on the head.

"Goodness gracious me!" said Henny Penny, "the sky is falling. I must go and tell the King."

So she went along and she went along and she went along until she met Cocky Locky.

"Where are you going, Henny Penny?" asked Cocky Locky.

"Oh," said Henny Penny, "the sky is falling and I am going to tell the King."

"May I go with you, Henny Penny?" asked Cocky Locky.

"Certainly," said Henny Penny.

So Henny Penny and Cocky Locky went to tell the King that the sky was falling.

They went along and they went along and they went along, until they met Ducky Daddles.

"Where are you going, Henny Penny and Cocky Locky?" asked Ducky Daddles.

"Oh, we are going to tell the King that the sky is falling," said Henny Penny and Cocky Locky.

"May I go with you?" asked Ducky Daddles.

"Certainly," said Henny Penny and Cocky Locky.

So Henny Penny, Cocky Locky, and Ducky Daddles went to tell the King that the sky was falling.

From *Chimney Corner Stories,* by Veronica Hutchinson, copyright 1925, 1953, by Veronica Hutchinson. Published by Minton, Balch & Company.

They went along and they went along and they went along until they met Goosey Poosey.

"Where are you going, Henny Penny, Cocky Locky, and Ducky Daddles?" asked Goosey Poosey.

"Oh, we are going to tell the King the sky is falling," said Henny Penny, Cocky Locky, and Ducky Daddles.

"May I go with you?" asked Goosey Poosey.

"Certainly," said Henny Pēnny, Cocky Locky, and Ducky Daddles.

So Henny Penny, Cocky Locky, Ducky Daddles, and Goosey Poosey went to tell the King that the sky was falling.

They went along and they went along and they went along until they met Turkey Lurkey.

"Where are you going, Henny Penny, Cocky Locky, Ducky Daddles, and Goosey Poosey?" asked Turkey Lurkey.

"Oh, we are going to tell the King the sky is falling," said Henny Penny, Cocky Locky, Ducky Daddles, and Goosey Poosey.

"May I go with you?" asked Turkey Lurkey.

"Certainly," said Henny Penny, Cocky Locky, Ducky Daddles, and Goosey Poosey.

So Henny Penny, Cocky Locky, Ducky Daddles, Goosey Poosey, and Turkey Lurkey went on to tell the King the sky was falling.

They went along and they went along and they went along until they met Foxy Woxy.

"Where are you going, Henny Penny, Cocky Locky, Ducky Daddles, Goosey Poosey, and Turkey Lurkey?" asked Foxy Woxy.

"Oh, we are going to tell the King the sky is falling," said Henny Penny, Cocky Locky, Ducky Daddles, Goosey Poosey, and Turkey Lurkey.

"Oh, but that is not the way to the King, Henny Penny, Cocky Locky, Ducky Daddles, Goosey Poosey, and Turkey Lurkey," said Foxy Woxy, "come with me and I will show you a short way to the King's Palace."

"Certainly," said Henny Penny, Cocky Locky, Ducky Daddles, Goosey Poosey, and Turkey Lurkey.

They went along and they went along and they went along until they reached Foxy Woxy's Cave. In they went after Foxy Woxy, and they never came out again.

To this day the King has never been told that the sky was falling.

Mr. and Mrs. Vinegar

BY FLORA ANNIE STEEL

Illustrations by Arthur Rackham

MR. and Mrs. Vinegar, a worthy couple, lived in a glass pickle-jar. The house, though small, was snug, and so light that each speck of dust on the furniture showed like a mole-hill; so while Mr. Vinegar tilled his garden with a pickle-fork and grew vegetables for pickling, Mrs. Vinegar, who was a sharp, bustling, tidy woman, swept, brushed, and dusted, brushed and dusted and swept to keep the house clean as a new pin. Now one day she lost her temper with a cobweb and swept so hard after it that bang! bang! the broom-handle went right through the glass, and crash! crash! clitter! clatter! there was the pickle-jar house about her ears all in splinters and bits.

She picked her way over these as best she might, and rushed into the garden.

"Oh, Vinegar, Vinegar!" she cried. "We are clean ruined and done for! Quit these vegetables! they won't be wanted! What is the use of pickles if you haven't a pickle-jar to put them in, and—I've broken ours—into little bits!" And with that she fell to crying bitterly.

But Mr. Vinegar was of different mettle; though a small man, he was a cheerful one, always looking at the best side of things, so he said, "Accidents will happen, lovey! But there are as good pickle-bottles in the shop as ever came out of it. All we need is money to buy another. So let us go out into the world and seek our fortunes."

"But what about the furniture," sobbed Mrs. Vinegar.

"I will take the door of the house with me, lovey," quoth Mr. Vinegar stoutly. "Then no one will be able to open it, will they?"

Mrs. Vinegar did not quite see how this fact would mend matters, but, being a good wife, she held her peace. So off they trudged into the world to seek their fortune, Mr. Vinegar bearing the door on his back like a snail carries its house.

Well, they walked all day long, but not a brass farthing did they make, and when night fell, they found themselves in a dark, thick forest. Now Mrs. Vinegar, for all she was a smart strong woman, was tired to death, and filled with fear of wild beasts, so she began once more to cry bitterly; but Mr. Vinegar was cheerful as ever.

"Don't alarm yourself, lovey," he said. "I will climb into a tree, fix the door firmly in a fork, and you can sleep there as safe and comfortable as in your own bed."

So he climbed the tree, fixed the door, and Mrs. Vinegar lay down on it, and being dead tired was soon fast asleep. But her weight tilted the door sideways, so, after a time, Mr. Vinegar, being afraid she might slip off, sat down on the other side to balance her and keep watch.

Now in the very middle of the night, just as he was beginning to nod, what should happen but that a band of robbers should meet beneath that very tree in order to divide their spoils. Mr. Vinegar could hear every word said quite distinctly, and began to tremble like an aspen as he listened to the terrible deeds the thieves had done to gain their ends.

"Don't shake so!" murmured Mrs. Vinegar, half asleep. "You'll have me off the bed."

"I'm not shaking, lovey," whispered back Mr. Vinegar in a quaking voice. "It is only the wind in the trees."

But for all his cheerfulness he was not really *very*

brave *inside*, so he went on trembling and shaking and shaking and trembling, till, just as the robbers were beginning to parcel out the money, he actually shook the door right out of the tree-fork, and down it came—with Mrs. Vinegar still asleep upon it—right on top of the robbers' heads!

As you may imagine, they thought the sky had fallen, and made off as fast as their legs would carry them, leaving their booty behind them. But Mr. Vinegar, who had saved himself from the fall by clinging to a branch, was far too frightened to go down in the dark to see what had happened. So up in the tree he sat like a big bird until dawn came.

Then Mrs. Vinegar woke, rubbed her eyes, yawned, and said, "Where am I?"

"On the ground, lovey," answered Mr. Vinegar, scrambling down.

And when they lifted up the door what do you think they found?

One robber squashed flat as a pancake and forty golden guineas all scattered about!

My goodness! How Mr. and Mrs. Vinegar jumped for joy!

"Now, Vinegar!" said his wife when they had gathered up all the gold pieces, "I will tell you what we must do. You must go to the next market-town and buy a cow; for, see you, money makes the mare to go, truly; but it also goes itself. Now a cow won't run away, but will give us milk and butter, which we can sell. So we shall live in comfort for the rest of our days."

"What a head you have, lovey," said Mr. Vinegar admiringly, and started off on his errand.

"Mind you make a good bargain," bawled his wife after him.

"I always do," bawled back Mr. Vinegar. "I made a good bargain when I married such a clever wife, and I made a better one when I shook her down from the tree. I am the happiest man alive!"

So he trudged on, laughing and jingling the forty gold pieces in his pocket.

Now the first thing he saw in the market was an old red cow.

"I am in luck to-day," he thought, "that is the very beast for me. I shall be the happiest of men if I get that cow." So he went up to the owner, jingling the gold in his pocket.

"What will you take for your cow?" he asked.

And the owner of the cow, seeing he was a simpleton, said, "What you've got in your pocket."

"Done!" said Mr. Vinegar, handed over the forty guineas and led off the cow, marching her up and down the market, much against her will, to show off his bargain.

Now, as he drove it about, proud as Punch, he noticed a man who was playing the bagpipes. He was followed about by a crowd of children who danced to the music, and a perfect shower of pennies fell into his cap every time he held it out.

"Ho, ho!" thought Mr. Vinegar. "That is an easier way of earning a livelihood than by driving about a beast of a cow! Then the feeding, and the milking, and the churning! Ah, I should be the happiest man alive if I had those bagpipes!"

So he went up to the musician and said, "What will you take for your bagpipes?"

"Well," replied the musician, seeing he was a simpleton, "it is a beautiful instrument and I make so much money by it, that I cannot take anything less than the red cow."

"Done!" cried Mr. Vinegar in a hurry, lest the man should repent of his offer.

So the musician walked off with the red cow, and Mr. Vinegar tried to play the bagpipes. But, alas, and alack! Though he blew till he almost burst, not a sound could

he make at first, and when he did at last, it was such a
terrific squeal and screech that all the children ran
away frightened, and the people stopped their ears.

But he went on and on, trying to play a tune, and
never earning anything, save hootings and peltings,
until his fingers were almost frozen with the cold, when
of course the noise he made on the bagpipes was worse
than ever.

Then he noticed a man who had on a pair of warm
gloves, and he said to himself, "Music is impossible
when one's fingers are frozen. I believe I should be the
happiest man alive if I had those gloves."

So he went up to the owner and said, "You seem, sir,
to have a very good pair of gloves." And the man replied,
"Truly, sir, my hands are as warm as toast this bitter
November day."

That quite decided Mr. Vinegar, and he asked at once
what the owner would take for them; and the owner,
seeing he was a simpleton, said, "As your hands seem
frozen, sir, I will, as a favour, let you have them for your
bagpipes."

"Done!" cried Mr. Vinegar, delighted, and made the
exchange.

Then he set off to find his wife, quite pleased with
himself. "Warm hands, warm heart!" he thought. "I'm
the happiest man alive!"

But as he trudged he grew very, very tired, and at last
began to limp. Then he saw a man coming along the
road with a stout stick.

"I should be the happiest man alive if I had that stick,"
he thought. "What is the use of warm hands if your feet
ache!" So he said to the man with the stick, "What will
you take for your stick?" and the man, seeing he was a
simpleton, replied:

"Well, I don't want to part with my stick, but as you are

so pressing I'll oblige you, as a friend, for those warm gloves you are wearing."

"Done for you!" cried Mr. Vinegar delightedly; and trudged off with the stick, chuckling to himself over his good bargain.

But as he went along a magpie fluttered out of the hedge and sate on a branch in front of him, and chuckled and laughed as magpies do. "What are you laughing at?" asked Mr. Vinegar.

"At you, forsooth!" chuckled the magpie, fluttering just a little further. "At *you*, Mr. Vinegar, you foolish man—

you simpleton—you blockhead! You bought a cow for
forty guineas when she wasn't worth ten, you exchanged
her for bagpipes you couldn't play—you changed the
bagpipes for a pair of gloves, and the pair of gloves for
a miserable stick. Ho, ho! Ha, ha! So you've nothing to
show for your forty guineas save a stick you might have
cut in any hedge. Ah, you fool! you simpleton! you
blockhead!"

And the magpie chuckled, and chuckled, and chuckled in such guffaws, fluttering from branch to branch as
Mr. Vinegar trudged along, that at last he flew into a
violent rage and flung his stick at the bird. And the stick
stuck in a tree out of his reach; so he had to go back to
his wife without anything at all.

But he was glad the stick had stuck in a tree, for Mrs.
Vinegar's hands were quite hard enough.

When it was all over Mr. Vinegar said cheerfully,
"You are too violent, lovey. You broke the pickle-jar, and
now you've nearly broken every bone in my body. I
think we had better turn over a new leaf and begin
afresh. I shall take service as a gardener, and you can
go as a housemaid until we have enough money to buy
a new pickle-jar. There are as good ones in the shop as
ever came out of it."

And that is the story of Mr. and Mrs. Vinegar.

The Three Billy Goats Gruff

RETOLD BY VERONICA HUTCHINSON

Illustration by Estelle Hollingworth

ONCE upon a time there were three Billy goats and their name was Gruff.

They were going up the mountain to get fat.

On their way up they had to cross a bridge and under this bridge there lived a Troll, with eyes as big as saucers and a nose as long as a broomstick.

The Billy goats did not know that the Troll lived there.

First of all came Little Billy Goat Gruff. He went trip-trap-trip-trap over the bridge.

The Troll poked up his head and said, "Who goes trip-trap-trip-trap-trip-trap over my bridge?"

The Little Billy goat said, "It is I, Little Billy Goat Gruff, and I'm going up the mountain to get fat."

"Oh, no, you're not," said the Troll, "because I'm going to eat you."

"Oh," said Little Billy Goat Gruff, "you wouldn't eat me, would you? I am so small, just wait for my brother, second Billy Goat Gruff and you eat him. He is much larger than I."

"Very well," said the Troll. "Be off with you," and trip-trap-trip-trap-trip-trap went Little Billy Goat Gruff.

Presently along came Second Billy Goat Gruff, and he went trip-trap! trip-trap! trip-trap! over the bridge. The Troll poked up his head and said, "Who goes trip-trap! trip-trap! trip-trap! over my bridge?"

The Second Billy Goat Gruff tried to make his voice sound very weak too, and he said, "It is I, Second Billy Goat Gruff, and I am going up to the mountain to get fat."

"Oh, no, you're not," said the Troll, "because I'm going to eat you."

Then the Second Billy Goat said, "Oh, you wouldn't eat me, would you? I am so small. You wait for my brother, Great Billy Goat Gruff, and you eat him. He is much larger than I."

"Very well then," said the Troll, "be off with you"; and trip-trap! trip-trap! trip-trap! went Second Billy Goat Gruff.

Last of all came Great Billy Goat Gruff. Oh, he was a great, large fellow. His great shaggy fur hung down to his feet. He had two large horns coming out of his forehead. When he walked the bridge just shook. He went Trip-Trop! Trip-Trop! Trip-Trop! "Oh!" went the bridge, he was so heavy.

The Troll poked up his head and said, "Who goes Trip-Trop! Trip-Trop! Trip-Trop! over my bridge?"

The Great Billy Goat stood there and said, "It is I, Great Billy Goat Gruff, and I'm going up the mountain to get fat."

"Oh, no, you're not," said the Troll, "because I am going to eat you."

"Come along then," said the Great Billy Goat Gruff, and up came the Troll. The Great Billy Goat caught him with his two horns and tossed him way up in the sky. That was the end of the Troll; and Trip-Trop! Trip-Trop! Trip-Trop! away he went over the bridge. By this time the three Billy goats are so fat that they couldn't come back even though they wanted to. So

"Snip Snap Snout
My tale is out."

Red Riding Hood

BY THE BROTHERS GRIMM

Translated by Mrs. E. V. Lucas,
Lucy Crane, and Marian Edwardes

Illustrations by Dagmar Wilson

ONCE upon a time there was a sweet little maiden
who was loved by all who knew her, but she was especially dear to her grandmother, who did not know how
to make enough of the child. Once she gave her a little
red velvet cloak. It was so becoming and she liked it
so much that she would never wear anything else, and
so she got the name of Red Riding Hood.

One day her mother said to her, "Come here, Red
Riding Hood! Take this cake and bottle of wine to
grandmother. She is weak and ill, and they will do her
good. Go quickly, before it gets hot. And don't loiter by
the way, or run, or you will fall down and break the
bottle, and there will be no wine for grandmother. When
you get there, don't forget to say 'Good morning' prettily,
without staring about you."

"I will do just as you tell me," Red Riding Hood promised her mother.

Her grandmother lived away in the wood, a good half
hour from the village. When she got to the wood she met
a wolf, but Red Riding Hood did not know what a
wicked animal he was, so she was not a bit afraid of him.

"Good morning, Red Riding Hood," he said.

"Good morning, wolf," she answered.

"Whither away so early, Red Riding Hood?"

From *Grimm's Fairy Tales*, by The Brothers Grimm, translated by Mrs. E. V.
Lucas, Lucy Crane, and Marian Edwardes.

"To grandmother's."

"What have you got in your basket?"

"Cake and wine. We baked yesterday, so I'm taking a cake to grandmother. She wants something to make her well."

"Where does your grandmother live, Red Riding Hood?"

"A good quarter of an hour farther into the wood. Her house stands under three big oak trees, near a hedge of nut trees which you must know," said Red Riding Hood.

The wolf thought, "This tender little creature will be a plump morsel! She will be nicer than the old woman. I must be cunning and snap them both up."

He walked along with Red Riding Hood for a while. Then he said, "Look at the pretty flowers, Red Riding Hood. Why don't you look about you? I don't believe you even hear the birds sing. You are just as solemn as if you were going to school. Everything else is so gay out here in the woods."

Red Riding Hood raised her eyes, and when she saw the sunlight dancing through the trees, and all the bright flowers, she thought, "I'm sure grandmother would be pleased if I took her a bunch of fresh flowers. It is still quite early. I shall have plenty of time to pick them."

So she left the path and wandered off among the trees to pick the flowers. Each time she picked one, she always saw another prettier one farther on. So she went deeper and deeper into the forest.

In the meantime the wolf went straight off to the grandmother's cottage and knocked at the door.

"Who is there?"

"Red Riding Hood, bringing you a cake and some wine. Open the door!"

"Lift the latch," called out the old woman. "I am too weak to get up."

The wolf lifted the latch and the door sprang open. He went straight in and up to the bed without saying a word, and ate up the poor old woman. Then he put on her nightdress and nightcap, got into bed and drew the curtains.

Red Riding Hood ran about picking flowers till she could carry no more, and then she remembered her grandmother again. She was astonished when she got to the house to find the door open, and when she entered the room everything seemed so strange.

She felt quite frightened but she did not know why. "Generally I like coming to see grandmother so much," she thought. "Good morning, grandmother," she cried. But she received no answer.

Then she went up to bed and drew the curtain back. There lay her grandmother, but she had drawn her cap down over her face and she looked very odd.

"Oh grandmother, what big ears you have," she said.

"The better to hear you with, my dear."

"Grandmother, what big eyes you have."

"The better to see you with, my dear."

"What big hands you have, grandmother."

"The better to catch hold of you with, my dear."

"But grandmother, what big teeth you have."

"The better to eat you up with, my dear."

Hardly had the wolf said this than he made a spring out of bed and swallowed poor little Red Riding Hood. When the wolf had satisfied himself he went back to bed, and he was soon snoring loudly.

A huntsman went past the house and thought, "How loudly the old lady is snoring. I must see if there is anything the matter with her."

So he went into the house and up to the bed, where he found the wolf fast asleep. "Do I find you here, you old sinner!" he said. "Long enough have I sought you!"

He raised his gun to shoot, when it just occurred to him that perhaps the wolf had eaten up the old lady, and that she might still be saved. So he took a knife and began cutting open the sleeping wolf. At the first cut he saw the little red cloak, and after a few more slashes, the little girl sprang out and cried, "Oh, how frightened I was! It was so dark inside the wolf." Next the old grandmother came out, alive but hardly able to breathe.

Red Riding Hood brought some big stones with which they filled the wolf, so that when he woke up and tried to spring away, the stones dragged him back and he fell down dead.

They were all quite happy now. The huntsman skinned the wolf and took the skin home. The grandmother ate the cake and drank the wine which Red Riding Hood had brought, and she soon felt quite strong. Red Riding Hood thought to herself, "I will never again wander off into the forest as long as I live, when my mother forbids it."

Cinderella

BY CHARLES PERRAULT

Adapted from the Andrew Lang translation

Illustrations by William Colrus

ONCE there was a gentleman who married, for his second wife, the proudest and most haughty woman that was ever seen. She had two daughters who were exactly like her in all things. He had a young daughter of unparalleled goodness and sweetness of temper, which she took from her mother, who was the best creature in the world.

No sooner were the ceremonies of the wedding over but the mother began to show her bad temper. She could not bear the good qualities of this pretty girl because they made her own daughters appear the more hateful. She employed her in the meanest work of the house: scouring the dishes and tables and scrubbing madam's room, also those of her daughters.

The girl slept in a sorry garret, upon a wretched straw bed, while her sisters lay in fine rooms, with floors all inlaid, upon beds of the very newest fashion, and where they had looking glasses so large they might see themselves at full length from head to foot.

The poor girl bore all patiently. When she had done her work, she used to go into the chimney corner and sit down among cinders and ashes, which caused her to be called Cinderwench. But the younger, who was not so rude and uncivil as the elder, called her Cinderella. However, Cinderella, in spite of her rags, was a hundred times prettier than her sisters, though they were always dressed very richly.

Adapted from the Blue Fairy Book, collected and edited by Andrew Lang. Published by Longmans, Green and Co., Ltd.

It happened that the king's son gave a ball and invited all persons of fashion to it. The two sisters were also invited, for they cut a very grand figure among the quality. They were delighted at this invitation and wonderfully busy in choosing such gowns, petticoats and headdresses as might become them. This was a new trouble to Cinderella, for it was she who ironed her sisters' linen and plaited their ruffles, while they talked all day long of nothing but how they should be dressed.

"For my part," said the elder, "I will wear my red-velvet suit with French trimming."

"And I," said the younger, "shall have my usual petticoat. But then, to make amends for that, I will put on my gold-flowered cloak, and my diamond ornament, which is far from being the most ordinary one in the world."

They sent for the best lady's maid they could get to make up their headdresses and adjust their double pinners, and they had their red brushes and patches from Mademoiselle de la Poche.

Cinderella was likewise consulted in all these matters, for she had excellent notions, and advised them always for the best and offered her services to dress their hair which they were very willing she should do. As she was doing this, they said to her:

"Cinderella, would you not like to go to the ball?"

"Alas," she said, "you only make fun of me. It is not for such as I to go there."

"You are in the right of it," replied they. "It would certainly make people laugh to see a cinderwench at a palace ball."

Anyone but Cinderella would have fixed their hair badly, but she was very good and dressed them perfectly. They went almost two days without eating, they were so happy. They broke above a dozen of laces in trying to be laced up close, that they might have a fine slender shape, and they were continually at their looking

glass. At last the happy day came. They went to court, and Cinderella followed them with her eyes as long as she could, and when she had lost sight of them, she fell a-crying.

Her godmother, who saw her all in tears, asked her what was the matter.

"I wish I could—I wish I could—" She was not able to speak the rest, being interrupted by her tears and sobbing.

This godmother of hers, who was a fairy, said to her, "You wish to go to the ball. Is it not so?"

"Yes," cried Cinderella, with a great sigh.

"Well," said her godmother, "be a good girl, and I will try to help you go." Then she said to her, "Run into the garden and bring me a pumpkin."

Cinderella went immediately to gather the finest one

and brought it to her godmother, not being able to imagine how this pumpkin could make her go to the ball. Her godmother scooped out all the inside of it, leaving nothing but the rind; which done, she struck it with her wand, and the pumpkin was instantly turned into a fine coach, gilded all over with gold.

She then went to look into her mousetrap, where she found six mice, all alive. She told Cinderella to lift up the little trap door, when, giving each mouse, as it went out, a little tap with her wand, the mouse was that moment turned into a fine horse. Altogether they made a very fine set of six horses of a beautiful mouse-coloured gray.

Being at a loss for a coachman, Cinderella said, "I will go and see if there is a rat in the rat-trap—we may make a coachman of him."

"You are right," replied her godmother. "Go and look."

Cinderella brought the trap to her, and in it there were three huge rats. The fairy chose the one which had the largest beard, and having touched him with her wand, he was turned into a fat, jolly coachman, who had the smartest whiskers eyes ever beheld. After that, she said to her:

"Go again into the garden, and you will find six lizards behind the watering pot; bring them to me."

Cinderella had no sooner done so than her godmother turned them into six footmen, who skipped up immediately behind the coach, with their liveries all covered with gold and silver. They clung as close behind each other as if they had done nothing else their whole lives. The fairy then said to Cinderella:

"Well, you see here carriage and horses and footmen fit to take you to the ball. Are you not pleased with it?"

"Oh, yes," cried Cinderella, "but must I go there as I am, in these old rags?"

Her godmother just touched her with her wand, and at the same instant her clothes were turned into cloth of gold and silver, all beset with jewels. This done, she gave her a pair of glass slippers, the prettiest in the whole world. Being thus decked out, Cinderella climbed into her coach, but her godmother, above all things, commanded her not to stay till after midnight, telling her, at the same time, that if she stayed one moment longer, the coach would be a pumpkin again, her horses mice, her coachman a rat, her footmen lizards, and her clothes would become just as they were before.

Cinderella promised her godmother she would not fail to leave the ball before midnight. And then away she drove, scarce able to contain herself for joy. The king's son, who was told that a great princess, whom nobody knew, had come, ran out to receive her. He gave her his hand as she alighted from the coach and led her into the hall, among all the company. There was immediate silence. They left off dancing, and the violins ceased to play, so eager was everyone to look at the singular beauties of the unknown newcomer. Nothing was heard but a confused noise of:

"Ha! How pretty she is! Ha! How pretty she is!"

The king himself, old as he was, could not help watching her and telling the queen softly that it was a long time since he had seen so beautiful and lovely a creature. All the ladies were busied in considering her clothes and headdress, that they might have some made next day after the same pattern, provided they could meet with such fine materials and find able hands to make them.

The king's son conducted her to the most honourable seat, and afterward took her out to dance with him, and she danced so gracefully that all more and more admired her. Fine refreshments were served, of which the young prince ate not a morsel, so intently was he gazing on Cinderella.

She sat down by her sisters, showing them a thousand civilities, giving them part of the oranges and citrons which the prince had presented her, which very much surprised them, for they did not know her. While Cinderella was thus amusing her sisters, she heard the clock strike eleven and three-quarters, whereupon she immediately made a curtsey to the company and hastened away as fast as she could.

Reaching home, she ran to seek out her godmother and, after having thanked her, said she could not but heartily wish she might go next day to the ball, because the king's son had asked her. As she was eagerly telling her godmother whatever had passed at the ball, her two sisters knocked at the door, which Cinderella ran and opened.

"How long you have stayed!" cried she, rubbing her eyes and stretching herself as if she had been just waked out of her sleep. She had not, however, had any inclination to sleep since they went from home.

"If you had been at the ball," said one of her sisters, "you would not have been tired with it. There we met the finest princess, the most beautiful ever seen with mortal eyes; she showed us a thousand civilities and gave us oranges and citrons."

Cinderella seemed very indifferent in the matter but asked them the name of the princess. They told her they did not know it and that the king's son would give all the world to know who she was. At this Cinderella, smiling, replied:

"She must, then, be very beautiful indeed. How happy you have been! Could not I see her? Ah, dear Miss Charlotte, do lend me your yellow clothes which you wear every day."

"Ay, to be sure," cried Miss Charlotte, "lend my clothes to a dirty cinderwench! I should be a fool."

Cinderella expected such an answer and was very glad of the refusal, for she would have been sadly put to it if her sister had done what she asked for jestingly.

The next day the two sisters were at the ball, and so was Cinderella, but dressed more magnificently than before. The king's son was always by her and never ceased his compliments and kind speeches to her. All this was so far from being tiresome that she quite forgot what her godmother had commanded her. At last, she counted the clock striking twelve when she took it to be no more than eleven. She then rose up and fled, as nimble as a deer. The prince followed but could not overtake her. She left behind one of her glass slippers, which the prince took up most carefully. Cinderella reached home, quite out of breath, and in her old clothes, having nothing left of all her finery but one of the little slippers, the mate to the one she had dropped.

The guards at the palace gate were asked if they had not seen a princess go out. They had seen nobody but a young girl, very meanly dressed, who had more the air of a poor country wench than a gentlewoman.

When the two sisters returned from the ball Cinderella asked them if they had been well entertained, and if the fine lady had been there. They told her, yes, but that she hurried away immediately when it struck twelve and with so much haste that she dropped one of her little glass slippers, the prettiest in the world. The king's son had taken it up. He had done nothing but look at her all the time at the ball, and most certainly he was very much in love with the beautiful girl who owned the glass slipper.

What they said was very true, for a few days afterward the king's son proclaimed, by sound of trumpet, that he would marry the girl whose foot this slipper would just fit. His servants began to try it upon the princesses, then the duchesses, and all the court, but in vain. It was brought to the two sisters, who each did all she possibly could to thrust her foot into the slipper. But they could not put on the slipper. Cinderella, who saw all this, and knew her slipper, said to them, laughing:

"Let me see if it will not fit me."

Her sisters burst out laughing and began to banter her. The gentleman who was sent to try the slipper looked earnestly at Cinderella and, finding her very handsome, said it was only fair that she should try, and that he had orders to let everyone make the attempt.

He obliged Cinderella to sit down, and putting the slipper to her foot, he found it went on easily and fitted her as if it had been made of wax. The astonishment of her two sisters was great, but still greater when Cinderella pulled out of her pocket the other slipper and put it on her foot. At that moment, in came her godmother who, having touched Cinderella's clothes with her wand, made them richer and more magnificent than any she had worn before.

And now her two sisters found her to be that fine, beautiful lady they had seen at the ball. They threw

themselves at her feet to beg pardon for all the ill-treat-ment they had made her undergo. Cinderella raised them up and, as she embraced them, cried that she for-gave them with all her heart and desired them always to love her.

She was conducted to the young prince. He thought her more charming than ever and, a few days after, married her. Cinderella, who was no less good than beautiful, gave her two sisters lodgings in the palace, and that very same day matched them with two great lords of the court.

The Three Bears

Illustrations by Robert Reed Macguire

ONCE upon a time there were Three Bears who lived together in a little house in the woods. One of them was a Little, Wee, Baby Bear, one was a Middle-Sized, Mother Bear, and one was a Great, Big, Father Bear. They each had a pot for their porridge: a little pot for the Little, Wee, Baby Bear, a middle-sized pot for the Middle-Sized, Mother Bear, and a great, big pot for the Great, Big, Father Bear. They each had a chair to sit in: a little chair for the Little, Wee, Baby Bear, a middle-sized chair for the Middle-Sized, Mother Bear, and a great, big chair for the Great, Big, Father Bear. They each had a bed to sleep in: a little bed for the Little, Wee, Baby Bear, a middle-sized bed for the Middle-Sized, Mother Bear, and a great, big bed for the Great, Big, Father Bear.

One morning after they had made porridge for breakfast and poured it into their porridge-pots, they went for a walk while the porridge was cooling.

While they were walking, a little girl named Goldilocks came to the house. First she looked in the window, then she peeped in the keyhole. Seeing nobody in the house, Goldilocks opened the door and went in. She saw the three bowls of porridge and set about helping herself.

First she tasted the great, big bowl of porridge, and that was too hot for her. Then she tasted the middle-sized bowl of porridge, and that was too cold for her. Then she tasted the little bowl of porridge, and that was just right. She liked it so much that she ate it all up.

Then Goldilocks sat down in the great, big chair belonging to the Great, Big, Father Bear, and that was too
hard for her. Then she sat down in the middle-sized chair
belonging to the Middle-Sized, Mother Bear, and that
was too soft for her. Then she sat down in the little chair
belonging to the Little, Wee, Baby Bear, and that was
just right. There she sat till the bottom of the chair came
out, and down she came upon the ground.

Then Goldilocks went upstairs to the bedroom where
the Three Bears slept. First she lay down on the bed of
the Great, Big, Father Bear, but that was too hard for
her. Next she lay down on the bed of the Middle-Sized,
Mother Bear, but that was too soft for her. Then she
lay down on the bed of the Little, Wee, Baby Bear.
That was neither too hard nor too soft, but just right. So
she covered herself up and fell fast asleep.

While Goldilocks was sleeping, the three Bears came
home for breakfast. The Great, Big, Father Bear, seeing
a spoon in his porridge, said in his great rough, gruff
voice,

"SOMEBODY HAS BEEN EATING MY PORRIDGE!"

When the Middle-Sized Bear saw a spoon in her porridge, she said in her middle-sized voice,

"SOMEBODY HAS BEEN EATING MY PORRIDGE!"

When the Little, Wee, Baby Bear looked at his bowl,
the porridge was all gone. Then the Little, Wee, Baby
Bear said in his little, wee voice,

"SOMEBODY HAS BEEN EATING MY PORRIDGE, AND HAS EATEN IT ALL UP!"

Then the Three Bears began to look about the house.
The Great, Big, Father Bear looked at his chair and said
in his great, rough, gruff voice,

"SOMEBODY HAS BEEN SITTING IN MY CHAIR!"

Then the Middle-Sized, Mother Bear said in her middle-sized voice,

"SOMEBODY HAS BEEN SITTING IN MY CHAIR!"

Then the Little, Wee, Baby Bear cried in his little, wee voice,

"SOMEBODY HAS BEEN SITTING IN MY CHAIR AND HAS SAT THE BOTTOM OUT!"

Then the Three Bears went upstairs to the bedroom. The Great, Big, Father Bear looked at his bed and said in his great, rough, gruff voice,

"SOMEBODY HAS BEEN LYING IN MY BED!"

Then the Middle-Sized Bear said in her middle-sized voice,

"SOMEBODY HAS BEEN LYING IN MY BED!"

And when the Little, Wee, Bear looked at his bed he cried, in his little wee voice,

"SOMEBODY HAS BEEN LYING IN MY BED—AND HERE SHE IS!"

Now the little, wee voice of the Little, Wee Bear was so sharp and shrill that it awakened Goldilocks at once. When she saw the Three Bears, she hopped out of bed, jumped out the window and ran away as fast as she could run.

The Little Red Hen and the Grain of Wheat

RETOLD BY VERONICA HUTCHINSON

Illustrations by Estelle Hollingworth

ONE day the Little Red Hen was scratching in the farmyard when she found a grain of wheat.

"Who will plant the wheat?" said she.

"Not I," said the duck.

"Not I," said the cat.

"Not I," said the dog.

"Very well then," said the Little Red Hen, "I will." So she planted the grain of wheat.

After some time the wheat grew tall and ripe.

"Who will cut the wheat?" asked the Little Red Hen.

"Not I," said the duck.

"Not I," said the cat.

"Not I," said the dog.

"Very well then, I will," said the Little Red Hen. So she cut the wheat.

"Now," she said, "who will thresh the wheat?"

"Not I," said the duck.

"Not I," said the cat.

"Not I," said the dog.

"Very well then, I will," said the Little Red Hen. So she threshed the wheat.

When the wheat was threshed, she said, "Who will take the wheat to the mill to have it ground into flour?"

"Not I," said the duck.

"Not I," said the cat.

"Not I," said the dog.

"Very well then, I will," said the Little Red Hen. So she took the wheat to the mill.

When the wheat was ground into flour, she said, "Who will make this flour into bread?"

"Not I," said the duck.

"Not I," said the cat.

"Not I," said the dog.

"Very well then, I will," said the Little Red Hen, and then baked a lovely loaf of bread.

Then she said, "Who will eat the bread?"

"Oh! I will," said the duck.

"Oh! I will," said the cat.

"Oh! I will," said the dog.

"Oh, no, you won't!" said the Little Red Hen. "I will." And she called her chicks and shared the bread with them.

The Three Little Pigs

Illustrations by Robert Reed Macguire

ONCE upon a time there was a mother Pig with three little Pigs, and as she had not enough to keep them, she sent them out to seek their fortune.

The first that went off met a Man with a bundle of straw, and said to him, "Please, Man, give me that straw to build a house"; the Man did, and the little Pig built a house with it. Presently came along a Wolf, and knocked at the door, and said, "Little Pig, little Pig, let me come in."

To which the little Pig answered, "No, no, by the hair of my chinny chin chin."

"Then I'll huff and I'll puff, and I'll blow your house in!" said the Wolf. So he huffed and he puffed, and he blew the house in, and ate up the little Pig.

The second Pig met a Man with a bundle of twigs and said, "Please, Man, give me those twigs to build a house"; the Man did, and the Pig built his house. Then along came the Wolf and said, "Little Pig, little Pig, let me come in."

"No, no, by the hair of my chinny chin chin."

"Then I'll puff and I'll huff, and I'll blow your house in!" said the Wolf. So he huffed and he puffed, and he puffed and he huffed, and at last he blew the house down, and ate up the second little Pig.

The third little Pig met a Man with a load of bricks, and said, "Please, Man, give me those bricks to build a house"; so the Man gave him the bricks, and he built his house with them. The Wolf came, as he did to the other little Pigs, and said, "Little Pig, little Pig, let me come in."

"No, no, by the hair of my chinny chin chin."

"Then I'll huff and I'll puff, and I'll blow your house in."

Well, he huffed and he puffed, and he huffed and he puffed, and he puffed and he huffed; but he could *not* get the house down. When he found that he could not,

with all his huffing and puffing, blow the house down, he said, "Little Pig, I know where there is a nice field of turnips."

"Where?" asked the little Pig.

"Oh, in 'Mr. Smith's field; and if you will be ready tomorrow morning, I will call for you, and we will go together and get some for dinner."

"Very well," said the Little Pig, "I'll be ready. What time do you mean to go?"

"At six o'clock," said the Wolf.

Well, the little Pig got up at five, got the turnips, and was home again before six. When the Wolf came he said, "Little Pig, are you ready?"

"*Ready?*" asked the little Pig. "I have been and come back again, and got a nice potful for dinner."

The Wolf felt very angry at this, but thought that he would be up to the little Pig somehow or other; so he said, "Little Pig, I know where there is a nice apple tree."

"Where?" asked the Pig.

"Down at Merry-Garden," replied the Wolf; "and if you will not deceive me, I will come for you, at five o'clock tomorrow, and we will go together and get some apples."

Well, the little Pig woke at four the next morning, and went off to get the apples, hoping to be back before the Wolf came; but he had farther to go, and had to climb the tree, so that just as he was coming down from it, he saw the Wolf coming. As you may suppose, that frightened him very much. When the Wolf came up he said:

"Little Pig, what! are you here before me? Are they nice apples?"

"Yes, very," said the little Pig; "I will throw you down one." And he threw it so far that, while the Wolf was gone to pick it up, the little Pig jumped down and ran home.

The next day the Wolf came again, and said to the
little Pig, "Little Pig, there is a Fair in the town this
afternoon: will you go?"

"Oh, yes," said the Pig, "I'll go; what time will you
be ready?"

"At three," said the Wolf.

So the little Pig went off as usual, early, got to the
Fair, bought a butter churn, and was on his way home
with it when he saw the Wolf coming. Then he could not
tell what to do. So he got into the churn to hide, and in
doing so turned it round, and it began to roll, and rolled
down the hill with the Pig inside it. This frightened the
Wolf so much that he ran home without going to the
Fair.

He went to the little Pig's house, and told him how
frightened he had been by a great round thing which
came down the hill past him.

Then the little Pig said, "Hah! I frightened you, did

I? I had been to the Fair and bought a butter churn, and when I saw you I got into it, and rolled down the hill."

Then the Wolf was very angry indeed, and declared he *would* eat up the little Pig, and that he would climb down the chimney after him.

When the little Pig saw what was about, he put a pot full of water in the fireplace, and made a blazing fire. Just as the Wolf was coming down the chimney, the little Pig took the cover off the pot, and in fell the Wolf! The little Pig put the cover on again, instantly boiled up the Wolf, and ate him for supper, and lived happily ever after.

BEST-LOVED POEMS

this happy day

This Happy Day

By Harry Behn

Illustration by William Colrus

Every morning when the sun
Comes smiling up on everyone,
It's lots of fun
To say good morning to the sun.
    Good morning, Sun!

Every evening after play
When the sunshine goes away,
It's nice to say,
Thank you for this happy day,
    This happy day!

I Sing All Day

By Ilo Orleans

Illustration by William Colrus

Music plays inside of me;
   And tunes are in my head
From waking time each morning
   Until I go to bed.

Music makes me happy;
   And things cannot go wrong
When I am filled with melody
   And sing my faith in song.

My Shadow

By Robert Louis Stevenson

Illustration by William Colrus

I have a little shadow that goes in and out with me,
And what can be the use of him is more than I can see.
He is very, very like me from the heels up to the head;
And I see him jump before me when I jump into my bed.

The funniest thing about him is the way he likes to
     grow—
Not at all like proper children, which is always very slow;
For he sometimes shoots up taller like an India-rubber
     ball,
And he sometimes gets so little that there's none of him
     at all.

He hasn't got a notion of how children ought to play,
And can only make a fool of me in every sort of way.
He stays so close beside me, he's a coward you can see;
I'd think shame to stick to nursie as that shadow sticks
     to me!

One morning very early before the sun was up,
I rose and found the shiny dew on every buttercup;
But my lazy little shadow, like an arrant sleepy-head,
Had stayed at home behind me and was fast asleep in
     bed.

The Cupboard

By Walter de la Mare

Illustration by William Colrus

I know a little cupboard,
With a teeny tiny key,
And there's a jar of Lollypops
   For me, me, me.

It has a little shelf, my dear,
As dark as dark can be,
And there's a dish of Banbury Cakes
   For me, me, me.

I have a small fat grandmamma,
With a very slippery knee,
And she's Keeper of the Cupboard,
   With the key, key, key.

And when I'm very good, my dear,
As good as good can be,
There's Banbury Cakes, and Lollypops
   For me, me, me.

The Land of Counterpane

By Robert Louis Stevenson

Illustration by William Colrus

When I was sick and lay a-bed,
I had two pillows at my head,
And all my toys beside me lay
To keep me happy all the day.

And sometimes for an hour or so
I watched my leaden soldiers go,
With different uniforms and drills,
Among the bed-clothes, through the hills;

And sometimes sent my ships in fleets
All up and down among the sheets;
Or brought my trees and houses out,
And planted cities all about.

I was the giant great and still
That sits upon the pillow-hill,
And sees before him, dale and plain,
The pleasant land of counterpane.

Animal Crackers

By Christopher Morley

Illustration by George J. Reilly

Animal crackers, and cocoa to drink,
That is the finest of suppers, I think;
When I'm grown up and can have what I please
I think I shall always insist upon these.
What do *you* choose when you're offered a treat?
When Mother says, "What would you like best to eat?"
Is it waffles and syrup, or cinnamon toast?
It's cocoa and animals that *I* love most!

The kitchen's the cosiest place that I know:
The kettle is singing, the stove is aglow,
And there in the twilight, how jolly to see
The cocoa and animals waiting for me.

Daddy and Mother dine later in state,
With Mary to cook for them, Susan to wait;
But they don't have nearly as much fun as I
Who eat in the kitchen with Nurse standing by;
And Daddy once said, he would like to be me
Having cocoa and animals once more for tea!

Hoppity

By A. A. Milne

Illustration by Ernest H. Shepard

Christopher Robin goes
Hoppity, hoppity,
Hoppity, hoppity, hop.
Whenever I tell him
Politely to stop it, he
Says he can't possibly stop.

If he stopped hopping, he couldn't go anywhere,
Poor little Christopher
Couldn't go anywhere . . .
That's why he *always* goes
Hoppity, hoppity,
Hoppity,
Hoppity,
Hop.

A Swing Song

By William Allingham

Illustration by Estelle Hollingworth

Swing, swing,
Sing, sing,
Here! my throne and I am a King!
Swing, sing,
Swing, sing,
Farewell, earth, for I'm on the wing!

Low, high,
Here I fly,
Like a bird through sunny sky;
Free, free,
Over the lea,
Over the mountain, over the sea!

Up, down,
Up and down,
Which is the way to London Town?
Where? Where?
Up in the air,
Close your eyes and now you are there!

Soon, soon,
Afternoon,
Over the sunset, over the moon;
Far, far,
Over all bar,
Sweeping on from star to star!

No, no,
Low, low,
Sweeping daisies with my toe.
Slow, slow,
To and fro,
Slow—
            slow—
                        slow—
                                    slow

The Land of Story-Books

By Robert Louis Stevenson

At evening when the lamp is lit,
Around the fire my parents sit;
They sit at home and talk and sing,
And do not play at anything.

Now, with my little gun, I crawl
All in the dark along the wall,
And follow round the forest track
Away behind the sofa back.

There, in the night, where none can spy,
All in my hunter's camp I lie,
And play at books that I have read
Till it is time to go to bed.

These are the hills, these are the woods,
These are my starry solitudes;
And there the river by whose brink
The roaring lions come to drink.

I see the others far away,
As if in firelit camp they lay,
And I, like to an Indian scout,
Around their party prowled about.

So, when my nurse comes in for me,
Home I return across the sea,
And go to bed with backward looks
At my dear land of Story-books.

Mud

By Polly Chase Boyden

Illustration by Willy Pogany

Mud is very nice to feel
All squishy-squash between the toes!
I'd rather wade in wiggly mud
Than smell a yellow rose.

Nobody else but the rosebush knows
How nice mud feels
Between the toes.

The Lost Doll

By Charles Kingsley

Illustration by Estelle Hollingworth

I once had a sweet little doll, dears,
The prettiest doll in the world;
Her cheeks were so red and white, dears,
And her hair was so charmingly curled.
But I lost my poor little doll, dears,
As I played on the heath one day;
And I cried for her more than a week, dears,
But I never could find where she lay.

I found my poor little doll, dears,
As I played on the heath one day;
Folks say she is terribly changed, dears,
For her paint is all washed away,
And her arms trodden off by the cows, dears,
And her hair not the least bit curled;
Yet for old sakes' sake, she is still, dears,
The prettiest doll in the world.

My Zipper Suit

By Mary Louise Allen

Illustration by Estelle Hollingworth

My zipper suit is bunny-brown—
The top zips up, the legs zip down.
I wear it every day.
My daddy brought it out from town.
Zip it up, and zip it down,
And hurry out to play.

People

By Lois Lenski

Illustration by William Colrus

Tall people, short people,
Thin people, fat,
Lady so dainty
Wearing a hat.
Straight people, dumpy people,
Man dressed in brown;
Baby in a buggy,
These make a Town.

The People

By Elizabeth Madox Roberts

The ants are walking under the ground,
And the pigeons are flying over the steeple,
And in between are the people.

Barber's Clippers

By Dorothy Baruch

Illustration by Irving Leveton

The barber snips and snips
My hair with his scissors
And then he zips on
His clippers.

It clips
Up and down
And around
My hair in back.

Ssss ssss
It swishes
On the sides
Behind my ears.

Ssss ssss
It tickles
As it slides
Straight up the middle
Of my neck.

Indian Children

By *Annette Wynne*

Illustration by William Dixon

Where we walk to school each day
Indian children used to play—
All about our native land,
Where the shops and houses stand.

And the trees were very tall,
And there were no streets at all,
Not a church and not a steeple—
Only woods and Indian people.

Only wigwams on the ground,
And at night bears prowling round—
What a different place today
Where we live and work and play!

The Twins

By *Elizabeth Madox Roberts*

Illustration by Irving Leveton

The two-ones is the name for it,
And that is what it ought to be,
But when you say it very fast
It makes your lips say *twins* you see.

When I was just a little thing,
About the year before the last,
I called it two-ones all the time,
But now I always say it fast.

The Ice-Cream Man

By Rachel Field

Illustration by Irving Leveton

When summer's in the city,
   And brick's a blaze of heat,
The Ice-Cream Man with his little cart
   Goes trundling down the street.

Beneath his round umbrella,
   Oh, what a joyful sight,
To see him fill the cones with mounds
   Of cooling brown or white:

Vanilla, chocolate, strawberry,
   Or chilly things to drink
From bottles full of frosty-fizz,
   Green, orange, white, or pink.

His car might be a flower bed
   Of roses and sweet peas,
The way the children cluster round
   A thick as honeybees.

My Policeman

By Rose Fyleman

Illustration by William Colrus

He is always standing there
At the corner of the Square;
He is very big and fine
And his silver buttons shine.

All the carts and taxis do
Everything he tells them to,
And the little errand boys
When they pass him make no noise.

Though I seem so very small
I am not afraid at all;
He and I are friends, you see,
And he always smiles at me.

Once I wasn't very good
Rather near to where he stood,
But he never said a word
Though I'm sure he must have heard.

Nurse has a policeman too
(Hers has brown eyes, mine has blue),
Hers is sometimes on a horse,
But I like mine best of course.

Boys' Names

By Eleanor Farjeon

Illustration by George J. Reilly

What splendid names for boys there are!
There's Carol like a rolling car,
And Martin like a flying bird,
And Adam like the Lord's First Word,
And Raymond like the Harvest Moon,
And Peter like a piper's tune,
And Alan like the flowing on
Of water. And there's John, like John.

Girls' Names

By Eleanor Farjeon

Illustration by George J. Reilly

What lovely names for girls there are!
There's Stella like the Evening Star,
And Sylvia like a rustling tree,
And Lola like a melody,
And Flora like a flowery morn,
And Sheila like a field of corn,
And Melusina like the moan
Of water. And there's Joan, like Joan.

Little

By Dorothy Aldis

Illustration by Estelle Hollingworth

I am the sister of him
And he is my brother.
He is too little for us
To talk to each other.

So every morning I show him
My doll and my book;
But every morning he still is
Too little to look.

Little Blue Shoes

By Kate Greenaway

Little Blue Shoes
Mustn't go
Very far alone, you know.
Else she'll fall down,
Or, lose her way.
Fancy—what
Would mamma say?
Better put her little hand
Under sister's wise command.
When she's a little older grown
Blue Shoes may go quite alone.

The Postman

By Laura E. Richards

Illustration by George J. Reilly

Hey! the little postman,
  And his little dog,
Here he comes a-hopping
  Like a little frog;
Bringing me a letter,
  Bringing me a note,
In the little pocket
  Of his little coat.

Hey! the little postman,
  And his little bag,
Here he comes a-trotting
  Like a little nag;
Bringing me a paper,
  Bringing me a bill,
From the little grocer
  On the little hill.

Hey! the little postman,
  And his little hat,
Here he comes a-creeping
  Like a little cat.
What is that he's saying?
  "Naught for you today!"
Horrid little postman!
  I wish you'd go away!

In Go-Cart So Tiny

By Kate Greenaway

Illustration by the author

In go-cart so tiny
   My sister I drew;
And I've promised to draw her
   The wide world through.

We have not yet started—
   I own it with sorrow—
Because our trip's always
   Put off till to-morrow.

The Dentist

By Rose Fyleman

I'd like to be a dentist with a plate upon the door
And a little bubbling fountain in the middle of the floor;
With lots of tiny bottles all arranged in coloured rows
And a page-boy with a line of silver buttons down his
   clothes.

I'd love to polish up the things and put them every day
Inside the darling chest of drawers all tidily away;
And every Sunday afternoon when nobody was there
I should go riding up and down upon the velvet chair.

ILLUSTRATION BY WILLIAM COLRUS

look for a lovely thing

Night

By Sara Teasdale

Stars over snow,
    And in the west a planet
Swinging below a star—
    Look for a lovely thing and you will find it,
It is not far—
    It never will be far.

White Season

By Frances Frost

In the winter the rabbits match their pelts to the earth.
With ears laid back, they go
Blown through the silver hollow, the silver thicket,
Like puffs of snow.

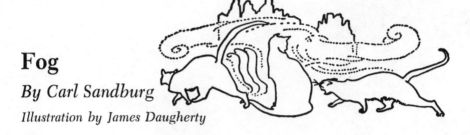

Fog

By Carl Sandburg

Illustration by James Daugherty

The fog comes
on little cat feet.

It sits looking
over harbor and city
on silent haunches
and then, moves on.

Autumn Fires

By Robert Louis Stevenson

Illustration by Jessie Wilcox Smith

In the other gardens
    And all up the vale,
From the autumn bonfires
    See the smoke trail!

Pleasant summer over
    And all the summer flowers,
The red fire blazes,
    The gray smoke towers.

Sing a song of seasons!
    Something bright in all!
Flowers in the summer,
    Fires in the fall!

Daffodils

By William Wordsworth

Illustration by H. J. Ford

I wander'd lonely as a cloud
That floats on high o'er vales and hills,
When all at once I saw a crowd,
A host of golden daffodils,
Beside the lake, beneath the trees
Fluttering and dancing in the breeze.

Continuous as the stars that shine
And twinkle on the milky way,
They stretch'd in never-ending line
Along the margin of a bay:
Ten thousand saw I at a glance
Tossing their heads in sprightly dance.

Where the Bee Sucks

By William Shakespeare

Illustration by George J. Reilly

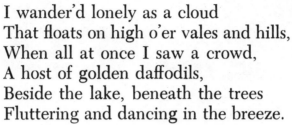

Where the bee sucks, there suck I;
In a cowslip's bell I lie;
There I couch when owls do cry.
On the bat's back I do fly
After summer, merrily:
Merrily, merrily shall I live now,
Under the blossom that hangs on the bough.

September Dusk

By Frances Frost

Illustration by Marguerite de Angeli

The soft puff-balls of thistles
And ground-pine turning gold
Are Summer's last word set upon
The glittering edge of cold.

Cycle

By Langston Hughes

Illustration by William Colrus

So many little flowers
Drop their tiny heads
But newer buds come to bloom
In their place instead.

I miss the little flowers
That have gone away.
But the newly budding blossoms
Are equally gay.

June Morning

By Frances Frost

Illustration by William Colrus

In the tangled grass of the sheep pasture,
Lying prone, I see
A grey grasshopper on a twig,
A green beetle teetering in a sun-glint,
Two ants fighting over a sliver of leaf,
A small bee swaying on a clover-blossom;
And my heart pounds softly against the turning earth.

It's Spring Again

By Ilo Orleans

Illustration by William Colrus

It's good to be back
   At the soil again;
Out in the garden
   To toil again.

It's good to plant
   And to sow again;
To dig and to rake
   And to hoe again.

A song of joy
   I sing again,
Because today,
   It's spring again.

The Moon's the North Wind's Cooky

By Vachel Lindsay

The Moon's the North Wind's cooky.
He bites it, day by day,
Until there's but a rim of scraps
That crumble all away.

The South Wind is a baker.
He kneads clouds in his den,
And bakes a crisp new moon that . . . greedy
North . . . Wind . . . eats . . . again!

Who Has Seen the Wind?

By Christina Rossetti

Illustration by George Richards

Who has seen the wind?
Neither I nor you:
But when the leaves hang trembling,
The wind is passing through.

Who has seen the wind?
Neither you nor I:
But when the trees bow down their heads
The wind is passing by.

Firefly

By Elizabeth Madox Roberts

Illustration by George J. Reilly

A little light is going by,
Is going up to see the sky,
A little light with wings.

I never could have thought of it,
To have a little bug all lit
And made to go on wings.

Dandelions

By Frances Frost

Illustration by George J. Reilly

Over the climbing meadows
Where swallow-shadows float,
These are the small gold buttons
On earth's green, windy coat.

105

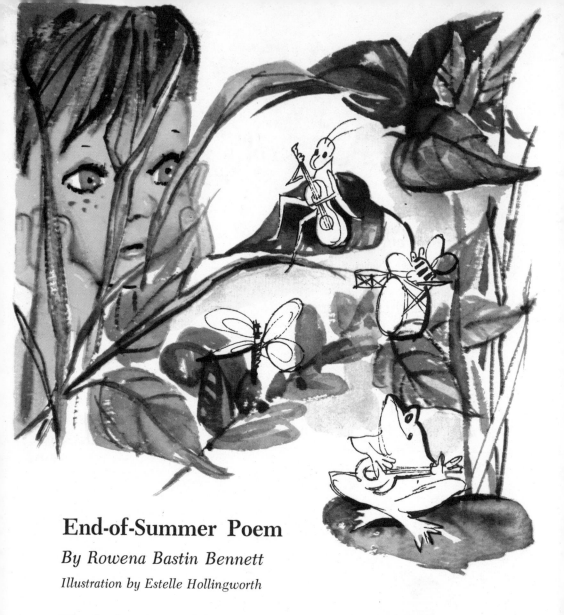

End-of-Summer Poem

By Rowena Bastin Bennett

Illustration by Estelle Hollingworth

The little songs of summer are all gone today.
The little insect instruments are all packed away:
The bumblebee's snare drum, the grasshopper's guitar,
The katydid's castanets—I wonder where they are.
The bullfrog's banjo, the cricket's violin,
The dragonfly's cello have ceased their merry din.
Oh, where is the orchestra? From harpist down to
    drummer
They've all disappeared with the passing of the summer.

The Animal Store

By Rachel Field

Illustration by Estelle Hollingworth

If I had a hundred dollars to spend,
    Or maybe a little more,
I'd hurry as fast as my legs would go
    Straight to the animal store.

I wouldn't say, "How much for this or that?"—
    "What kind of a dog is he?"
I'd buy as many as rolled an eye,
    Or wagged a tail at me!

I'd take the hound with the drooping ears
    That sits by himself alone;
Cockers and cairns and wobbly pups
    For to be my very own.

I might buy a parrot all red and green,
    And the monkey I saw before,
If I had a hundred dollars to spend,
    Or maybe a little more.

A Little Squirrel

By a child in a Winnetka nursery

Illustration by George J. Reilly

I saw a little squirrel,
Sitting in a tree;
He was eating a nut
And wouldn't look at me.

I Love Little Pussy

By Jane Taylor

Illustration by Marguerite de Angeli

I love little Pussy,
   Her coat is so warm,
And if I don't hurt her,
   She'll do me no harm;
So I'll not pull her tail,
   Nor drive her away,
But Pussy and I
   Very gently will play.

Chickadee

By Hilda Conkling

Illustration by George J. Reilly

The chickadee in the appletree
Talks all the time very gently.
He makes me sleepy.
I rock away to the sea-lights.
Far off I hear him talking
The way smooth bright pebbles
Drop into water . . .
Chick-a-*dee-dee-dee* . . .

Mice

By Rose Fyleman

Illustration by George J. Reilly

I think mice
Are rather nice.

Their tails are long,
Their faces small,
They haven't any
Chins at all.
Their ears are pink,
Their teeth are white,
They run about
The house at night.
They nibble things
They shouldn't touch
And no one seems
To like them much.

But *I* think mice
Are nice.

Trot Along, Pony

*By Marion Edey
and Dorothy Grider*

Illustration by William Colrus

Trot along, pony.
　　Late in the day,
Down by the meadow
　　Is the loveliest way.

The apples are rosy
　　And ready to fall.
The branches hang over
　　By Grandfather's wall.

But the red sun is sinking
　　Away out of sight.
The chickens are settling
　　Themselves for the night.

Your stable is waiting
　　And supper will come.
So turn again, pony,
　　Turn again home.

The Seals

By Dorothy Aldis

Illustration by William Colrus

The seals all flap
Their shining flips
And bounce balls on
Their nosey tips,
And beat a drum,
And catch a bar,
And wriggle with
How pleased they are.

The Monkeys

By Edith Osborne Thompson

Illustration by William Colrus

Sing a song of monkeys,
A jolly bunch of monkeys!
Leaping, swinging in their cages
Looking wise as ancient sages,
Nonchalant and carefree manner,
Nibbling peanuts or banana,
Every day is just another
To a monkey or his brother.

Sing a song of monkeys,
Happy, merry monkeys,
If you're ever tired or blue
I can tell you what to do!
Let the monkeys at the Zoo
Make a monkey out of you!

The Tree Toad

By Monica Shannon

Illustration by William Colrus

The Tree Toad is a creature neat,
With tidy rubbers on his feet.
Embarrassment is all he knows—
His color comes, his color goes.

The Tree Toad is quite small, at least,
Unless his girth has just increased.
The truth is always hard to seek,
For things are changing every week.

The Extraordinary Dog

By Nancy Byrd Turner

Illustration by Estelle Hollingworth

When Mother takes me calling
I say, "Oh, please and please
Let's visit with the folks who own
The funny Pekinese!"

I walk around him softly
Upon my tipsy-toes;
He sits so queer and solemn there,
So scornful in the nose.

I wonder very often:
Suppose I gave a sneeze,
A loud "Kerchoo!"—what would he do,
The pompous Pekinese?

The Ordinary Dog

By Nancy Byrd Turner

Illustration by Estelle Hollingworth

When Brother takes me walking
I cry, "Oh, hip, hooray!
We're sure to see the jolly pup
That joins us every day!"

His ears are raggy-shaggy;
His coat's a dusty brown;
He meets me like a cannon ball
And nearly knocks me down.

He tells me all his secrets,
With joyful jumpings-up.
I wish the pompous Pekinese
Could know the Jolly Pup!

The Hairy Dog

By Herbert Asquith

Illustration by William Colrus

My dog's so furry I've not seen
His face for years and years:
His eyes are buried out of sight,
I only guess his ears.

When people ask me for his breed,
I do not know or care:
He has the beauty of them all
Hidden beneath his hair.

Little Lady Wren

By Tom Robinson

Illustration by William Colrus

Little Lady Wren,
Hopping from bough to bough,
Bob your tail for me,
Bob it now!

You carry it so straight
Up in the air and when
You hop from bough to bough
You bob it now and then.

Why do you bob your tail,
Hopping from bough to bough,
And will not bob it when I say,
"Bob it now!"?

114

What Is It?

By Marie Louise Allen

Illustration by William Colrus

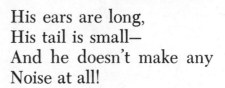

Tall ears,
Twinkly nose,
Tiny tail,
And—hop, he goes!

What *is* he—
Can you guess?
I feed him carrots
And watercress.

His ears are long,
His tail is small—
And he doesn't make any
Noise at all!

Tall ears,
Twinkly nose,
Tiny tail,
And—hop, he goes!

The Sea Gull Curves His Wings

By Elizabeth Coatsworth

Illustration by William Colrus

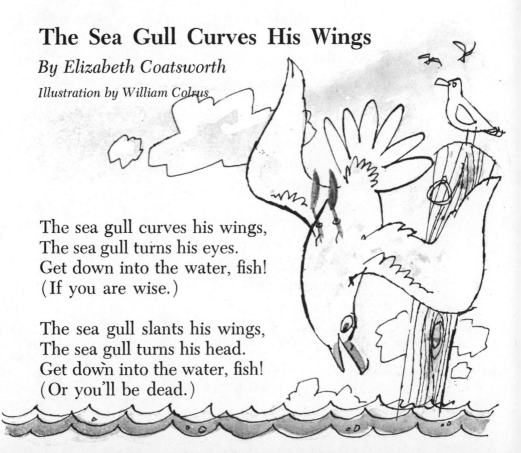

The sea gull curves his wings,
The sea gull turns his eyes.
Get down into the water, fish!
(If you are wise.)

The sea gull slants his wings,
The sea gull turns his head.
Get down into the water, fish!
(Or you'll be dead.)

A Kitten

By Eleanor Farjeon

Illustration by Estelle Hollingworth

He's nothing much but fur
And two round eyes of blue,
He has a giant purr
And a midget mew.

He darts and pats the air,
He starts and cocks his ear,
When there is nothing there
For him to see and hear.

He runs around in rings,
But why we cannot tell;
With sideways leaps he springs
At things invisible—

Then half-way through a leap
His startled eyeballs close,
And he drops off to sleep
With one paw on his nose.

The Backwards Boy

By Leslie Thompson

Illustration by Estelle Hollingworth

There's a funny thing in Funny Town—
It's a backwards boy who's upside down.
His feet are where his head should be;
And there is this that puzzles me:
If his head is always on the ground,
Is it flat instead of round?
And when he says "Yes," does he nod his head,
Or does he wiggle his toes instead?
When he wants some food to eat,
Does he take it with fingers or with feet?
I've pondered this with puzzled frown:
Does he button his overalls up—or down?

Alas, that we should never know
How the answers to these questions go!
We might as well just give it up.
This backwards boy—I made him up!

Hiding

By Dorothy Aldis

Illustration by George J. Reilly

I'm hiding, I'm hiding,
And no one knows where;
For all they can see is my
Toes and my hair.

And I just heard my father
Say to my mother—
"But darling, he must be
Somewhere or other;

Have you looked in the INKWELL?"
And Mother said, "Where?"
"In the INKWELL," said Father. But
I was not there.

Then "Wait!" cried my mother—
"I think that I see
Him under the carpet." But
It was not me.

118

"Inside the mirror's
A pretty good place,"
Said Father and looked, but saw
Only his face.

"We've hunted," sighed Mother,
"As hard as we could
And I AM so afraid that we've
Lost him for good."

Then I laughed out aloud
And I wiggled my toes
And Father said—"Look, dear,
I wonder if those

Toes could be Benny's.
There are ten of them. See?"
And they WERE so surprised to find
Out it was me!

Tired Tim

By *Walter de la Mare*

Illustration by George J. Reilly

Poor tired Tim! It's sad for him.
He lags the long bright morning through,
Ever so tired of nothing to do;
He moons and mopes the livelong day,
Nothing to think about, nothing to say;
Up to bed with his candle to creep,
Too tired to yawn, too tired to sleep:
Poor tired Tim! It's sad for him.

The Owl and the Pussy-Cat

By Edward Lear

Illustration by the author

The Owl and the Pussy-Cat went to sea
   In a beautiful pea-green boat;
They took some honey, and plenty of money
   Wrapped up in a five-pound note.
The Owl looked up to the moon above,
   And sang to a small guitar:
"O lovely Pussy! O Pussy, my love,
   What a beautiful Pussy you are,
      You are,
      You are!
   What a beautiful Pussy you are!"

Pussy said to the Owl: "You elegant fowl,
   How charmingly sweet you sing!
Oh, let us be married—too long we have tarried—
   But what shall we do for a ring?"
They sailed away for a year and a day
   To the land where the bong tree grows;
And there in a wood, a piggy-wig stood
   With a ring at the end of his nose,
      His nose,
      His nose.
   With a ring at the end of his nose.

"Dear Pig, are you willing to sell for one shilling
   Your ring?" Said the piggy, "I will."
So they took it away, and were married next day
   By the turkey who lives on the hill.
They dined upon mince and slices of quince,
   Which they ate with a runcible spoon,
And hand in hand on the edge of the sand
   They danced by the light of the moon,
      The moon,
      The moon.
   They danced by the light of the moon.

The End

By A. A. Milne

Illustration by Ernest H. Shepard

When I was One,
I had just begun.

When I was Two,
I was nearly new.

When I was Three,
I was hardly me.

When I was Four,
I was not much more.

When I was Five,
I was just alive.

But now I am Six, I'm as clever as clever.
So I think I'll be six now for ever and ever.

The Duel

By Eugene Field

Illustration by Warren Chappell

The gingham dog and the calico cat
Side by side on the table sat;
'Twas half-past twelve, and (what do you think!)
Nor one nor t'other had slept a wink!
  The old Dutch clock and the Chinese plate
  Appeared to know as sure as fate
There was going to be a terrible spat.
  (*I wasn't there; I simply state*
  What was told me by the Chinese plate!)

The gingham dog went "Bow-wow-wow!"
And the calico cat replied "Mee-ow!"
The air was littered, an hour or so,
With bits of gingham and calico,
  While the old Dutch clock in the chimney-place
  Up with its hands before its face,
For it always dreaded a family row!
  (*Now mind: I'm only telling you*
  What the old Dutch clock declares is true!)

The Chinese plate looked very blue,
And wailed, "Oh, dear! what shall we do?"
But the gingham dog and the calico cat
Wallowed this way and tumbled that,
  Employing every tooth and claw
  In the awfullest way you ever saw—
And, Oh! How the gingham and calico flew!
  (*Don't fancy I exaggerate!*
  I got my news from the Chinese plate!)

122

Next morning, where the two had sat,
They found no trace of dog or cat;
And some folks think unto this day
That burglars stole that pair away!
    But the truth about the cat and pup
    Is this: they ate each other up!
Now what do you really think of that!
    (*The old Dutch clock it told me so,*
    And that is how I came to know.)

The Frog

By Hilaire Belloc

Illustration by George J. Reilly

Be kind and tender to the Frog,
    And do not call him names,
As "Slimy-skin," or "Polly-wog,"
    Or likewise, "Uncle James,"

Or "Gape-a-grin," or "Toad-gone-wrong,"
    Or "Billy Bandy-knees":
The Frog is justly sensitive
    To epithets like these.

No animal will more repay
    A treatment kind and fair,
At least so lonely people say
Who keep a Frog (and, by the way,
    They are extremely rare).

The Yak

By Hilaire Belloc

As a friend to the children, commend me the Yak;
    You will find it exactly the thing;
It will carry and fetch, you can ride on its back,
    Or lead it about with a string.

The Tartar who dwells on the plains of Thibet
    (A desolate region of snow),
Has for centuries made it a nursery pet,
    And surely the Tartar should know!

Then tell your papa where the Yak can be got,
    And if he is awfully rich,
He will buy you the creature—or else he will not,
    (I cannot be positive which).

Holding Hands

By Lenore M. Link

Illustration by George J. Reilly

Elephants walking
Along the trails

Are holding hands
By holding tails.

Trunks and tails
Are handy things

When elephants walk
In Circus rings.

Elephants work
And elephants play

And elephants walk
And feel so gay.

And when they walk—
It never fails

They're holding hands
By holding tails.

there are elves and fairies yet

Children, Children, Don't Forget

By Dora Owen

Illustration by Irving Leveton

Children, children, don't forget
There are elves and fairies yet;
Where the knotty hawthorn grows
Look for prints of fairy toes.
Where the grassy rings are green
Moonlight dances shall be seen.
Watch and wait: O lucky you,
If you find a fairy shoe:
For a ransom he will pay,
Hobbling barefoot all the day,
Lay it on his mushroom seat,
Wish your wish and go your way
If your wish should be discreet
Never fear but he will pay.

A Fairy Went A-Marketing

By Rose Fyleman

Illustration by Irving Leveton

A Fairy went a-marketing—
   She bought a little fish;
She put it in a crystal bowl
   Upon a golden dish.
An hour she sat in wonderment
   And watched its silver gleam,
And then she gently took it up
   And slipped it in a stream.

A fairy went a-marketing—
   She bought a colored bird;
It sang the sweetest, shrillest song
   That ever she had heard.
She sat beside its painted cage
   And listened half the day,
And then she opened wide the door
   And let it fly away.

A fairy went a-marketing—
   She bought a winter gown
All stitched about with gossamer
   And lined with thistledown.
She wore it all afternoon
   With prancing and ·delight,
Then gave it to a little frog
   To keep him warm at night.

126

A fairy went a-marketing—
  She bought a gentle mouse
To take her tiny messages,
  To keep her tiny house.
All day she kept its busy feet
  Pit-patting to and fro
And then she kissed its silken ears,
  Thanked it, and let it go.

I Keep Three Wishes Ready

By Annette Wynne

Illustration by Irving Leveton

I keep three wishes ready,
Lest I should chance to meet,
Any day a fairy
Coming down the street.

I'd hate to have to stammer,
Or have to think them out,
For it's very hard to think things up
When a fairy is about.

And I'd hate to lose my wishes,
For fairies fly away,
And perhaps I'd never have a chance
On any other day.

So I keep three wishes ready
Lest I should chance to meet,
Any day a fairy
Coming down the street.

The Visitor

By Rachel Field

Illustration by the author

Feather-footed and swift as a mouse
An elfin gentleman came to our house;
Knocked his wee brown knuckles upon our door;
Bowed till his peaked cap swept the floor.
His shiny eyes blinked bright at me
As he asked for bread and a sup of tea,
"And plenty of honey, please," he said,
"For I'm fond of honey on my bread!"
Cross-legged he sat, with never a word,
But the old black kettle sang like a bird;
The red geranium burst in bloom
With the blaze of firelight in the room,
The china rattled on every shelf,
And the broom danced merrily all by itself.
Quick to the pantry then I ran
For to serve that elfin gentleman.
I brewed him tea, I brought him bread
With clover honey thickly spread.
One sip he took, one elfin bite,
But his ears they twitched with sheer delight.
He smacked his lips and he smiled at me.
"May good luck follow you, child!" said he.
He circled me round like a gay green flame
Before he was off the way he came,
Leaving me there in the kitchen dim,
Sighing and staring after him,
With the fire low and the tea grown cold,
And the moon through the window sharp and old,
Only before me—instead of honey,
That bread was golden with thick-spread money!

Have You Watched the Fairies?

By Rose Fyleman

Have you watched the fairies when the rain is done
Spreading out their little wings to dry them in the sun?
 I have, I have! Isn't it fun?

Have you heard the fairies all among the limes
Singing little fairy tunes to little fairy rhymes?
 I have, I have, lots and lots of times!

Have you seen the fairies dancing in the air,
And dashing up behind the stars to tidy up their hair?
 I have, I have; I've been there!

The Little Elfman

By John Kendrick Bangs

Illustration by Irving Leveton

I met a little Elfman once,
 Down where the lilies blow.
I asked him why he was so small,
 And why he didn't grow.

He slightly frowned, and with his eye
 He looked me through and through—
"I'm just as big for me," said he,
 "As you are big for you!"

The Goblin

By Rose Fyleman

Illustration by George J. Reilly

A goblin lives in *our* house, in *our* house, in *our* house,
A goblin lives in *our* house all the year round.
He bumps
And he jumps
And he thumps
And he stumps.
He knocks
And he rocks
And he rattles at the locks.
A goblin lives in *our* house, in *our* house, in *our* house,
A goblin lives in *our* house all the year round.

Brownie

By A. A. Milne

Illustration by Ernest H. Shepard

In a corner of the bedroom is a great big curtain,
    Someone lives behind it but I don't know who;
I think it is a Brownie, but I'm not quite certain.
    (Nanny isn't certain, too.)

I looked behind the curtain, but he went so quickly—
    Brownies never wait to say, "How do you do?"
They wriggle off at once because they're all so tickly.
    (Nanny says they're tickly, too.)

Could It Have Been a Shadow?

By Monica Shannon

Illustration by George J. Reilly

What ran under the rosebush?
    What ran under the stone?
Could it have been a shadow,
    Running away alone?

Maybe a fairy's shadow,
    Slipping away at dawn
To guard a gleaming pot of gold
    For a busy leprechaun.

The Fairies

By William Allingham

Illustration by Boris Artzybasheff

> Up the airy mountain
>   Down the rushy glen,
> We daren't go a-hunting,
>   For fear of little men;
> Wee folk, good folk,
>   Trooping all together;

Green jacket, red cap,
　And white owl's feather.
Down along the rocky shore
　Some make their home,
They live on crispy pancakes
　Of yellow tide-foam;
Some in the reeds
　Of the black mountain-lake,
With frogs for their watch-dogs,
　All night awake.

High on the hill-top
　The old King sits;
He is now so old and gray
　He's nigh lost his wits.
With a bridge of white mist
　Columbkill he crosses,
On his stately journeys
　From Slieveleague to Rosses;
Or going up with music,
　On cold starry nights,
To sup with the Queen,
　Of the gay Northern Lights.

They stole little Bridget
　For seven years long;
When she came down again
　Her friends were all gone.
They took her lightly back
　Between the night and morrow;
They thought she was fast asleep,
　But she was dead with sorrow.
They have kept her ever since
　Deep within the lake,
On a bed of flag leaves,
　Watching till she wake.

By the craggy hill-side,
  Through the mosses bare,
They have planted thorn trees
  For pleasure here and there.
Is any man so daring
  As dig them up in spite?
He shall find the thornies set
  In his bed at night.

Up the airy mountain,
  Down the rushy glen,
We daren't go a-hunting
  For fear of little men;
Wee folk, good folk,
  Trooping all together;
Green jacket, red cap,
  And white owl's feather.

Fairies

By Hilda Conkling

Illustration by William Colrus

I cannot see fairies.
I dream them.
There is no fairy can hide from me;
I keep on dreaming till I find him:
There you are, Primrose! I see you, Black Wing!

City Streets and Country Roads

By Eleanor Farjeon

Illustration by William Colrus

The city has streets—
    But the country has roads.
In the country one meets
    Blue carts with their loads
Of sweet-smelling hay,
    And mangolds, and grain:
Oh, take me away
    To the country again!

In the city one sees
    Big trams rattle by,
And the breath of the chimneys
    That blot out the sky,
And all down the pavements
    Stiff lamp-posts one sees—
But the country has hedgerows,
    The country has trees.

As sweet as the sun
    In the country is rain:
Oh, take me away
    To the country again!

135

Ducks' Ditty

By Kenneth Grahame

Illustration by William Colrus

All along the backwater,
Through the rushes' tall,
Ducks are a-dabbling,
Up tails all!

Ducks' tails, drakes' tails,
Yellow feet a-quiver,
Yellow bills all out of sight
Busy in the river.

Slushy green undergrowth
Where the roach swim—
Here we keep our larder,
Cool and full and dim.

Everyone for what he likes!
We like to be
Heads down, tails up,
Dabbling free!

High in the blue above
Swifts whirl and call—
We are down a-dabbling
Up tails all!

136

F Is the Fighting Firetruck

By Phyllis McGinley

Illustration by George J. Reilly

F is the fighting Firetruck
   That's painted a flaming red.
When the signals blast
It follows fast
   When the chief flies on ahead.
And buses pull to the curbing
   At the siren's furious cry,
For early or late
They have to wait
   When the Firetruck passes by.

Bridges

By Rhoda W. Bacmeister

Illustration by Irving Leveton

I like to look for bridges
Everywhere I go,
Where the cars go over
With water down below.

Standing by the railings
I watch the water slide
Smoothly under to the dark,
And out the other side.

City

By Langston Hughes

Illustration by George J. Reilly

In the morning the city
Spreads its wings
Making a song
In stone that sings.

In the evening the city
Goes to bed
Hanging lights
About its head.

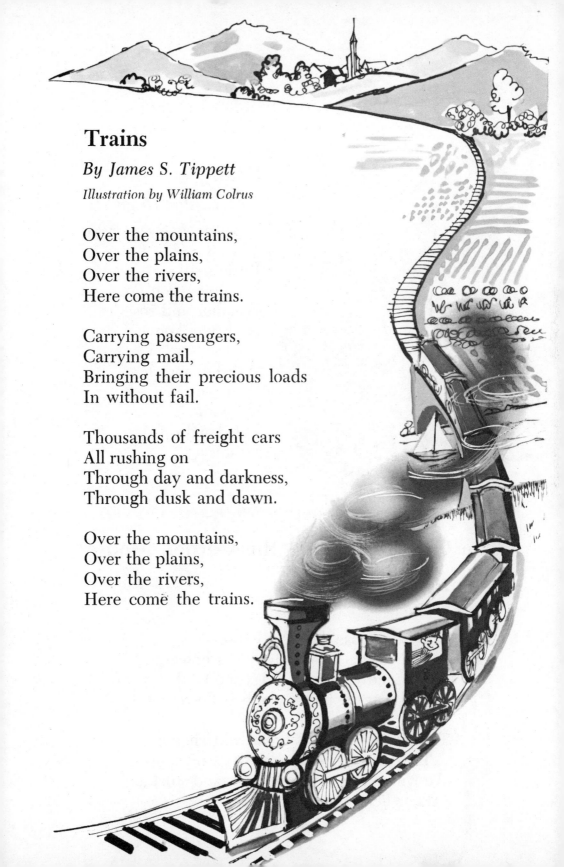

Trains

By James S. Tippett

Illustration by William Colrus

Over the mountains,
Over the plains,
Over the rivers,
Here come the trains.

Carrying passengers,
Carrying mail,
Bringing their precious loads
In without fail.

Thousands of freight cars
All rushing on
Through day and darkness,
Through dusk and dawn.

Over the mountains,
Over the plains,
Over the rivers,
Here come the trains.

Snail

By Langston Hughes

Illustration by George J. Reilly

Little snail,
Dreaming you go.
Weather and rose
Is all you know.

Weather and rose
Is all you see,
Drinking
The dewdrop's
Mystery.

The City Mouse and the Garden Mouse

By Christina Rossetti

The city mouse lives in a house—
   The garden mouse lives in a bower,
He's friendly with the frogs and toads,
   And sees the pretty plants in flower.

The city mouse eats bread and cheese—
   The garden mouse eats what he can;
We will not grudge him seeds and stocks,
   Poor little timid furry man.

Taking Off

Anonymous

Illustration by George J. Reilly

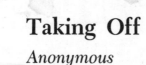

The airplane taxis down the field
And heads into the breeze,
It lifts its wheels above the ground,
It skims above the trees,
It rises high and higher
Away up toward the sun,
It's just a speck against the sky
—And now it's gone!

Butterfly

By Hilda Conkling

Illustration by George J. Reilly

As I walked through my garden
I saw a butterfly light on a flower.
His wings were pink and purple:
He spoke a small word . . .
It was *Follow!*
"I cannot follow,"
I told him,
"I have to go the opposite way."

Stop–Go

By Dorothy Baruch

Illustration by George J. Reilly

Automobiles
In
  a
    row
Wait to go
While the signal says:
    STOP

Bells ring
Tingaling
Red light's gone!
Green light's on!
Horns blow!
And the row
Starts to
    GO

The Cow

By Robert Louis Stevenson

The friendly cow all red and white,
　　I love with all my heart:
She gives me cream with all her might,
　　To eat with apple-tart.

She wanders lowing here and there,
　　And yet she cannot stray;
All in the pleasant open air,
　　The pleasant light of day;

And blown by all the winds that pass
　　And wet with all the showers,
She walks among the meadow grass
And eats the meadow flowers.

The Chickens

By Rose Fyleman

Illustration by George J. Reilly

What a fearful battle,
What a dreadful storm!
Five little chickens
Fighting for a worm.

When the worm had vanished
They all said—Peep—and then
The five little chickens
Were all good friends again.

Motor Cars

By Rowena Bastin Bennett

Illustration by Estelle Hollingworth

From a city window, 'way up high,
I like to watch the cars go by.
They look like burnished beetles black,
That leave a little muddy track
Behind them as they slowly crawl.
Sometimes they do not move at all
But huddle close with hum and drone
As though they feared to be alone.
They grope their way through fog and night
With the golden feelers of their light.

Good Night

By Victor Hugo

Illustration by Irving Leveton

Good night! Good night!
Far flies the night;
But still God's love
Shall flame above,
Making all bright.
Good night! Good night!

Sleep, Baby, Sleep!

Anonymous

Sleep, baby, sleep!
Thy father watches the sheep;
Thy mother is shaking the dream-land tree,
And down falls a little dream on thee:
Sleep, baby, sleep!

Sleep, baby, sleep!
The large stars are the sheep,
The wee stars are the lambs, I guess,
The fair moon is the shepherdess:
Sleep, baby, sleep!

145

Old Gaelic Lullaby

Anonymous

> Hush! the waves are rolling in,
> White with foam, white with foam;
> Father toils amid the din;
> But baby sleeps at home.
>
> Hush! the winds roar hoarse and deep—
> On they come, on they come!
> Brother seeks the wandering sheep;
> But baby sleeps at home.
>
> Hush! the rain sweeps o'er the knowes,
> Where they roam, where they roam;
> Sister goes to seek the cows;
> But baby sleeps at home.

Cradle Hymn

By Martin Luther

Away in a manger, no crib for a bed,
The little Lord Jesus laid down his sweet head.
The stars in the bright sky looked down where he lay—
The little Lord Jesus asleep on the hay.

The cattle are lowing, the baby awakes,
But little Lord Jesus, no crying he makes.
I love thee, Lord Jesus! look down from the sky,
And stay by my cradle till morning is nigh.

Before Sleeping

Anonymous

Illustration by Marguerite de Angeli

Matthew, Mark, Luke, and John,
Bless the bed that I lie on.
Before I lay me down to sleep
I give my soul to Christ to keep.
Four corners to my bed,
Four angels there aspread,
Two to foot, and two to head,
And four to carry me when I'm dead.
I go by sea, I go by land,
The Lord made me with His right hand.
If any danger come to me,
Sweet Jesus Christ deliver me.
He's the branch and I'm the flower,
Pray God send me a happy hour,
And if I die before I wake,
I pray that Christ my soul will take.

Wynken, Blynken, and Nod

By Eugene Field

Illustration by William Colrus

Wynken, Blynken, and Nod one night
   Sailed off in a wooden shoe—
Sailed on a river of crystal light,
   Into a sea of dew.
"Where are you going, and what do you wish?"
   The old moon asked the three.
"We have come to fish for the herring fish
   That live in this beautiful sea;
   Nets of silver and gold have we!"
      Said Wynken,
      Blynken,
      And Nod.

The old moon laughed and sang a song,
   As they rocked in the wooden shoe,
And the wind that sped them all night long
   Ruffled the waves of dew.
The little stars were the herring fish
   That lived in that beautiful sea—
"Now cast your nets wherever you wish—
   Never afeard are we!"
   So cried the stars to the fishermen three,
      Wynken,
      Blynken,
      And Nod.

All night long their nets they threw
   To the stars in the twinkling foam—
Then down from the skies came the wooden shoe,
   Bringing the fishermen home;
'Twas all so pretty a sail it seemed
   As if it could not be,
And some folks thought 'twas a dream they'd dreamed
   Of sailing that beautiful sea—
   But I shall name you the fishermen three:
      Wynken,
      Blynken,
      And Nod.

Wynken and Blynken are two little eyes,
   And Nod is a little head,
And the wooden shoe that sailed the skies
   Is a wee one's trundle-bed.
So shut your eyes while mother sings
   Of the wonderful sights that be,
And you shall see the beautiful things
   As you rock in the misty sea,
   Where the old shoe rocked the fishermen three—
      Wynken,
      Blynken,
      And Nod.

Sleep

By John Tabb

      When he is a little chap,
         We call him *Nap*.
      When he somewhat older grows,
         We call him *Doze*.
      When his age by hours we number,
         We call him *Slumber*.

Vespers

By A. A. Milne

Illustration by Irving Leveton

Little Boy kneels at the foot of the bed,
Droops on the little hands little gold head.
Hush! Hush! Whisper who dares!
Christopher Robin is saying his prayers.

God bless Mummy. I know that's right.
Wasn't it fun in the bath tonight?
The cold's so cold and the hot's so hot.
Oh! *God bless Daddy*—I quite forgot.

If I open my fingers a little bit more,
I can see Nanny's dressing-gown on the door
It's a beautiful blue, but it hasn't a hood.
Oh! *God bless Nanny and make her good.*

Mine has a hood, and I lie in bed,
And pull the hood right over my head,
And I shut my eyes, and I curl up small,
And nobody knows that I'm there at all.

Oh! *Thank you, God, for a lovely day.*
And what was the other I had to say?
I said "Bless Daddy," so what can it be?
Oh! Now I remember. *God bless me.*

Little Boy kneels at the foot of the bed,
Droops on the little hands little gold head.
Hush! Hush! Whisper who dares!
Christopher Robin is saying his prayers.

Lullaby of an Infant Chief

By Sir Walter Scott

Illustration by William Colrus

O hush thee, my baby, thy sire was a knight,
Thy mother a lady both lovely and bright;
The woods and the glens from the tower which we see,
They all are belonging, dear baby, to thee.

O, fear not the bugle, though loudly it blows,
It calls but the warders that guard thy repose;
Their bows would be bended, their blades would be red,
Ere the step of a foeman draws near to thy bed.

O, hush thee, my baby, the time will soon come
When thy sleep shall be broken by trumpet and drum;
Then hush thee, my darling, take rest while you may,
For strife comes with manhood, and waking with day.

STORIES FOR FUN

The ABC Bunny

BY WANDA GÁG

Illustrations by the author

A for Apple, big and red

B for Bunny, snug a-bed

C for Crash!

D for Dash!

E for Elsewhere in a flash

F for Frog—he's fat and funny

"Looks like rain," says he to Bunny

G for Gale!

H for Hail!

Hippy-hop goes Bunny's tail

I for Insects here and there

J for Jay with jaunty air

K for Kitten, catnip-crazy

L for Lizard—look how lazy

M for Mealtime—munch, munch, munch!

M-m-m! these greens are good for lunch

N for Napping in a Nook

O for Owl with bookish look

P for prickly Porcupine

Pins and needles on his spine

Q for Quail

R for Rail

S for Squirrel Swishy-tail

T for Tripping back to Town

U for Up and Up-side-down

V for View

Valley too

W "We welcome you!"

X   for eXit—off, away!

That's enough for us today

Y   for You, take one last look

Z   for Zero, close the book!

For an alphabet book with a lively story read The Hullabaloo A B C, by Beverly Cleary, published by Henry Z. Walck, Inc. A fun-filled counting book is Dancing in the Moon, by Fritz Eichenberg, published by Harcourt, Brace & World.

Scaredy Cat

BY PHYLLIS KRASILOVSKY

Illustrations by Ninon

ONCE there was a little black kitten.
He was as black as a Halloween night.
As black as coal.
As black as a deep dark hole.
As black as windows when nobody's home.
As black as Daddy's shoes.

He was as black as his mother who was a big black cat. But he did have green eyes, and it's a good thing he did, because they were a warning to anyone who thought he was a piece of black fur that might be stepped on!

This little black kitten at first belonged to an old lady. But since she had no room for him in her house, she gave him to two little children who wanted a pet.

How happy they were to have him! They squeezed him all the way home, but the poor little kitten didn't know they were loving him and he was frightened.

When they got to their house he ran right under the couch and wouldn't come out.

The children wanted to call him Blacky, or Spooky, or Midnight, or Halloween, or some name like that, but he looked too scared to HAVE a name! He looked too scared to be called anything but Scaredy Cat. So that was what they named him—SCAREDY CAT.

Scaredy Cat was scared of everything.
He was scared of footsteps.
He was scared of the children who wanted to hold him.
He was scared of the children's mother who wanted to
    feed him.
He was scared of the children's father who had a big
    deep voice.

He was scared of the daytime and hid under the couch almost all day long. Sometimes he hid under one of the beds. The children were always crawling on their hands and knees trying to coax him to come out. But he just wouldn't. He was too scared.

He was scared of the nighttime, too. You could tell by
the way his green eyes shone in the dark, looking big
and frightened.

He was scared of the vacuum cleaner and the carpet
    sweeper and the broom.
He was scared when the dog next door barked at him
    through the window.

He was scared of EVERYTHING! And when he was
scared, his back arched like half a circle and his tail
stood straight up in the air like a black flag.

The children were very sad for they wanted the kitten
to love them. They tried to whisper and to walk softly
and to be gentle, but no matter what they did, Scaredy
Cat huddled against the wall with his back arched and
his tail up like a flag.

Their mother said, "Don't worry. As soon as he gets used to us he won't be scared any more."

One day the family went for a ride in their car and left Scaredy Cat all alone in the house. It seemed very quiet with everyone gone and Scaredy Cat poked his head out from under the couch to see what was the matter.

No one reached out to hold him. No one tried to feed him. There were no footsteps to scare him. So he poked his head out a little farther and looked all around. Sunbeams were dancing on the rug. He reached his paw out and tried to catch one. And then he tried to catch another! Soon he was dancing all over the living room trying to catch the sunbeams. This was FUN!

Scaredy Cat walked around the house carefully examining things. He was scared at first when he saw the vacuum cleaner in the hall. But it didn't move or make a noise at all. He walked slowly around it and even rubbed his back against it!

Then he looked outside the window and saw the dog next door. But he didn't run to hide the way he usually did. "Meeeeeow!" he said, and made frightening faces at the dog through the window.

Scaredy Cat found a saucerful of milk that the children's mother had left for him on the kitchen floor. He lapped it up with his pink tongue. How good it tasted!

Then he found a ball in the living room. He put his paw out to touch it and it rolled. He put his paw out again and it rolled some more. A fine game! Soon he was chasing the ball all over the house.

When Scaredy Cat got tired of playing, he tried out all the chairs in the living room looking for the most comfortable one. He decided Mother's chair was the softest one and soon he was all curled up on it. He was lonesome now and wished the children were home to love him. Then he went to sleep.

Soon the family came home. When Mother saw Scaredy Cat she said, "My goodness, I left my black fur muff on the big chair!"

But when she went to pick it up, Scaredy Cat opened his big green eyes and Mother saw it wasn't her muff at all! "Why you sleepy little Scaredy Cat!" she said, "You're not hiding from us! You're not scared any more, are you?"

Scaredy Cat only purred. He was glad to have the family come home and love him. Now that he had looked around and had such fun and seen how nice everything was, he liked his new home. Maybe some OTHER cat would be scared . . .

But not SCAREDY CAT!

Other books by Phyllis Krasilovsky that you will love are The Cow Who Fell in the Canal, *and* Very Little Girl, *both published by Doubleday & Company, Inc.*

The Wide-Awake Owl

BY LOUIS SLOBODKIN

Illustrations by the author

OLGA, the little owl, could not sleep. She was wide awake.

She tried to sleep, like all owls do, during the daytime. But she could not sleep a wink.

She tried sleeping with only one eye shut the way owls do.

Then she tried sleeping with the other eye shut. And at last she shut both eyes as tight as she could for a long, long, time. But it was no use. The little owl could not sleep. She was wide awake.

"What shall I do?" she said to herself. "I must sleep. Everyone has to sleep."

At last Olga decided to ask the wise old owl who lived nearby what to do. She flew over to the oak tree where the wise old owl lived.

The wise old owl, with only one eye shut, was sound asleep in the bright sunlight.

"Excuse me," said Olga gently. The wise old owl kept right on sleeping.

"Excuse me," said Olga again in a louder voice.

But the old owl kept right on sleeping.

"EXCUSE me!" screeched Olga as loud as she could.

"WHO . . . WHO . . . What's the matter?" said the wise old owl as he woke up.

"I can't sleep," said Olga.

"Well I CAN!" said the wise old owl and went right back to sleep again.

"Please help me," said Olga. "What shall I do? I can't sleep a wink."

The wise old owl grumbled and half-opened his eyes. "Did you try sleeping with one eye shut?" he asked. "Yes," said Olga.

"Try it again . . . right now!" said the wise old owl.

Again Olga shut one eye tight and tried to sleep. The wise old owl watched her a moment.

"Asleep yet?" he asked.

"No," said Olga.

"Try sleeping with the other eye shut."

Olga tried that too and after another moment the old owl asked:

"Asleep yet?"

"No," said Olga.

The old owl thought a few minutes.

"Well then," he said . . . "I don't like to advise this because owls do not usually sleep this way . . . but try sleeping with both eyes shut."

Olga shut both her eyes as tight as she could. The wise old owl watched her carefully for two long minutes. Then he shouted:

"ASLEEP YET?"

Olga's eyes popped open. She sadly shook her head.

"Well, there's no more I can do for you," said the wise old owl. And he shut one eye again and promptly went back to sleep.

Olga flew back to her own tree and perched on a branch.

"Dear me, what shall I do? What shall I do?" said Olga.

"What do you want to do?" asked somebody.

Olga turned her head. It was a friendly chipmunk who lived higher up in her tree.

"I want to sleep," said Olga, "but I can't."

"Did you try sleeping all curled up like this?" asked the friendly chipmunk. "This is the way I sleep."

The chipmunk curled up like a tight ball of fur and fell asleep at once.

Olga curled up as best she could, closed her eyes . . . and she almost fell off the branch.

"I can't sleep that way," she said.

Just then a young possum came down the tree.

"Of course you can't sleep like that," said the possum. "I can't either. Try sleeping like this. I always do."

The possum curled his long tail firmly around the branch of the tree and hung head down. Then he smiled gently, closed his eyes and in a flash he was sound asleep.

Since Olga had no long curly tail, she took a firm grip on the branch with her claws and let herself tumble forward until she hung upside down too.

She closed one eye.

Then she closed the other eye.

Then she closed both eyes tight. She tried very hard to sleep but she could not.

And again she opened her eyes.

"I can't sleep that way either," she said.

A bluejay who had been watching said, "Of course you can't. No bird can sleep like that. Here, try sleeping this way."

The bluejay tucked her head under her wing and in no time at all she was fast asleep.

Olga tried tucking her head under her wing. But her neck was so short and her head so big her wing hardly covered one eye.

"Dear me, dear me, will I ever sleep again," sighed Olga.

A robin who had been flying by stopped and sat on a twig.

"I have a good way to sleep," said the robin. "Try standing on one leg on a springy twig like this. It will rock you to sleep. Watch me."

The robin stood on one leg and the twig rocked up and down once . . . twice and before anyone could count to three fast . . . the robin was asleep.

Olga looked along the branch where she stood until she saw another little twig. She hopped onto the twig and stood on one leg. Then she bounced to make the twig rock. She bounced once . . . then twice, and on the third bounce, because Olga was too heavy for the twig . . . the twig broke!

And Olga went crashing down through the branches of the tree! And she could not get her wings spread in time to keep from bumping on the ground when she landed.

A little thrush flew down from somewhere.

"What happened?" he cried. "Find something good to eat?"

"I wasn't looking for something to eat," said Olga. "I was trying to fall asleep."

"That's a funny way to fall asleep," said the thrush— "falling down through a tree that way."

By this time the little animals and birds who had been showing Olga how to go to sleep were awakened by the sound of her fall and they all rushed down from the tree.

"Are you hurt?" they cried.

Olga shook her head. "No, I'm not . . . And I still haven't been able to go to sleep."

Then Olga quickly explained to the thrush all the ways she had tried to go to sleep. . . . Like the chipmunk all curled up and like the bluejay with her head tucked under her wing and like the robin standing one-legged on a swinging twig. . . .

"Oh," said the thrush, "so you want to GO to sleep! I know the best way to GO to sleep. . . . Come on back up into the tree."

So Olga and the other birds and animals went back up into the tree with the thrush.

The sun was just beginning to set and the woods were beginning to darken.

"Now," said the thrush, when they were all settled, "this is the best time of the day to go to sleep. And this is the best way to go to sleep . . . Go to sleep singing. Sing a low, sweet song and you will go to sleep in a jiffy."

Then the thrush began to sing a low, sweet song and all the others joined in:

And Olga and the other birds and animals never learned the end of the thrush's song because she and all the others fell fast asleep.

From then on, whenever Olga the little owl was wide awake and found it hard to go to sleep, she half-closed her eyes and sang softly to herself the thrush's song . . . or as much of the song as she knew.

And she always fell asleep before she came to the end of the song so she never really had to know how it ended.

Other stories that will make you love bedtime are Goodnight Moon, by Margaret Wise Brown, and Bedtime for Frances, by Russell Hoban, both published by Harper & Brothers, and Switch on the Night, by Ray Bradbury, published by Pantheon Books, Inc.

The Circus Baby

BY MAUD AND MISKA PETERSHAM

Illustrations by the authors

ONCE there was a Mother Elephant who lived with
a circus. Her baby marched beside her in every parade.
Sometimes when the sun was very very hot, the tired
little elephant would stop short. He would not take
another step. For Mother Elephant this was most em-
barrassing. She had to pick him up with her long trunk
and carry him. But all in all Mother Elephant was very
proud of her baby.

Mother Elephant was friendly with all the people in
the circus. Best of all she loved Zombie the clown and
his family. She spent much of the time with her head
poked through the flap of Zombie's tent.

Her tiny black eyes saw everything. Her ears were
so big she could hear everything.

She liked to watch the clowns when they were eating. Mr. Clown sat at one end of the table with Mrs. Clown at the other end. The baby clown, with a pretty bib tied around his neck, sat in a high-chair in the middle.

Mother Elephant decided that her baby must learn to eat properly just as the circus people did.

One day when Mr. and Mrs. Clown were still in the big circus tent, Mother Elephant awakened her child. "Shush," she said to the sleepy baby. "Come with me, but don't make any noise."

The little elephant took hold of his mother's tail. Stepping softly, they made their way across the circus grounds. They tiptoed right up to the clowns' empty tent.

After Mother Elephant and her baby were both inside the tent, she was surprised at how little space there was. But she was very careful not to break anything. She held her big flappy ears close to her head and she made herself just as small as possible.

She sat her baby up on Mr. Clown's stool. The baby clown's high-chair was much too small.

She tied Mrs. Clown's apron around his neck for a bib. In front of him she placed a bowl of beans and the largest spoon she could find.

Now the little elephant always tried to do what his mother wanted. But he just could not manage that spoon.

He tried with one foot and then with another. His trunk was always in the way. At last he held the spoon with his trunk.

The beans spilled all over the apron-bib and all over Mrs. Clown's nice clean tablecloth. Mother Elephant coaxed him to try once more.

He put his foot out to hold the bowl. The bowl tipped and clattered off the table.

Then Mr. Clown's stool gave a loud creak and split into many pieces. The Baby Elephant went tumbling to the floor.

Just at that moment they heard Mr. and Mrs. Clown coming home. Poor Mother Elephant!

She was so excited, she reared straight up.

The tent collapsed right over her head and right over the little elephant. Then the surprised Mr. and Mrs. Clown saw their tent

walk

away.

The next day Mr. and Mrs. Clown were given a beautiful new tent. Mother Elephant promised never to go into it.

And she said to her baby, "My child, you do not have to learn to eat as the circus people do because, after all, *you* are an ELEPHANT."

More favorite picture books by the Petershams are The Rooster Crows—*an American Mother Goose collection, and* An American ABC, *both published by The Macmillan Company.*

Angus and the Cat

BY MARJORIE FLACK

Illustrations by the author

EACH day as Angus grew older he grew

L O N G E R

but not much

HIGHER.

Scottie dogs grow that way.

Now as Angus grew older and longer he learned

MANY THINGS.

He learned it is best to stay in one's own yard

and FROGS can jump

but NOT to jump after them

and BALLOONS go POP!

Angus also learned NOT to lie on the sofa and NOT to take SOMEBODY ELSE'S food and things like that.

But there was SOMETHING outdoors Angus was very curious about but had NEVER learned about, and that was CATS.

The leash was TOO short.

Until one day WHAT should Angus find INDOORS lying on the SOFA but a strange little CAT!
Angus came closer—
The CAT sat up.
Angus
came
closer—

UP jumped the CAT onto the arm of the sofa. Angus came closer and—

SISS-S-S-S-S-S!!!

That little CAT boxed
Angus's ears!
Woo-oo-oof—Woo-oo-oof!
said Angus.

UP jumped the CAT onto the sofa back, up to the mantel—and Angus was not

HIGH

enough to reach her!

But at lunch time down she came to try and take Angus's food—though not for long.
UP she jumped onto the table, and Angus was not

HIGH

enough to reach her!

At nap time there she was sitting in Angus's own special square of sunshine—

WASHING HER FACE,

though not for long.

UP she jumped onto the window sill, and Angus was not

HIGH

enough to reach her!

For THREE whole days Angus was very busy chasing THAT CAT, but she always went up out of reach until on the fourth day he chased her

UP-THE-STAIRS

into the

BEDROOM

and she was completely

GONE!

Angus looked under the bed—no CAT was there. Angus looked out of the window into his yard, into the next yard—no CAT could he see

ANYWHERE.

Angus went

DOWN-THE-STAIRS

He looked on the sofa—no CAT was there. He looked on the mantel—no CAT was there. Angus looked on the table and on the window sills—no CAT was indoors ANYWHERE.

So Angus was ALL-ALONE.

There was no CAT to box his ears. There was no CAT to take his food. There was no CAT to sit in his sunshine. There was no CAT to chase away. So Angus was

ALL-ALONE.

and he had

NOTHING-TO-DO!

Angus missed the little CAT. But—at lunch time he heard this noise:

P U R R R R R —

and there she was again.

And Angus knew
 and the CAT knew
  that Angus knew
   that—
Angus was GLAD the cat came back!

Angus, that amusing Scotch terrier, has more fun in the country in Marjorie Flack's Angus and the Ducks, and Angus Lost, both published by Doubleday.

Kiki Dances

BY CHARLOTTE STEINER

Illustrations by the author

KIKI was a little girl who liked to dress up and pretend. Most of the time she pretended she was

a grown-up lady.

But when she went to the rodeo she decided she would rather be a cowboy. That was all right until her dog Rover decided he did not want to be

a bucking bronco.

Then Kiki went to a magic show. She watched the magician put eggs into his hat and bring out live rabbits and live birds. It looked easy but—

When Kiki tried to be a magician at home for her dolls, the eggs did not turn into rabbits and birds.

They broke.

And nobody but Muffy the cat liked *that*.

When Kiki went to the circus, she liked the tightrope walker best of all. At home she was sure she could walk a tightrope, but the chair kept falling down.

Poor Kiki!

Then Kiki's mother took her to the ballet. Kiki loved the dancers in their beautiful costumes. She imagined just how she would look in a fluffy ballet skirt with a crown on her head.

Kiki could hardly wait to get home so she could dress up and be a ballet dancer.

But somehow she didn't look at all like a dancer. She was very sad until her mother told her she could go to ballet school and learn to dance.

But when Kiki went to dancing school she was surprised. No one was dressed in pretty costumes. Instead, the other little girls wore funny tights or jerseys called leotards.

The piano player wasn't dressed up, either,

Nor even the dancing teacher. And then right away Kiki was so busy learning to dance that she forgot all about the pretty costumes. *Everything was fun—*

Doing *pliés* at the bar—And learning the positions, and practicing the positions at home even when she was

> brushing her teeth,
>   or drinking water,
>   or getting a book.

Learning to be ballet dancer was so much fun that Kiki didn't think about playing dress up or pretend.

Then one day she got an invitation to a party. The invitation said, *"Come dressed up as somebody you'd like to be."*

At once Kiki knew what costume she wanted to wear. Her mother started making it that very day.

The party was great fun. All of Kiki's friends were there.

Bobby came as a cowboy, Betsy was a witch, and somebody was a ghost, Peter was a clown, Ann was a little Dutch girl, and Bill was a cook.

But Kiki was the best surprise of all, because Kiki was dressed as a ballet dancer,

And Kiki danced!

Kiki has many delightful times in a series of books about her, written by Charlotte Steiner and published by Doubleday. Among these are Kiki and Muffy, Kiki Goes to Camp, Kiki is an Actress, and Kiki Loves Music.

The Box with Red Wheels

BY MAUD AND MISKA PETERSHAM

Illustrations by the authors

UNDER a tree in the garden stood a strange looking box with red wheels.

The gate leading into the garden was wide open.

The curious animals marched through the open gate and walked straight up to the box to find out what it was.

First the cow looked in. She looked and she looked. "Moo! Moo!" she called. "What's this? Moo-oo-oo-oo!"

Next came the little fat pony and he looked down into the box. But then he shook his head. He didn't know.

Up hopped a rabbit. Hoppity Hop. He jumped so high that he flopped right into the box. Then out he jumped. He did not know what it was, in that box with the bright red wheels.

Mother Duck waddled up with her four little ducks.
She stretched out her long neck until she could see.

"Shush! —   Quack, Quack!"
she said to her four ducklings.
"S-H-U-S-H!
Whatever it is, it is sleeping.
Quack, Quack,
Q-U-A-C-K!"

"Meow! Meow! Meow! Meow! Let me look!" cried the
fuzzy black kitten. And she climbed up and peeked over
the edge. But all she said was,
"Purr! Purr! Purr-r-r-r!" Then
around and around the box she
walked purring softly.

A little dog with long curly ears came running into the garden. "Bow Wow! What's all the fuss?" he barked. He looked very wise. He knew, so he sat down close beside the box.

Suddenly up out of the box, popped—a little round head. It was a baby.

"Mama! Mama!" the baby called. "What's this? And what's this?" And the curious baby looked from one friendly animal to the other.

Mother came running from the house. She waved her apron and she shouted "Shoo! Shoo! Shoo! S-H-O-O!"

All the animals ran out of the garden.

Mother carefully closed the gate. The animals were very, very sad. They wanted to play with the baby.

Mother looked at the sad baby.

She looked at the very, very, very sad animals.

and then——

Quickly she opened the gate and let them all come into the garden again.

The gentle cow, the friendly pony, the shy rabbit, the purring kitten, the dog with the curly ears, Mother duck, and her four little ducks all played together with that baby in the garden.

If you have enjoyed reading about the farm animals in this story, you will want to read the adventures of the animals in Cock-A-Doodle-Doo, by Berta & Elmer Hader, published by The Macmillan Company, and Will Spring Be Early? Or Will Spring Be Late? by Crockett Johnson, published by Crowell.

The Velveteen Rabbit

BY MARGERY WILLIAMS

Illustrations by William Nicholson

THERE was once a velveteen rabbit, and in the beginning he was really splendid. He was fat and bunchy, as a rabbit should be; his coat was spotted brown and white, he had real thread whiskers, and his ears were lined with pink sateen. On Christmas morning, when he sat wedged in the top of the Boy's stocking, with a sprig of holly between his paws, the effect was charming.

There were other things in the stocking, nuts and oranges and a toy engine, and chocolate almonds and a clockwork mouse, but the Rabbit was quite the best of all. For at least two hours the Boy loved him, and then Aunts and Uncles came to dinner, and there was a great rustling of tissue paper and unwrapping of parcels, and in the excitement of looking at all the new presents the Velveteen Rabbit was forgotten.

For a long time he lived in the toy cupboard or on the nursery floor, and no one thought very much about him. He was naturally shy, and being only made of velveteen, some of the more expensive toys quite snubbed him. The mechanical toys were very superior, and looked down upon every one else; they were full of modern ideas, and pretended they were real. The model boat, who had lived through two seasons and lost most of his paint, caught the tone from them and never

The Velveteen Rabbit, by Margery Williams, is published by Doubleday & Company, Inc.

missed an opportunity of referring to his rigging in technical terms. The Rabbit could not claim to be a model of anything, for he didn't know that real rabbits existed; he thought they were all stuffed with sawdust like himself, and he understood that sawdust was quite out-of-date and should never be mentioned in modern circles. Even Timothy, the jointed wooden lion, who was made by the disabled soldiers, and should have had broader views, put on airs and pretended he was connected with Government. Between them all the poor little Rabbit was made to feel himself very insignificant and commonplace, and the only person who was kind to him at all was the Skin Horse.

The Skin Horse had lived longer in the nursery than any of the others. He was so old that his brown coat was bald in patches and showed the seams underneath, and most of the hairs in his tail had been pulled out to string bead necklaces. He was wise, for he had seen a long succession of mechanical toys arrive to boast and swagger, and by-and-by break their mainsprings and pass away, and he knew that they were only toys, and would never turn into anything else. For nursery magic is very strange and wonderful, and only those playthings that are old and wise and experienced like the Skin Horse understand all about it.

"What is REAL?" asked the Rabbit one day, when they were lying side by side near the nursery fender, before Nana came to tidy the room. "Does it mean having things that buzz inside you and a stick-out handle?"

"Real isn't how you are made," said the Skin Horse. "It's a thing that happens to you. When a child loves you for a long, long time, not just to play with, but REALLY loves you, then you become Real."

"Does it hurt?" asked the Rabbit.

"Sometimes," said the Skin Horse, for he was always

truthful. "When you are Real you don't mind being hurt."

"Does it happen all at once, like being wound up," he asked, "or bit by bit?"

"It doesn't happen all at once," said the Skin Horse. "You become. It takes a long time. That's why it doesn't often happen to people who break easily, or have sharp edges, or who have to be carefully kept. Generally, by the time you are Real, most of your hair has been loved off, and your eyes drop out and you get loose in the joints and very shabby. But these things don't matter at all, because once you are Real you can't be ugly, except to people who don't understand."

"I suppose *you* are Real?" said the Rabbit. And then he wished he had not said it, for he thought the Skin Horse might be sensitive. But the Skin Horse only smiled.

"The Boy's Uncle made me Real," he said. "That was a great many years ago; but once you are Real you can't become unreal again. It lasts for always."

The Rabbit sighed. He thought it would be a long time before this magic called Real happened to him. He longed to become Real, to know what it felt like; and yet the idea of growing shabby and losing his eyes and whiskers was rather sad. He wished that he could become it without these uncomfortable things happening to him.

There was a person called Nana who ruled the nursery. Sometimes she took no notice of the playthings lying about, and sometimes, for no reason whatever, she went swooping about like a great wind and hustled them away in cupboards. She called this "tidying up," and the playthings all hated it, especially the tin ones. The Rabbit didn't mind it so much, for wherever he was thrown he came down soft.

One evening, when the Boy was going to bed, he couldn't find the china dog that always slept with him. Nana was in a hurry, and it was too much trouble to hunt for china dogs at bedtime, so she simply looked about her, and seeing that the toy cupboard door stood open, she made a swoop.

"Here," she said, "take your old Bunny! He'll do to

sleep with you!" And she dragged the Rabbit out by one ear, and put him into the Boy's arms.

That night, and for many night after, the Velveteen Rabbit slept in the Boy's bed. At first he found it rather uncomfortable, for the Boy hugged him very tight, and sometimes he rolled over on him, and sometimes he pushed him so far under the pillow that the Rabbit could scarcely breathe. And he missed, too, those long moonlight hours in the nursery, when all the house was silent, and his talks with the Skin Horse. But very soon he grew to like it, for the Boy used to talk to him, and made nice tunnels for him under the bedclothes that he said were like the burrows the real rabbits lived in. And they had splendid games together, in whispers, when Nana had gone away to her supper and left the nightlight burning on the mantelpiece. And when the Boy dropped off to sleep, the Rabbit would snuggle down close under his little warm chin and dream, with the Boy's hands clasped close round him all night long.

And so time went on, and the little Rabbit was very happy—so happy that he never noticed how his beautiful velveteen fur was getting shabbier and shabbier, and his tail coming unsewn, and all the pink rubbed off his nose where the Boy had kissed him.

Spring came, and they had long days in the garden, for wherever the Boy went the Rabbit went too. He had rides in the wheelbarrow, and picnics on the grass, and lovely fairy huts built for him under the raspberry canes behind the flower border. And once, when the Boy was called away suddenly to go out to tea, the Rabbit was left out on the lawn until long after dusk, and Nana had to come and look for him with the candle because the Boy couldn't go to sleep unless he was there. He was wet through with the dew and quite earthy from diving into the burrows the Boy had made for him in the flower bed, and Nana grumbled as she rubbed him off with a corner of her apron.

"You must have your old Bunny!" she said. "Fancy all that fuss for a toy!"

The Boy sat up in bed and stretched out his hands.

"Give me my Bunny!" he said. "You mustn't say that. He isn't a toy. He's REAL!"

When the little Rabbit heard that he was happy, for

he knew that what the Skin Horse had said was true at last. The nursery magic had happened to him, and he was a toy no longer. He was Real. The Boy himself had said it.

That night he was almost too happy to sleep, and so much love stirred in his little sawdust heart that it almost burst. And into his boot-button eyes, that had long ago lost their polish, there came a look of wisdom and beauty, so that even Nana noticed it next morning when she picked him up, and said, "I declare if that old Bunny hasn't got quite a knowing expression!"

That was a wonderful Summer!

Near the house where they lived there was a wood, and in the long June evenings the Boy liked to go there after tea to play. He took the Velveteen Rabbit with him, and before he wandered off to pick flowers, or play at brigands among the trees, he always made the Rabbit a little nest somewhere among the bracken, where he would be quite cosy, for he was a kind-hearted little boy and he liked Bunny to be comfortable. One evening, while the Rabbit was lying there alone, watching the ants that ran to and fro between his velvet paws in the grass, he saw two strange beings creep out of the tall bracken near him.

They were rabbits like himself, but quite furry and brand-new. They must have been very well made, for their seams didn't show at all, and they changed shape in a queer way when they moved; one minute they were long and thin and the next minute fat and bunchy, instead of always staying the same like he did. Their feet padded softly on the ground, and they crept quite close to him, twitching their noses, while the Rabbit stared hard to see which side the clockwork stuck out, for he knew that people who jump generally have something to wind them up. But he couldn't see it. They were evidently a new kind of rabbit altogether.

They stared at him, and the little Rabbit stared back. And all the time their noses twitched.

"Why don't you get up and play with us?" one of them asked.

"I don't feel like it," said the Rabbit, for he didn't want to explain that he had no clockwork.

"Ho!" said the furry rabbit. "It's as easy as anything." And he gave a big hop sideways and stood on his hind legs.

"I don't believe you can!" he said.

"I can!" said the little Rabbit. "I can jump higher than anything!" He meant when the Boy threw him, but of course he didn't want to say so.

"Can you hop on your hind legs?" asked the furry rabbit.

That was a dreadful question, for the Velveteen Rabbit had no hind legs at all! The back of him was made all in one piece, like a pincushion. He sat still in the bracken, and hoped that the other rabbits wouldn't notice.

"I don't want to!" he said again.

But the wild rabbits have very sharp eyes. And this one stretched out his neck and looked.

"He hasn't got any hind legs!" he called out. "Fancy a rabbit without any hind legs!" And he began to laugh.

"I have!" cried the little Rabbit. "I have got hind legs! I am sitting on them!"

"Then stretch them out and show me, like this!" said the wild rabbit. And he began to whirl round and dance, till the little Rabbit got quite dizzy.

"I don't like dancing," he said. "I'd rather sit still!"

But all the while he was longing to dance, for a funny new tickly feeling ran through him, and he felt he would give anything in the world to be able to jump about like these rabbits did.

The strange rabbit stopped dancing, and came quite close. He came so close this time that his long whiskers brushed the Velveteen Rabbit's ear, and then he wrinkled his nose suddenly and flattened his ears and jumped backwards.

"He doesn't smell right!" he exclaimed. "He isn't a rabbit at all! He isn't real!"

"I *am* Real!" said the little Rabbit. "I am Real! The Boy said so!" And he nearly began to cry.

Just then there was a sound of footsteps, and the Boy ran past near them, and with a stamp of feet and a flash of white tails the two strange rabbits disappeared.

"Come back and play with me!" called the little Rabbit. "Oh, do come back! I *know* I am Real!"

But there was no answer, only the little ants ran to and fro, and the bracken swayed gently where the two strangers had passed. The Velveteen Rabbit was all alone.

"Oh, dear!" he thought. "Why did they run away like that? Why couldn't they stop and talk to me?"

For a long time he lay very still, watching the bracken, and hoping that they would come back. But they never returned, and presently the sun sank lower and the little white moths fluttered out, and the Boy came and carried him home.

Weeks passed, and the little Rabbit grew very old and shabby, but the Boy loved him just as much. He loved him so hard that he loved all his whiskers off, and the pink lining to his ears turned grey, and his brown spots faded. He even began to lose his shape, and he scarcely looked like a rabbit any more, except to the Boy. To him he was always beautiful, and that was all that the little Rabbit cared about. He didn't mind how he looked to other people, because the nursery magic had made him Real, and when you are Real shabbiness doesn't matter.

And then, one day, the Boy was ill.

His face grew very flushed, and he talked in his sleep, and his little body was so hot that it burned the Rabbit when he held him close. Strange people came and went in the nursery, and a light burned all night and through it all the little Velveteen Rabbit lay there, hidden from sight under the bedclothes, and he never stirred, for he was afraid that if they found him some one might take him away, and he knew that the Boy needed him.

It was a long weary time, for the Boy was too ill to play, and the little Rabbit found it rather dull with nothing to do all day long. But he snuggled down patiently, and looked forward to the time when the Boy should be well again, and they would go out in the garden amongst the flowers and the butterflies and play splendid games in the raspberry thicket like they used to. All sorts of delightful things he planned, and while the Boy lay half asleep he crept up close to the pillow and whispered them in his ear. And presently the fever turned, and the Boy got better. He was able to sit up in bed and look at picture books, while the little Rabbit cuddled close at his side. And one day, they let him get up and dress.

It was a bright, sunny morning, and the windows stood wide open. They had carried the Boy out on to the balcony, wrapped in a shawl, and the little Rabbit lay tangled up among the bedclothes, thinking.

The Boy was going to the seaside tomorrow. Everything was arranged, and now it only remained to carry out the doctor's orders. They talked about it all, while the little Rabbit lay under the bedclothes, with just his head peeping out, and listened. The room was to be disinfected, and all the books and toys that the Boy had played with in bed must be burnt.

"Hurrah!" thought the little Rabbit. "Tomorrow we shall go to the seaside!" For the Boy had often talked of the seaside, and he wanted very much to see the big waves coming in, and the tiny crabs, and the sand castles.

Just then Nana caught sight of him.

"How about his old Bunny?" she asked.

"*That?*" said the doctor. "Why, it's a mass of scarlet

fever germs!—Burn it at once. What? Nonsense! Get
him a new one. He mustn't have that any more!"

And so the little Rabbit was put into a sack with the
old picture-books and a lot of rubbish, and carried out
to the end of the garden behind the fowl-house. That
was a fine place to make a bonfire, only the gardener

was too busy just then to attend to it. He had the potatoes to dig and the green peas to gather, but next morning he promised to come quite early and burn the whole lot.

That night the Boy slept in a different bedroom, and he had a new bunny to sleep with him. It was a splendid bunny, all white plush with real glass eyes, but the Boy was too excited to care very much about it. For tomorrow he was going to the seaside, and that in itself was such a wonderful thing that he could think of nothing else.

And while the Boy was asleep, dreaming of the seaside, the little Rabbit lay among the old picture-books in the corner behind the fowl-house, and he felt very lonely. The sack had been left untied, and so by wriggling a bit he was able to get his head through the opening and look out. He was shivering a little, for he had always been used to sleeping in a proper bed, and by this time his coat had worn so thin and threadbare from hugging that it was no longer any protection to him. Near by he could see the thicket of raspberry canes, growing tall and close like a tropical jungle, in whose shadow he had played with the Boy on bygone mornings. He thought of those long sunlit hours in the garden—how happy they were—and a great sadness came over him. He seemed to see them all pass before him, each more beautiful than the other, the fairy huts in the flower-bed, the quiet evenings in the wood when he lay in the bracken and the little ants ran over his paws; the wonderful day when he first knew that he was Real. He thought of the Skin Horse, so wise and gentle, and all that he had told him. Of what use was it to be loved and lose one's beauty and become Real if it all ended like this? And a tear, a real tear, trickled down his little shabby velvet nose and fell to the ground.

And then a strange thing happened. For where the tear had fallen a flower grew out of the ground, a mysterious flower, not at all like any that grew in the garden. It had slender green leaves the colour of emeralds, and in the centre of the leaves a blossom like a golden cup. It was so beautiful that the little Rabbit forgot to cry, and just lay there watching it. And presently the blossom opened, and out of it there stepped a fairy.

She was quite the loveliest fairy in the whole world. Her dress was of pearl and dewdrops, and there were flowers round her neck and in her hair, and her face was like the most perfect flower of all. And she came close to the little Rabbit and gathered him up in her arms and kissed him on his velveteen nose that was all damp from crying.

"Little Rabbit," she said, "don't you know who I am?"

The Rabbit looked up at her, and it seemed to him that he had seen her face before, but he couldn't think where.

"I am the nursery magic Fairy," she said. "I take care of all the playthings that the children have loved. When they are old and worn out and the children don't need them any more, then I come and take them away with me and turn them into Real."

"Wasn't I Real before?" asked the little Rabbit.

"You were Real to the Boy," the Fairy said, "because he loved you. Now you shall be Real to every one."

And she held the little Rabbit close in her arms and flew with him into the wood.

It was light now, for the moon had risen. All the forest was beautiful, and the fronds of the bracken shone like frosted silver. In the open glade between the tree-trunks the wild rabbits danced with their shadows on the velvet grass, but when they saw the Fairy they all stopped dancing and stood round in a ring to stare at her.

"I've brought you a new playfellow," the Fairy said. "You must be very kind to him and teach him all he needs to know in Rabbitland, for he is going to live with you for ever and ever!"

And she kissed the little Rabbit again and put him down on the grass.

"Run and play, little Rabbit!" she said.

But the little Rabbit sat quite still for a moment and never moved. For when he saw all the wild rabbits dancing around him he suddenly remembered about his hind legs, and he didn't want them to see that he was made all in one piece. He did not know that when the Fairy kissed him that last time she had changed him altogether. And he might have sat there a long time, too shy to move, if just then something hadn't tickled his nose, and before he thought what he was doing he lifted his hind toe to scratch it.

And he found that he actually had hind legs! Instead of dingy velveteen he had brown fur, soft and shiny, his ears twitched by themselves, and his whiskers were so long that they brushed the grass. He gave one leap and the joy of using those hind legs was so great that he went springing about the turf on them, jumping sideways and whirling round as the others did, and he grew so excited that when at last he did stop to look for the Fairy she had gone.

He was a Real Rabbit at last, at home with the other rabbits.

Other stories about very real days are The Blue Day, *by René Guillot, published by Abelard-Schuman, and* Impunity Jane, *by Rumer Godden, published by Viking.*

The Poppy Seed Cakes

BY MARGERY CLARK

Illustrations by Maud and Miska Petersham

ONCE upon a time there was a little boy and his name was Andrewshek. His mother and his father brought him from the old country when he was a tiny baby.

Andrewshek had an Auntie Katushka and she came from the old country, too, on Andrewshek's fourth birthday.

Andrewshek's Auntie Katushka came on a large boat. She brought with her a huge bag filled with presents for Andrewshek and his father and his mother. In the huge bag were a fine feather bed and a bright shawl and five pounds of poppy seeds.

From *The Poppy Seed Cakes*, by Margery Clark. Copyright 1954 by Doubleday & Company, Inc.

The fine feather bed was made from the feathers of her old green goose at home. It was to keep Andrewshek warm when he took a nap.

The bright shawl was for Andrewshek's Auntie Katushka to wear when she went to market.

The five pounds of poppy seeds were to sprinkle on little cakes which Andrewshek's Auntie Katushka made every Saturday for Andrewshek.

One lovely Saturday morning Andrewshek's Auntie Katushka took some butter and some sugar and some flour and some milk and seven eggs and she rolled out some nice little cakes. Then she sprinkled each cake with some of the poppy seeds which she had brought from the old country.

While the nice little cakes were baking, she spread out the fine feather bed on top of the big bed, for Andrewshek to take his nap. Andrewshek did not like to take a nap.

Andrewshek loved to bounce up and down and up and down on his fine feather bed.

Andrewshek's Auntie Katushka took the nice little cakes out of the oven and put them on the table to cool; then she put on her bright shawl to go to market. "Andrewshek," she said, "please watch these cakes while

you rest on your fine feather bed. Be sure that the kitten and the dog do not go near them."

"Yes, indeed! I will watch the nice little cakes," said Andrewshek. "And I will be sure that the kitten and the dog do not touch them." But all Andrewshek really did was to bounce up and down and up and down on the fine feather bed.

"Andrewshek!" said Andrewshek's Auntie Katushka, "how can you watch the poppy seed cakes when all you do is to bounce up and down and up and down on the fine feather bed?" Then Andrewshek's Auntie Katushka, in her bright shawl, hurried off to market.

But Andrewshek kept bouncing up and down and up and down on the fine feather bed and paid no attention to the little cakes sprinkled with poppy seeds.

Just as Andrewshek was bouncing up in the air for the ninth time, he heard a queer noise that sounded like "Hs-s-s-s-sss," at the front door of his house.

"Oh, what a queer noise!" cried Andrewshek. He jumped down off the fine feather bed and opened the front door. There stood a great green goose as big as Andrewshek himself. The goose was very cross and was scolding as fast as he could. He was wagging his head and was opening and closing his long red beak.

"What do you want?" said Andrewshek. "What are you scolding about?"

"I want all the goose feathers from your fine feather bed," quacked the big green goose. "They are mine."

"They are not yours," said Andrewshek. "My Auntie Katushka brought them with her from the old country in a huge bag."

"They are mine," quacked the big green goose. He waddled over to the fine feather bed and tugged at it with his long red beak.

"Stop, Green Goose!" said Andrewshek, "and I will give you one of Auntie Katushka's poppy seed cakes."

"A poppy seed cake!" the green goose quacked in delight. "I love nice little poppy seed cakes! Give me one and you shall have your feather bed."

But one poppy seed cake could not satisfy the greedy green goose.

"Give me another!" Andrewshek gave the green goose another poppy seed cake.

"Give me another!" the big green goose hissed and frightened Andrewshek nearly out of his wits.

Andrewshek gave him another and another and another till all the poppy seed cakes were gone.

Just as the last poppy seed cake disappeared down the long neck of the green goose, Andrewshek's Auntie Katushka appeared at the door, in her bright shawl. "Boo! hoo!" cried Andrewshek. "See! that naughty green goose has eaten all the poppy seed cakes."

"What? All my nice little poppy seed cakes?" cried Andrewshek's Auntie Katushka. "The naughty goose!"

The greedy goose tugged at the fine feather bed again with his long red beak and started to drag it to the door. Andrewshek's Auntie Ka-  tushka ran after the green goose and just then there was a dreadful explosion. The greedy goose who had stuffed himself with poppy seed cakes had burst and his feathers flew all over the room.

"Well! well!" said Andrewshek's Auntie Katushka, as she gathered up the pieces of the big green goose. "We soon shall have two fine feather pillows for your fine feather bed."

Other stories in this book tell about Andrewshek, a white goat, and a pair of red-topped boots. You'll enjoy them all.

Sneakers,
that Rapscallion Cat

BY MARGARET WISE BROWN

Illustrations by Jean Charlot

ONCE there was a little fat cat, and his name was
Sneakers. His mother called him Sneakers because he
had four white paws and the rest of him was inky black.
All her other kittens were inky black all over.

The first time that his mother saw Sneakers lying with
his four white paws waving in the air, she thought he
must have gone wading in a saucer of milk.

She picked him out of her pile of kittens by the scruff
of his neck. Then she lay down and held him, squirming
between her two front paws, while she tried to clean
the milk off his tiny white feet and make them inky
black like all her other kittens' feet.

She licked and she licked and she purred a song while
she licked. But the milk would not come off!

And she licked and she licked, and she purred and she purred, but still he had four white paws.

Just then the mother cat saw the little boy running toward her. It was the first warm day in the year, and he had on a pair of brand-new, clean white sneakers.

The mother cat looked at the little boy's sneakers. And she blinked at her kitten with its four white paws. And then she purred and she purred and she purred. And the little kitten was called Sneakers from then on.

Now Sneakers was a rapscallion cat from the time he was born. The other kittens stayed in the box until they grew up enough. But Sneakers was off even before he grew up enough.

Sneakers went off after little black bugs. He chased butterfly shadows across the ground. He pounced on people's shoelaces if they were the least bit hanging. Sneakers went *pounce, pounce, pounce,* all day long. And then he went *pounce* into his bed at night. And, curling his little white feet under him into a warm fur ball, he went *pounce* to sleep.

His mother always knew that, no matter how much he went pouncing off, he would always come pouncing back, so she didn't worry about him.

But she did think, over and over again, "By the incredible velvet that grows on my nose, this is a funny little cat!"

One day his mother licked his little face all clean and smooth. And she said, "Now Sneakers, my kitten, my little fur cat, away you go!

"You are to live in the house with the little boy, and make him laugh, and chase away the mice, and never knock anything off the tables.

"I am a barn cat, and my home is here, in the barn in the hay.

"But you will be a house cat, and you will sleep before the fire and only come out here in the daytime.

"Now off you go to the house, and keep your little paws clean as the milk you drink every morning." So off Sneakers went to live in the big house and be the little boy's kitten.

At first, it seemed very quiet in the house at night after the barn. Sneakers missed the sound of the horses stomping in their stalls and the mice squeaking and squealing in the hay loft.

Then, at table one day, purely by accident, the little boy knocked over a plate of peaches. They rolled all over the floor in every direction—little round peaches rolling away.

"My, but I'm glad this happened," thought the funny little kitten. And he batted one of the peaches around on the floor.

"I do wish that lots of things would come spilling all over the floor for me to chase every day."

Everyone laughed so hard to see Sneakers scooting around after the peaches with his paw they forgot who knocked the peaches over.

The little boy laughed, too.

But the little kitten never knocked things off himself. He just prowled round and round with one eye cocked and waited for things to happen.

One afternoon the cook came back from town all dressed up in a brand-new hat—a brand-new hat with red feathers on it.

She met Sneakers in the pantry.

"Where are you going, you little Sneaker cat?" she said to him.

"Just *prowling around, prowling around*," answered Sneakers. (Or at least that's what it sounded like, as he purred and blinked his bright yellow eyes.)

Whiff! The wind came blowing in at the kitchen door. It blew the cook's hat off with all its red feathers.

Pounce went Sneakers!

Pounce on the feathers and the brand-new hat.

And he slid across the floor.

"Oh, Sneakers, you kitten, you rapscallion cat! Give me back my brand-new hat!"

But Sneakers was having fun, and he knew the cook moved slowly.

He batted the hat with his paw.

"My, but I'm glad this happened!" he thought. And he skidded the hat under the table.

The cook had to chase Sneakers all over the kitchen and into the sink before she could get her brand-new hat.

She put it back on her head—right on top of her head. And she stood there, looking at Sneakers.

Sneakers just sat by the side of the sink—where he wasn't supposed to be—and licked his milk-white paws.

"Oh, Sneakers," said the cook, "the minute I saw you, I knew you were in here just waiting to get into some kind of mischief."

"No," said Sneakers, "I was just *prowling around, prowling around.*" (Or that is what he seemed to be saying.)

And he walked out of the kitchen on his four white paws to find the little boy.

The little boy was at the barn, making the harness soft and clean with saddle soap and a wet sponge.

"Hello, Sneaker cat," said the little boy. "Where are you going?"

"Just *prowling around, prowling around,*" said Sneakers. And he rubbed his fur back against the little boy's bare leg.

Then he sat down to wait for something to happen—for the sponge to drop, or something to spill.

For Sneakers was a rapscallion cat.

Margaret Wise Brown has written many fun-filled books about animal adventures. Three you will want to read are Poodle and the Sheep, Young Kangaroo, and Runaway Bunny.

Evie and the Wonderful Kangaroo

BY IRMENGARDE EBERLE

Illustrations by Louis Slobodkin

A kangaroo makes a wonderful playmate, as Evie Dell discovered. Especially a kangaroo that carries a lace-edged handkerchief in her pocket!

EVIE Dell had a kangaroo for a pet. Her name was Cookie, and she and Evie liked each other very much. When the Dells first got her, the people in the small California town where they lived were surprised at such a pet. But they soon got used to it. And they were always interested in her because she was a wonderful, remarkable kangaroo.

Cookie had once been a zoo kangaroo and had learned many things from people because she had seen and heard so many every day. The Dells had bought her when the town had to give up its zoo. They saw right away that she was unusually friendly and smart. But just how smart and friendly Cookie was they couldn't know then. They found that out later.

The Dells had built her a little house on the lawn beside their own house in Valley Town. There she lived very quietly at first. She quickly became a great pet to the whole family though, and especially to Evie, who was seven years old.

Evie used to peek into Cookie's house sometimes. And she was surprised how neat and orderly she always kept it.

Cookie liked Evie, and often played ball or other games with her. Sometimes Cookie went with Evie to play with other children in the neighborhood. She even went to the near-by store with Evie when she had to shop for her mother. Usually Evie let her hold the money because Cookie never lost things. The kangaroo kept the coins in the handy private pocket she had in her front.

Once when Mrs. Dell was in a store with them, Cookie made it clear that she wanted a lace-edged handkerchief that lay on the counter. So Mrs. Dell bought it and gave it to her. After that Cookie always wore it tucked into her private pocket with the lace edge showing.

One summer evening when it was nearly dinnertime, Evie and Cookie came home together from a neighbor's. They had brought back some roller skates Evie had left there the day before. They went right to the kitchen where Mrs. Dell was cooking dinner.

"Bring the chairs up to the table, please," she called to Evie. "Dinner will be ready in a minute."

While Evie went to the dining room to do that, Mrs. Dell gave Cookie her supper, which was a large bowl full of crisp lettuce and cabbage leaves. Cookie preferred this to any other kind of dinner, and she bowed her thanks and took the bowl out to the back porch and began to eat.

The Dells went into the dining room and sat down at the table. As Daddy began putting slices of baked ham and potatoes on the plates, Mother said:

"Grandma Ware telephoned today. She said she had baked a lovely layer cake with coconut frosting for Grandpa's birthday, which is tomorrow, as you know. She said she wished we could come over and spend the

afternoon and eat cake and celebrate Grandpa's birthday with them."

"Let's do!" Evie cried. "We could go early in the morning and stay all day."

"Daddy can't go, of course," Mother said. "He has to
go to work as usual. And I can't go either, because I
promised Daddy I'd help him in his office."

Evie asked: "Can I go alone, please?"

"Oh, no," Mother said. "It's too long a walk for that."

Daddy said: "Of course you can't go alone, Evie.
After all, you're just seven."

Evie said: "But Grandpa will be so disappointed if
none of us goes to see him on his birthday. And so will
Grandma."

Mother said: "It's a good thing we sent Grandpa his
birthday present by mail. Now it won't matter so much
if none of us can go."

"But I love Grandpa. And I like coconut layer cake,"
Evie put in.

"I know," said Daddy, "and I'm sorry, Evie, but it can't
be helped."

"Oh *Daddy!*" Evie wailed.

There came a loud *plop, plop, plop* from the back
porch. It was Cookie, of course, pounding with her tail
the way she did when she wanted them to pay attention
to her. They looked toward the back door and there she
stood, her eyes bright, pointing to herself with a dainty
hand.

"Why look," Daddy said, "Cookie means that *she* can
take Evie to Grandma and Grandpa Ware's."

"Of course!" Mother said. "Why didn't we think of that
ourselves! I don't know of anyone I'd trust more than
Cookie. She's smart, and strong, and she's Evie's friend.
She'll take care of Evie."

Evie was delighted. "Then I can go!" she cried, smiling at Cookie. "Oh, Cookie, we'll have fun." And she

said to her mother: "I hope Cookie stays with me the rest of my life. She's such a wonderful kangaroo."

After dinner Mother went to telephone Grandpa and Grandma that Evie and Cookie were coming tomorrow.

The next morning Evie dressed in her fresh blue cotton dress. She put on a pink sweater, as the spring morning was cool. And she gathered a few things she wanted to take along to play with. She took her favorite blue-eyed doll, June, and her doll suitcase with some little clothes in it. She took her bubble pipe just in case she might want to make soap bubbles. And she took her small blue and white umbrella.

"Well," said Daddy, watching her come down the stairs, "you surely won't need all those things just for a day's visit at Grandma's and Grandpa's."

But Evie wanted to take the things along, and Daddy said: "All right."

Mother made up a small snack for Evie and Cookie. She knew they would like to have just a little picnic somewhere along the way, before they got to Grandma's for lunch.

Cookie brushed herself to make herself neat. She put her favorite rubber ball in the pocket on her front, and tucked in her lace-trimmed handkerchief so that it just showed at the edge.

Then at eight-thirty Evie and Cookie were ready. They said good-by to Daddy and Mother who were leaving the house to go in the other direction in the car; and they set off northward.

They walked for two blocks stopping briefly as people they passed said hello to them. Then they turned east. Cookie sometimes took long leaps, because that was the most comfortable way for a kangaroo to go on so long a trip. But after each leap she waited for Evie as usual. They went along the tree-shaded street for awhile, and then came to a part where there were no trees at all, only wide green lawns. The sun, which was rising higher and higher in the sky, became so warm that Evie said she had to take off her sweater. When they stopped to do that, they stayed a little while, sitting in the grass at the edge of a lawn. Then some children they knew came along and talked with them.

Soon Evie and Cookie went on, however. They had walked quite a way when Cookie noticed that Evie didn't have her sweater with her. Cookie whacked the sidewalk with her strong, hard tail—*plop, plop, plop.* But Evie was thinking of other things and didn't know what Cookie meant. So Cookie herself turned and went leaping back to the place where they had sat on the lawn.

Evie leaned against a tree beside the walk and waited. In a minute Cookie came bounding back with the sweater.

"Oh, thank you," Evie cried. "How did I ever forget my sweater!"

Cookie shrugged her shoulders.

They had gone another block when Evie said: "Oh, Cookie, where's my umbrella?"

Cookie looked at her and saw that she truly didn't have her little umbrella. So she and Evie went back together to the tree against which Evie had leaned a little while before. And there stood her little blue and white umbrella. Cookie took it and hung it over her own arm by its cord loop.

"I guess this is one of my forgetting days," Evie said. "I wish it wasn't. We want to hurry and get to Grandpa's and Grandma's."

Cookie nodded her head and she pounded the sidewalk hard with her tail to show she agreed, but it really sounded as though she were getting a little impatient. It worried Evie.

As they went on once more, she thought: "Maybe Cookie would feel better again if we stopped and ate our lunch about now." So she started to look for a nice place to sit down. By and by they came to a brook. There was a bridge for cars and people to go over. Below, there were green, grassy banks along the water's edge.

Evie said: "Look, Cookie, isn't this a nice place! Let's stop and have our picnic here."

Cookie liked the idea, and so they went down and put all their things on the grassy bank and made themselves comfortable. Evie took off her sandals and pink socks and waded, and Cookie of course came in too. After a few minutes they stopped playing in the brook, and sat in the grass on the bank and unwrapped Evie's sandwiches and Cookie's lettuce. They were just beginning to eat when a truck came along. It was about to cross the bridge when the driver saw Evie and Cookie.

He swung his truck to the side of the road and stopped it. He leaned far out and looked more carefully. "Well, well," he cried. "As I live! It's a kangaroo!"

Cookie smiled and bobbed her head at him.

Evie told him, "Yes, she's our pet kangaroo, Cookie. Everybody around here is used to her."

"I'm not from around here," the man said. "And seeing a kangaroo is a treat to me. Do you mind if I stop with you a minute? I'd like to chat with Cookie."

"Of course," said Evie.

Again Cookie nodded vigorously.

"Thank you," said the man. "I'm an Australian, you see. And I haven't talked to a kangaroo since I left that country five years ago. Just looking at this one makes me homesick. My, my, a kangaroo from home!"

He backed his car off the bridge, and parked it at the side of the road, and leaned out and talked to Evie and Cookie. Evie offered him one of her sandwiches, and Cookie offered him some lettuce. But he wouldn't take any. He just wanted to talk.

He told Cookie where he used to live in Australia, and how much he liked it there. He talked about the many kangaroos he used to see far out in the wild country. And he told about the towns and cities and the people there. Cookie kept nodding her head and looking pleased and interested.

After a while the man from Australia said: "Well, I'll have to be going now. It's been nice talking over old times, Cookie. Good-by, Miss."

Cookie and Evie went up the bank and stood at the edge of the road and waved as he drove away.

Cookie's big eyes were bright, and she almost looked as though she were smiling.

Evie said: "You certainly like that man from Australia, don't you, Cookie?"

Cookie nodded her head vigorously.

Evie said: "He's a very nice man."

It was lovely there by the brook, and they would have liked to stay longer. But even more they wanted to get to Grandpa's and Grandma's. So Cookie went in the water just once more and got her feet and tail good and wet and cool. Then they gathered their things together, and went out into the road, and over the bridge eastward—the same way the truck had gone.

Evie looked at Cookie's feet and tail. All along them the dust of the road was mixing with the water and making a fine mud. She pointed it out to Cookie, and Cookie shook her feet a little but then walked on, shrugging her narrow shoulders.

They hadn't gone far when Evie stopped and said: "Oh, Cookie, I left my pink socks behind."

Cookie looked really disgusted. She had just made a fine long jump forward, but she came back again. She plopped her tail hard on the ground, as she often did when she was cross, and she had a little frown on her forehead. But there was nothing else to do. She and Evie had to go back and get the socks.

After that nothing more happened for a while, and they came to Sun Pond Park with its tall trees, its lawns, and benches. Across the road there was a small shopping center. Nearest the corner stood a stationery store, then the grocery store, and a post office sub-station, and a bank, and about a block farther on there stood a small restaurant.

Cookie and Evie stood looking at this interesting place for a minute. They had been here several times before, but it was just far enough from home to feel a little strange and freshly interesting. They saw a few people walking along. Some knew them and called out, "Hello." Some were strangers to them and stared at Cookie because she was a kangaroo. They were surprised to see her walking along with a little girl. But most of the people knew her quite well and weren't surprised.

Evie saw some children, about a block away, turning into the park. They were carrying some kind of an interesting-looking toy, all yellow and red. She was eager to see what it was, so she told Cookie she was going to play with the children a minute. She asked Cookie if she didn't want to come along. But Cookie shook her head. She did go into the park a little way with Evie, but she was just looking for a place to sit down. She found one that suited her on a bench beside a drinking fountain. Here she made herself comfortable and motioned to Evie to put her things down on the grass. She would take care of them till Evie came back.

Evie put everything down and said, "I won't be but a minute, Cookie," and skipped away. She joined the children far on the other side of the park, and she played with them and their red and yellow toy, which was a new kind of kite. She stayed about half an hour.

Then she remembered Grandma and Grandpa and

the birthday. So, saying good-by to the children, she hurried away. She made a short-cut across the grass to get back to the road, and aimed at a point beyond the little shopping center, which put her well ahead on the way to Grandma's house.

She was going along this road singing to herself, when she suddenly had an uncomfortable feeling. Had she forgotten something? She had! And this time it was Cookie!

How could she forget Cookie, even for a minute? And where had she left her? Oh, yes, over at the other end of the park by the bench and the drinking fountain. She ran back there as fast as she could.

After a while she came to the place where she had left Cookie. But Cookie wasn't there! At first Evie thought maybe she had made a mistake about the place. But there was the bench, and just a few feet away from it, the drinking fountain. She looked in the grass behind the bench and saw a pair of her doll's socks laid out neatly side by side. So this was the right place, after all. But certainly Cookie hadn't forgotten the doll's socks.

Evie thought: "Cookie never forgets my things like I do. She must have left those little doll socks as a sign to me—to tell me she left on purpose. She must be very angry at me."

Evie felt terribly sad, and she was worried too. Where could Cookie have gone?

Evie went to the street. A woman was passing, and she asked her: "Have you seen a tame, very neat, very polite kangaroo around here?"

"No," said the woman. "Certainly not."

Then Evie asked a young man, and he answered: "Yes, I saw one coming out of the park with an armful of stuff a while ago. And with a lace-edged handkerchief in her pocket. I was so surprised, it made me laugh. I don't know where she went."

Evie thanked him and went on. She crossed the street and went into the stationery store. A big, heavy man with a rosy face leaned over the counter and asked her what she wanted.

"Please, Mister," Evie asked, "have you seen a kangaroo anywhere around here?"

"Yes indeed I have," said the man. "She was in here about twenty minutes ago. She bought some heavy brown paper and some twine, and a shopping bag."

"She did?" Evie was puzzled. "What did she do with them?"

"Why," said the man, "she had a lot of stuff with her— a doll, a doll suitcase, a little umbrella, a sweater, and I don't know what all. She wrapped them up in the brown paper and tied the package up with the string. Made a very neat package, really. She tried to put the package in the pouch on her front, but it was too big. Wouldn't go in. So then she bought the shopping bag to carry the package in."

"Those were my things," Evie explained. "I wonder if . . ."

The man went on: "Then the kangaroo went off toward the post office. But I don't know how she was going to mail the package unless she got somebody who knew you to address it to you some way."

Evie was moving back toward the door while he explained the last of this. Now she said: "That was a very strange thing for Cookie to do."

If Cookie was trying to mail the things home to her it must be because she wasn't coming back to be Evie's pet and friend any more. That would be *terrible!* She must find Cookie as quickly as possible, and get her to come back. Surely she would come when she saw how much Evie cared about her.

"Good-by," she said to the stationery store man, and darted out the door.

Just a few steps farther on Evie came to the grocery store. She turned in there and asked for Cookie. But the two men who were waiting on the customers said that no kangaroo had come in that morning. Where could Cookie be?

Next, Evie looked into the post office, but Cookie hadn't been there yet to mail her stuff home. Evie was relieved to hear that. But she must find Cookie. She hurried on to the restaurant half a block away. As soon as she stepped up to the screen door she saw Cookie inside.

Cookie was sitting at a table with the man from Australia who had stopped his truck to talk to them by the brook. There was a white cloth on the table, and a teapot and cups, and they were drinking tea and talking and looking very content. On the floor beside Cookie lay the brown shopping bag. There were two men at another table, and they were staring at the kangaroo just exactly as if they had never seen one in a restaurant before, which was probably true.

Evie opened the door and came in. "Cookie!" she cried. "I'm so glad to find you. I've been looking everywhere for you. I thought I'd lost you."

Cookie looked up and smiled and motioned her to come to the table.

The Australian said: "Hello there." He got up and brought a chair over from another table for Evie. "Cookie and I were talking about Australia," he said. "And if you'll excuse me we'll go on with our conversation."

Evie nodded solemnly. And the man turned back to the kangaroo.

"I don't blame you, Cookie," he said. "I know how you feel."

"How does she feel?" Evie asked anxiously.

"She feels even the best friendship there is gets kind of stretched and yanked out of shape if one friend always makes a lot of trouble by forgetting things, leaving things behind. It's uncomfortable for Cookie, you see. And when you forgot Cookie herself, well—" He gave a wry grin. "Anyway, she came here looking for me a little while ago. She asked me if I knew of a way she could get back to Australia. And as I'm sailing on a ship that leaves San Francisco next Wednesday, I'm offering to take her along."

Evie was horrified. "Cookie, you wouldn't go?" she cried.

Cookie looked sad, but she nodded her head.

Evie turned to the Australian. "But Cookie does still like me, doesn't she?"

Before he could answer, Cookie nodded vigorously. And then the Australian said: "Oh, very much."

Evie leaned close to her kangaroo and said: "Please stay with me, Cookie."

Cookie looked at her with a sweet smile on her face. But then she turned her eyes away, and put her hands over her ears. She liked Evie so much that she was afraid she would go back to her if she listened to her. And she didn't want to spend all her life picking things up. It just wouldn't be any fun.

The two men in the restaurant had heard most of this conversation, and now they came over to join in.

One of them said: "I sure hope you won't go off to the other side of the world and leave this little girl, Kangaroo."

The other said: "Friendship's a nice thing, Kangaroo. It's worth trying to save yours and Evie Dell's."

The waitress came out of the kitchen bringing a sandwich for the Australian. She asked: "Who tracked all that mud in here?" and pointed to the big marks on the floor which Cookie's feet and tail had made.

Cookie looked embarrassed.

The waitress did not notice that and went on: "What's all this talk about the Kangaroo leaving? Of course you can't leave your friend Evie, Cookie."

The Australian bit into his sandwich. Cookie shrugged her shoulders and looked sad.

Then the Australian said: "You people don't understand kangaroos. You can't just tell Cookie what to do. You've got to make a plan."

"A plan?" Evie asked. "What kind of a plan?"

"Why, a plan that will make things more comfortable for Cookie, of course," said the Australian.

"I still want to know," the waitress said, "who muddied the floor." Cookie hung her head. And the waitress went off about her work with a knowing smile. "I won't make a fuss, no matter who it was," she flung back. "But if it's the kangaroo, all I've got to say is she needn't be so cross about Evie's forgetting things."

Cookie looked at her, with her big eyes bright, and nodded her head. At first she nodded slowly, and then more and more vigorously. She seemed to have an idea, and she looked very pleased.

Suddenly she got off her chair and picked up the shopping bag and took the package out. Everyone watched her to see why she was doing this.

Cookie pointed to her pouch, in which she was carrying a number of articles. She pointed to Evie and patted her front to show that Evie had no pouch. She shook her head sadly.

Then with a *plop, plop, plop* of her tail, and a happy expression on her face that looked like someone who is saying, "I've got a plan!", she hung the strap of the shopping bag around Evie's neck. The bag hung over Evie's front, making just about as convenient a pouch as Cookie herself had. Now Evie could carry all her things in there.

Everyone was pleased at Cookie's gift to Evie. "That's it," said the Australian slapping his knee.

"Why didn't *I* think of that," the waitress exclaimed.

"A fine idea," said one of the men. "I think that's what Evie needs. And I'll say Cookie is fair and square."

The Australian had finished his sandwich and the last of his tea, and he pushed back his chair. Cookie put down the money for her part of the tea. She hopped off her chair and motioned to Evie to come. Evie picked up the brown paper package and unwrapped it and put her doll, June, her small umbrella, sweater, bubble pipe, and doll suitcase in her own shopping bag pouch. Then she and Cookie started to leave.

"Good-by, good-by!" they said to everybody, and to the Australian particularly.

"Thank you for not taking Cookie away," Evie told him.

"It was a pleasure," he said. "Though of course I'm

sorry not to have her for company on my voyage next Wednesday."

He, too, paid the waitress for his tea, and then he put on his cap and went ahead of Evie and Cookie and held the screen door open for them. "Good wishes," he said, and whistling gaily, went to his truck and drove away.

Evie and Cookie were out on the sidewalk when the waitress came running after them.

"Here, wait a minute!" she cried. "I've got a present for Cookie." She handed the kangaroo a rather new coconut mat that had been lying before the front door.

Cookie was delighted. She gave the waitress a broad smile and tucked the mat under her arm. Then she plopped her tail enthusiastically.

"She's saying thank you," Evie explained.

Everyone said good-by once more. Evie and Cookie, feeling fine, started back toward the road they had left more than an hour ago.

Evie looked at the clock over the bank as they passed. It was a quarter past ten. She said: "Oh Cookie, Grandma and Gandpa will be looking for us. They'll wonder what's happened to us. We'd better hurry."

Cookie plopped the ground with her strong tail to show that she agreed, and that *she* was going to hurry. She made two extra long hops, and then waited. Evie hurried after her.

Evie's new pouch suited her just fine, and she marched along singing a little tune and bumping her knees against the full bag, making a nice rhythm.

They were soon out in the open country. They passed a big truck garden on one side and an orchard on the other. After the next curve in the road they came to Grandma's and Grandpa's house.

Grandma and Grandpa were on the front lawn waiting for them.

Grandma called out: "Look, Grandpa!" She hurried

to meet them. "At last they're here," she went on, "Evie and her wonderful kangaroo!"

"It's fine to see you, Evie," Grandpa said. "And you too, Cookie. But what kept you so long on the road?"

Evie explained just a little. Then she started to go inside. But Cookie stopped and laid the coconut mat down before the door and wiped her feet and tail, which were a little muddy and dusty.

"Look at Cookie wiping her feet," Evie said to Grandma and Grandpa.

"How neat," said Grandma.

Cookie grinned happily.

"Well, I never!" Grandpa exclaimed. "No, I really never saw such a smart, wonderful kangaroo in all my life."

Cookie picked up her mat and shook it out, and they all went indoors.

In the bedroom Evie put down her shopping bag with all the things in it, and Cookie put her mat right beside it, so she wouldn't forget it when she went home later on.

Grandma gave them a cool drink of orangeade to freshen them up after their long walk, and then they all went outdoors again so that they could visit with each other, and so that Evie and Cookie could play on the lawn.

At lunch time they celebrated Grandpa's birthday and ate the coconut layer cake, all but Cookie who preferred leaves, of course.

In the same book you can read what happened when Evie's family tried to go away on vacation without Cookie. There are more stories in a second book, Evie and Cookie, published by Alfred A. Knopf, Inc.

Rosa-Too-Little

BY SUE FELT

Illustrations by the author

IT was winter. The snow was piled in shapeless mounds
along 110th Street.

But it wasn't the snow that bothered Rosa as she followed Margarita up the library steps into the warm indoors.

For as long as she could remember Rosa had been
following her big sister, Margarita, to the library.

And every time Rosa waited while Margarita returned
her books.

And every time she waited Rosa was sad. She wanted very much to have books of her own to return.

"Please, Margarita," she would say, "when can I join?"

"You are too little, Rosa. You have to write your name and get a card before you can take books out."

"It is always the same. Last winter I was too little. Last summer I was too little. Why am I always too little to have my own books?" Rosa sighed.

Rosa was big enough to help her mother at home while Margarita and Antonio were at school. But whenever Margarita came from school to take her to the library, Rosa was ready.

Always before Margarita chose new books she would hold Rosa up to press her face against the cool glass to look into that small other world of the PEEP SHOW.

"Oh, there is Peter Rabbit in bed," Rosa would say, "and there is Mrs. Rabbit making him some Camomile Tea and Flopsy, Mopsy, and Cottontail are eating bread and milk and blackberries."

On Fridays Margarita and Antonio went to STORY

HOUR upstairs while Rosa, who was too little, sat in the READING ROOM looking at Picture Books. She looked at the pictures until she knew every one by heart. This made Rosa sad, too. She was certain that if she could only have her own library card and take home her own books she would be able to read them. She wanted so much to go to STORY HOUR, too, and hear the library teacher tell fairy tales. Sometimes Margarita told Rosa the stories or read them to her at home. But Rosa knew it was not quite the same as hearing them at STORY HOUR. She was sure she must be nearly big enough to make a wish and help blow out the candle after STORY HOUR. Antonio had told her about that part, too.

"Oh, how I would like to do that. Why am I always too little?" Rosa sighed.

The snow melted. After light spring rains the trees in Central Park were fringed with baby green leaves.

Margarita carried her jump rope to school and often played double Dutch on the sidewalks in the evenings as the nights grew warmer.

And Rosa was too little for jump rope.

When Margarita wasn't jumping rope she was roller skating. And Mother said Rosa was too little for roller skates.

It seemed to Rosa she was too little for anything. Antonio and his friends once again were training their pigeons on the rooftops. Antonio and his friends didn't want her on the roof. And Antonio was too busy to take her to the library. No one would take her to the library. And that was what Rosa wanted to do most of all.

She was sad.

Rosa begged and begged her mother to let her go alone to the library.

Finally one day her mother said yes.

Rosa could go all by herself. She remembered to wait for the green lights crossing the street. She remembered to wait in line. She was very proud to do it all alone.

But when at last she reached the desk and the library teacher asked for her books, Rosa suddenly remembered something else.

Rosa Maldonado did not have any books; she did not even have a library card. She was too little to join. Poor little Rosa covered her face, pushed her way out of the line, and ran down the stairs, out the door, and all the way home.

"Rosa, little dear, what is the matter, *chiquita?*" her mother asked. Rosa sobbed louder, but at last her mother understood.

"Rosa," she comforted, "we will make a plan, a secret for you and me!"

And Rosa was not quite so sad!

The next day was hot, but Rosa and her mother didn't mind. They started their plan.

All through the long, hot, city summer Rosa worked on her plan except for the days when the street-cleaning men turned on the water hydrant, *the Pompa,* Rosa, Margarita, and Antonio called it. Then they rushed through the fast, cold spray of water. The pavement was cool on the soles of their feet.

Most of the children forgot about books, but not Rosa.

Sometimes in the afternoon Margarita took Rosa to hear the Picture Books read in the library. Everything was quiet in the summer. There were not so many children, for some of them were in camp and some were in the country and all the rest were too hot and sticky to do much of anything.

Rosa listened to the stories and smiled inside with her secret.

And every day Rosa worked on her plan in a special corner at home so that Margarita and Antonio wouldn't guess.

One day Mama said:

"When school starts in September, Rosa may go with Margarita and Antonio."

Then Rosa smiled. She was not too little any more. She could hardly wait.

The last day before school was to begin the little penny merry-go-round came. *La machina,* the children called it. Everyone on 110th Street who had pennies had a ride, and the others followed the music. But they weren't so happy as when *la machina* had been there in

the spring. Playtime was over—no more long days of
jump rope, marbles, skating, and stoopball.

But Rosa skipped with joy.

On Monday school started, and Rosa walked with
Margarita and Antonio—quiet and proud. It was very
exciting to be in school, but there was something else
Rosa wanted to do, too.

At three o'clock she waited by the playground gate till
Margarita and Antonio came out and then Rosa pulled
her sister's hand.

"Margarita, Margarita, today may I go?"

"Rosa, what are you talking about? How do you like
school?" said Margarita.

"It's wonderful. But Margarita, today may I go to the
library with you?" asked Rosa, still pulling her sister's
hand.

"But Rosa," said Margarita, "why today? I have home-work to do."

"Please, Margarita." And finally Margarita gave in to Rosa's pleading and they went together to the library.

Lots of boys and girls were back again to get their cards after the summer. Soon Rosa's turn came.

"What do you want, Rosa?" asked the librarian, who had seen Rosa so many times she knew her name.

"I want to join, please," said Rosa.

"Oh, but Rosa, you are very little. You must be able to write your name you know."

"I can write my name," Rosa said proudly.

The library lady smiled and took a white slip of paper from a drawer, dipped a pen in the inkwell, and said: "Write your name on this line, Rosa."

Rosa held tight to the pen and carefully, carefully made the letters.

The pen scratched. Rosa wasn't used to ink, and she wasn't sure the librarian could read her name, but when Rosa looked up, the library lady smiled.

"That's fine, Rosa," she said.

"Why, Rosa," Margarita said, "that's wonderful!" and she wrote in the address and school and Rosa's grade and age.

"Rosa, take this home and have your mother fill out the other side, then bring it back," the librarian said.

Rosa ran down the stairs and out the door. She ran all the way home and into the kitchen where her mother was preparing dinner.

"Mama, Mama, I joined, I joined! I wrote my name and you must sign the paper so I can get my card."

Her mother smiled proudly and kissed Rosa's hot little face. She signed her name and Rosa's father's name on the back of the paper.

The librarian was surprised to see Rosa back so soon.

"I ran," Rosa said, and showed her mother's name on the paper. Then the librarian gave Rosa a blue slip of paper and Rosa wrote her name again. All the time Rosa saw her name on a brand-new card. It would be all her own. The library teacher helped her read the pledge:

When I write my name in this book, I promise to take good care of the books I use in the library and at home and to obey the rules of the library.

Then Rosa stood on a stool and wrote her name in the big book. That was the best moment of all, because now Rosa Maldonado's name was in the book, the big black book where all the other children who could write had signed their names.

She listened to the rules carefully, although she already knew them. She promised to take good care of her books and to bring them back on time and always to have her hands clean!

Then Rosa walked over to the EASY BOOKS and found the two books she wanted. She knew just where to find them.

Rosa then waited in line to have her books stamped. She smiled back at the library teacher. Then she walked down the library stairs and out into the brisk evening. She squeezed her very own books.

"I am not too little any more," said Rosa.

She was very happy.

If you have enjoyed this story of Rosa's adventures in the library, you will love Jean Fritz's How to Read a Rabbit, a tale about a very unusual kind of library.

Billy and Blaze

BY C. W. ANDERSON

Illustrations by the author

BILLY was a little boy who loved horses more than anything else in the world. Whenever he had a chance to ride some farmer's horse he used to pretend that it was a prancing pony.

One birthday morning his father said to him, "Out on the lawn you will find your birthday present."

And there stood a beautiful bay pony with four white feet and a white nose. Billy had never been so happy.

No boy was ever more proud and happy than Billy when he went out for his first ride. Right from the very start Billy and his new pony seemed to like and understand each other.

After thinking for a long time about many names Billy decided to call the pony Blaze because he had a white blaze down his face.

Before going to bed that first night he took a flash light and went down to the stable to see if Blaze was all right. Already Blaze seemed to feel at home and he was glad to see him.

As soon as it was daylight Billy was up cleaning and brushing Blaze so they could take a long ride after breakfast.

It was not long before Blaze would come galloping whenever Billy called, for he knew there would be a carrot or a piece of sugar for him as well as much petting. And he, too, enjoyed the rides through the woods where there was so much to see.

One day when they were riding along a path through the woods they came to a tree fallen across the path and Blaze jumped quickly over it. Billy was so surprised he almost fell off. But it was very exciting and he decided to try it again. So when they came to the next small fence he leaned forward and gripped with his knees and over they sailed. It felt like flying.

One day in the woods they heard a dog howling as if in pain. They rode to the spot and there they found a dog caught in a trap that had probably been set for some wild animals.

Although the dog was badly hurt he seemed to know that Billy was trying to help him. He stood very still while Billy opened the trap and set him free. And then he limped along home with Billy and Blaze.

When they got home Billy bandaged the dog's foot and gave him something to eat. He was very hungry. The dog seemed to have no home. No one could find out where he came from, so Billy's father let him keep him. He named the dog Rex and wherever Billy went there you were sure to find Rex too.

Rex and Blaze were great friends. He went down to the stable to see Blaze very often and usually slept there with him.

One day when Billy and Blaze were out riding they saw a sign on a tree telling about a Horse Show and a silver cup that was to be given to the best pony. "Let's try for it," said Billy to Blaze.

When Billy got to the show with Blaze and Rex and saw how many fine ponies were there he began to be afraid that he might not win the cup after all. But one pony after another knocked down the rail when he jumped and Billy began to feel that Blaze might win after all. He knew that he and Blaze had often jumped over fences almost as high as these.

At last Billy's turn came. Blaze jumped perfectly and Rex jumped beside him. Everybody clapped and cheered. Rex was not supposed to jump but everybody liked to see a dog jump so well.

"You have a fine pony," said the judge as he gave Billy a silver cup almost too big for him to hold. A man came out and took a picture of all three of them. Then the judge pinned a blue ribbon on Blaze's bridle, with "first prize" printed in gold letters on it.

The grass and trees looked very green and the birds sang very gaily as they rode home. Blaze seemed to know he had done well for he carried his head very high and pranced all the way.

Billy was as happy as any boy could be. For Blaze's supper that evening he brought many carrots and much sugar, and Rex had the finest bone in the house.

Billy set the silver cup up in his room. Every time he looked at it, he was very, very proud of Blaze. His pony was his best friend.

If you have enjoyed reading Billy and Blaze, *you will want to read* Blaze and the Forest Fire, Blaze and the Gypsies, *and* Blaze Finds the Trail, *by C. W. Anderson, published by* The Macmillan Company.

Peter Churchmouse

BY MARGOT AUSTIN

Illustrations by the author

Up jumped Peter!
S-N-A-P! went the snap-rat!
Poor little Peter Churchmouse raised his eyebrows
the way he always did when he made a poem,

> "I wish the cheese I ate
> Were on a plate
> That wouldn't snap at me
> Because I DON'T LIKE IT!"

Then Peter sat right down on the big wooden snap-rat
and ate his cheese. Every last bit.

"Now," said Peter, "I shall bite another big hole in
something so that Parson Pease-Porridge will put more
cheese on the snap-rat for tomorrow."

So Peter ate a great big hole in the red felt that lined
Parson Pease-Porridge's best collection basket.

"There," said Peter, "Parson Pease-Porridge will be
sure to notice that!"

"I'll be twitched," said Parson Pease-Porridge next
morning when he saw the great big hole that Peter had
made in the best collection basket.

"These holes will be the ruination of me. I must do
something drastic! I'll show these rats—I'll get a *cat!!*"

"Oh-h-h," said Peter Churchmouse. "Oh-h-h, poor me!"

Then Peter Churchmouse raised his eyebrows the way
he always did when he thought of a poem,

"I believe I heard
That terrible word
I'm scared to tell it
So I'll only spell it—
C-A-T!"

Next day Peter looked for cheese on the snap-rat as usual.

But the snap-rat was gone and in its place was a bowl of milk. And beside the bowl of milk was Gabriel.

"Hello," said Peter stepping bravely from behind the organ, "I'm afraid of cats. Are you a cat?"

"Who? Me?" said Gabriel sitting up. "I'm not a cat. I'm a kitten and my name's Gabriel. Are you a rat?"

"Of course not," said Peter. "I'm a poor Churchmouse and my name is Peter."

"Hello, Peter," said Gabriel. "I'm to scare the rats away. The rats who've been eating big holes in things. Do you know how to scare rats?"

"No I don't," said Peter. "And if I did it wouldn't help you because there aren't any rats here at all. There's only poor me. I pretend I'm rats. *I* bite the great big holes in everything!"

"You don't!" said Gabriel.

"I do," said Peter. "Once I even ate a hymn book. It tasted awful."

"For pity's sake," said Gabriel in a shocked voice. "Cover and all?"

"Cover and all," said Peter. "And I didn't like to do it."

"Then why *did* you do it?" asked Gabriel.

"Because I was hungry," said Peter. "I'm *always* hungry!"

"How sad for you," said Gabriel. "Parson Pease-Porridge gives *me* lots to eat."

"That's because you're a big kitten and he can see you," cried poor Peter. "But I'm a little mouse and he

can't see me at all. He's too near-sighted! He doesn't
even know I live here. And now that you've come even
the snap-rat is gone. All I ever got to eat was the cheese
on the snap-rat and I wouldn't have got that if Parson
Pease-Porridge didn't think I was rats that make the
holes *I* bite in things. Fuss, fuss, fuss. Oh, I don't like it!"

"How very sad," said Gabriel. "How very, very sad."

"Sad indeed," said Peter, "I even make poems about
it."

"I'd like to hear one, please," said Gabriel.

"Gladly," said Peter, raising his eyebrows. "One goes
like this—

> Snap, whack, bang,
> Goes the snap-rat bang,
> Goes snap bang,
> Goes whack bang,
> Fuss, fuss, fuss!"

"It's a beautiful poem," said Gabriel admiringly. "I
could listen and listen and listen."

"Thank you kindly," said Peter.

"Maybe I can help you think of a way to let Parson
Pease-Porridge know he has a poor hungry Churchmouse," said Gabriel. "So you'll get lots to eat like I do."

"But how?" said Peter.

"I really don't know," said Gabriel. "I'll think very
hard."

"Please do," said Peter. "Think hard while I have a lick
of your milk."

So Peter played hide-behind-the-hymn-book on the
shelf where the hymn books were kept. And Gabriel
played chew-the-toe with Parson Pease-Porridge's old
black slipper. And they both played slide-up-and-down
the pew bench.

And all the while Peter longed and longed for cheese.
And all the while Gabriel thought and thought about

how he could help poor Peter. But Gabriel couldn't think of a single way.

"Listen, Gabriel," said Peter at last.

"I am," said Gabriel. "I'm listening."

"That's fine," said Peter, "because I have an idea about how I can get Parson Pease-Porridge to notice me."

"And get some cheese," added Gabriel.

"Well," said Peter. "I've heard Parson Pease-Porridge say that little children who drink lots of milk grow up to be big children, and you're a big kitten so it must be because you drink lots of milk. So *maybe* if I drink lots of milk I'll grow so big that Parson Pease-Porridge will be able to see me!"

"I *am* a big kitten," admitted Gabriel. "So that must be the reason. Help yourself to some more of my milk."

"Thank you," said Peter between licks, "I much prefer cheese but I'll take anything, even milk, if only Parson Pease-Porridge will notice me!"

"I'll be twitched," remarked Parson Pease-Porridge. "I never knew a kitten to drink so much milk!"

For Peter drank and drank Gabriel's milk every day. And every day he asked Gabriel if he had grown any bigger. And every day he looked in the mirror over the organ to see if he looked any bigger. And every day Gabriel measured him alongside Parson Pease-Porridge's ink bottle to see if he stretched any bigger—but he didn't. Not one bit.

"Except," said Gabriel, "your waist is nearly as round as the ink bottle."

"It's no use," said poor Peter, "no use at all."

"Make a poem about it," said Gabriel.

"Very well," said Peter, lifting his eyebrows—

> "Drink, drink, drink,
> To make me bigger;
> But all I do
> Is lose my figure.
> Fuss, fuss, fuss!"

"How beautiful," said Gabriel. "I could listen and listen."

Peter stopped dancing on the black notes of the organ and looked over the edge of the keyboard at Gabriel.

"Gabriel, do you know what?" asked Peter.

Gabriel stopped sharpening his nails on the organ's green carpet pedals and looked up at Peter.

"I don't," said Gabriel.

"I have another idea, that's what!" said Peter. "About how I can get Parson Pease-Porridge to notice me."

"And get some cheese," added Gabriel.

"If," said Peter, waving his arms, "Parson Pease-Porridge saw my nice red knitted bed he'd know it was much too small for rats to sleep in. So he'd know right off that a little Churchmouse slept in it. Wouldn't he?"

"Quite true," agreed Gabriel. "And it's such a beautiful bed, too."

"It *is* a nice bed," said Peter. "We'll put it beside his black leather book so he'll be sure to see it."

"We'll do it right now," said Gabriel, "because I've heard Parson Pease-Porridge say 'never put off till tomorrow what you can do right now.'"

So Peter and Gabriel laid the red knitted bed right beside the big black leather book.

"There," said Peter, "Parson Pease-Porridge will be *sure* to notice that!"

"I'll be twitched," said Parson Pease-Porridge when he saw Peter's knitted bed beside his black leather book.

"How in the world did my old red mitten get here? I've been hunting for that good red mitten for ages. Hem-mmp! I'm a forgetful old man! So I'll just put this mitten in my pocket so I won't lose it again. Hemp, hemp-p-p!"

And away went Parson Pease-Porridge with Peter's bed.

"How very, very sad," said Gabriel. "Now your bed's gone."

"It's the only bed I had," said poor little Peter. "The only bed I *ever* had."

"You *should* make a poem about it," encouraged Gabriel.

"I will," said Peter lifting his eyebrows—

> "I had a bed,
> My bed was red.
> Now it's gone,
> I have no place to rest my head.
> It's gone—my lovely bed!"

"It's a beautiful poem," said Gabriel. "It's so sad, I could listen and listen and listen."

"Peter, do you know what?" asked Gabriel.

"I do not," said Peter who was sniffing the flowers that stood on Parson Pease-Porridge's desk.

"I have an idea," answered Gabriel, "that will be *sure* to get Parson Pease-Porridge to notice you."

"So I'll get some cheese," said Peter. "Hurry and tell me."

"It's this," said Gabriel. "If you stood right under Parson Pease-Porridge's nose he'd have to see you. Wouldn't he?"

"True," said Peter. "But how *can* I stand right under Parson Pease-Porridge's nose? He's much too tall."

"It's really quite simple," said Gabriel. "When Parson Pease-Porridge sits at his desk to read his big black book it's right under his nose. So if you jump out of those flowers, plop, onto the big black book you'll be right under his nose, too. Then if you'll stand very still he'll be sure to notice you."

"True, true," said Peter. "I'll climb into the flowers right now."

"Do hurry," whispered Gabriel. "Parson Pease-Porridge is coming!"

"Hum-mp," said Parson Pease-Porridge sitting down at his desk.

"Hemp, hem-mmp," said Parson Pease-Porridge opening his black leather book.

"Now," whispered Peter to himself. "Now is the time!"

So plop, jumped Peter, plump in the middle. Right under Parson Pease-Porridge's nose!

"And *now*," said Peter to himself, "Parson Pease-Porridge will be *sure* to notice me."

"I'll be twitched," said Parson Pease-Porridge, pushing up his spectacles. "What's this? Oh, I'm a bothered old man.

"I'll be twitched," said Parson Pease-Porridge pushing his spectacles down again. "I see a grey spot before my eyes!

"I must have my glasses changed," said he, closing his big book with a terrible—

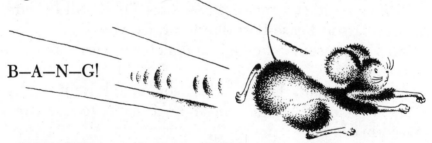

B—A—N—G!

"Oh-h-h," gasped Peter. "Oh-h, poor me."

"He thought you were a grey spot," said Gabriel.

"I might have been," said Peter.

"Very true," said Gabriel. "How awful!"

"I shall make a poem about it," said Peter raising his eyebrows—

> "I jumped quick
> When the book closed whang.
> I learned the trick
> On the snap-rat bang.
> Fuss, fuss, fuss!"

"Very lovely," sighed Gabriel. "I could listen and listen."

"I have another idea," said Gabriel.

"About how I can get Parson Pease-Porridge to notice me so I'll get cheese?" asked Peter.

"That's right," said Gabriel.

"Then please stop playing jump-over-the-pew-bench," said Peter, "because I'm listening."

"It's this," said Gabriel. "I'll spill Parson Pease-Porridge's ink bottle. Then you can walk in the ink and make foot-prints on his big white blotter, and when he sees your little foot-prints he'll know you're a little Churchmouse."

"Then I'll get cheese," said Peter. "Cheese!"

"Quite true," said Gabriel. "Follow me."

So up they jumped onto Parson Pease-Porridge's desk. Gabriel gave the ink bottle a big push. Over it went and out came the ink.

"Now," said Gabriel. "Make some tracks."

"I will," said Peter running right through the ink and right onto Parson Pease-Porridge's clean white blotter. And he went round and round and round.

"Stop, Peter!" cried Gabriel. "Stop!"

"Why?" asked Peter.

"Because," cried Gabriel, "look what's happening!"

For every step poor Peter took on the blotter was spreading bigger and bigger.

"Don't make more prints. Parson Pease-Porridge will think I've done it," cried Gabriel. "Quick! Dry your feet on something!"

"I'll dry my feet here," said Peter, jumping from the blotter to the sermon that Parson Pease-Porridge had finished writing that very morning.

"Hurry, hurry," cried Gabriel. "Here comes Parson Pease-Porridge. We'd better go!"

"Fuss, fuss, fuss," said Peter wiping his feet very hard all along the bottom of Parson Pease-Porridge's sermon.

"I'll be twitched," said Parson Pease-Porridge, "Gabriel has spilled my ink! Tut, tut, look at his big tracks on my blotter!

"Tut, tut, *tut*," said Parson Pease-Porridge looking from the blotter to his sermon, "I'm a bothered old man. It seems I've made foot-notes on the bottom of my sermon, but I can't seem to read them. Hem-mp! That settles it. I *must* have my glasses changed this *very* day.

"A pretty pass!" said Parson Pease-Porridge as he hurried away. "Can't even read my *own* foot-notes!"

"It's no use," said Peter. "Parson Pease-Porridge will never notice me. Never."

"And you'll never get any cheese," added Gabriel.

"But I *must* have cheese," cried Peter.

"How sad for you," said Gabriel. "Make a poem about it."

"I shall," said Peter lifting his eyebrows—

> "Oh, please, please,
> I want cheese.
> I'm sad, sad,
> I wish I had
> Cheese, Cheese, CHEESE!"

"Lovely," said Gabriel. "I could listen and listen."

"Gabriel," said Peter, "I'm going to bite a hole in something!"

"Oh, do!" encouraged Gabriel. "Do bite something!"

"I will," said Peter. "I'll bite a hole right through the middle of Parson Pease-Porridge's sermon! Then he'll notice me!"

So Peter began to bite and bite right through the middle of Parson Pease-Porridge's sermon.

"Oh my, it's the biggest hole I've ever seen," admired Gabriel, when Peter had finished.

"It's the biggest hole I ever bit," said Peter.

The next day Parson Pease-Porridge had a new pair of spectacles that were three times as thick and three times as strong as his old ones.

"Hem-mp," said he. "It's fine to have new spectacles. I can see everything. I believe I'll have a look at my sermon!

"I'll be twitched," cried Parson Pease-Porridge when he saw the *tremendous* hole in the middle of his sermon. "Oh ruination! Oh, I'm a bothered old man!"

And *then* Parson Pease-Porridge looked at the foot-notes that he couldn't read the day before.

"Upon my soul," cried Parson Pease-Porridge. "These are *not* foot-notes, these are foot-prints! Little foot-prints! I have a Churchmouse! Poor little thing he's eaten all these holes to show me he's hungry!"

"Hem-m-mp," said Parson Pease-Porridge. "Owing to this slight accident (here Parson Pease-Porridge looked at the hole in his sermon) I must abandon the text I prepared for today. So I shall speak about KINDNESS instead. KINDNESS to very little animals.

"And now," smiled Parson Pease-Porridge, "never put off till tomorrow what you can do right now!

"I must get CHEESE for my Churchmouse!"

"Oh-h, Gabriel," whispered Peter. "Did you hear that?"

"I did," said Gabriel. "Parson Pease-Porridge has noticed you at last!"

"Oh, poor me," cried Peter. "I'm going to get cheese after all!"

"Quite true," replied Gabriel.

"I'll make a little poem about it," said Peter lifting his eyebrows the way he always did—

> "Cheese,
> Cheese, cheese,
> Cheese, cheese, cheese,
> C—H—E—E—S—E!"

"How beautiful," sighed Gabriel. "I could listen and listen and listen."

Peter Churchmouse's other adventures can be read in Margot Austin's *Churchmouse Stories.* Miss Austin has also written more about Gabriel in *Gabriel Churchkitten,* and *Gabriel Churchkitten and the Moths.* All three are published by E. P. Dutton.

The Five Chinese Brothers

BY CLAIRE HUTCHET BISHOP

Illustrations by the author

ONCE upon a time there were Five Chinese Brothers and they all looked exactly alike. They lived with their mother in a little house not far from the sea.

The First Chinese Brother could swallow the sea.
The Second Chinese Brother had an iron neck.
The Third Chinese Brother could stretch and stretch
and stretch his legs.
The Fourth Chinese Brother could not be burned.
And
The Fifth Chinese Brother could hold his breath
indefinitely.

Every morning the First Chinese Brother would go fishing, and whatever the weather, he would come back to the village with beautiful and rare fish which he had caught and could sell at the market for a very good price.

One day, as he was leaving the market place, a little boy stopped him and asked him if he could go fishing with him.

"No, it could not be done," said the First Chinese Brother.

But the little boy begged and begged and finally the First Chinese Brother consented. "Under one condition," said he, "and that is that you shall obey me promptly."

"Yes, yes," the little boy promised.

Early next morning, the First Chinese Brother and the little boy went down to the beach.

"Remember," said the First Chinese Brother, "you must obey me promptly. When I make a sign for you to come back, you must come at once."

"Yes, yes," the little boy promised.

Then the First Chinese Brother swallowed the sea. And all the fish were left high and dry at the bottom of the sea. And all the treasures of the sea lay uncovered.

The little boy was delighted. He ran here and there stuffing his pockets with strange pebbles, extraordinary shells and fantastic algae.

Near the shore the First Chinese Brother gathered some fish while he kept holding the sea in his mouth. Presently he grew tired. It is very hard to hold the sea. So he made a sign with his hand for the little boy to come back. The little boy saw him but paid no attention.

The First Chinese Brother made great movements with his arms that meant "Come back!" But did the little boy care? Not a bit and he ran further away.

Then the First Chinese Brother felt the sea swelling inside him and he made desperate gestures to call the little boy back. But the little boy made faces at him and fled as fast as he could.

The First Chinese Brother held the sea until he thought he was going to burst. All of a sudden the sea forced its way out of his mouth, went back to its bed . . . and the little boy disappeared.

When the First Chinese Brother returned to the village, alone, he was arrested, put in prison, tried and condemned to have his head cut off.

On the morning of the execution he said to the judge:
"Your Honor, will you allow me to go and bid my
mother good-bye?"

"It is only fair," said the judge.

So the First Chinese Brother went home . . . and
the Second Chinese Brother came back in his place.

All the people were assembled on the village square
to witness the execution. The executioner took his sword
and struck a mighty blow.

But the Second Chinese Brother got up and smiled.
He was the one with the iron neck and they simply could
not cut his head off. Everybody was angry and they decided that he should be drowned.

On the morning of the execution, the Second Chinese
Brother said to the judge:

"Your Honor, will you allow me to go and bid my
mother good-bye?"

"It is only fair," said the judge.

So the Second Chinese Brother went home . . . and
the Third Chinese Brother came back in his place.

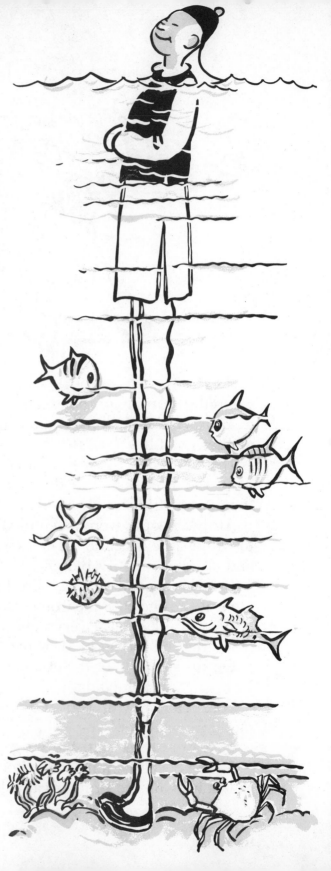

He was pushed on a boat which made for the open sea.

When they were far out on the ocean, the Third Chinese Brother was thrown overboard.

But he began to

S-T-R-E-T-C-H

and

S–T–R–E–T–C–H

and

S—T—R—E—T—C—H

his legs,
way down
to the bottom
of the sea,
and all the time
his smiling face
was bobbing up
and down
on the crest
of the waves.

He simply could not be drowned.

Everybody was very angry, and they all decided that he should be burned.

On the morning of the execution, the Third Chinese Brother said to the judge:

"Your Honor, will you allow me to go and bid my mother good-bye?"

"It is only fair," said the judge.

So the Third Chinese Brother went home . . . and the Fourth Chinese Brother came back in his place.

He was tied up to a stake. Fire was set to it and all the people stood around watching it. In the midst of the flames they heard him say:

"This is quite pleasant."

"Bring some more wood!" the people cried.

The fire roared higher.

"Now it is quite comfortable," said the Fourth Chinese Brother, for he was the one who could not be burned. Everybody was getting more and more angry every minute and they all decided to smother him.

On the morning of the execution, the Fourth Chinese Brother said to the judge:

"Your Honor, will you allow me to go and bid my mother good-bye?"

"It is only fair," said the judge.

So the Fourth Chinese Brother went home . . . and the Fifth Chinese Brother came back in his place. A large brick oven had been built on the village square and it had been all stuffed with whipped cream. The Fifth Chinese Brother was shovelled into the oven, right in the middle of the cream, the door was shut tight, and everybody sat around and waited.

They were not going to be tricked again! So they stayed there all night and even a little after dawn, just to make sure.

Then they opened the door and pulled him out. And he shook himself and said, "My! That was a good sleep!"

Everybody stared open-mouthed and round-eyed.

But the judge stepped forward and said, "We have tried to get rid of you in every possible way and somehow it cannot be done. It must be that you are innocent."

"Yes, yes," shouted all the people. So they let him go and he went home.

And

The Five Chinese Brothers and their mother all lived together happily for many years.

You won't want to miss three other exciting stories that take place in China. They are The Story About Ping, by Marjorie Flack, published by The Viking Press, Mei Li, by Thomas Handforth, published by Doubleday & Company, Inc., and The Pointed Brush, by Patricia M. Martin, published by Lothrop, Lee & Shepard Co., Inc.

Any Old Junk Today?

BY CAROLYN HAYWOOD

Illustrations by the author

> *Although only seven years old, Eddie is quite a businessman. And what business could possibly be more fun than the junk business?*

NEVER a week went by without Eddie bringing home some piece of what Eddie called "valuable property," and his father called "junk."

The family always knew when Eddie had brought home a new treasure. Eddie would always announce at dinner, "I had a very enjoyable day today." When Eddie said this, his father would look at his mother and say, "Uh! Oh!"

After dinner his father would go down to the basement, and there he would find another piece of junk added to Eddie's collection.

"Now, see here, Edward!" said his father one evening. "This junk collecting has reached the limit. What happens every week? I'll tell you. On Friday night every man in this neighborhood puts his rubbish out for the rubbish collectors, and every Saturday a large part of it lands in our basement. Now, I am tired of it. The basement looks like a junk shop, or worse. It looks like a dump. This thing has got to stop."

Eddie looked very downcast as he said, "You were glad when I brought home the telegraph pole, weren't you?"

"Well, that was different," said his father. "Moreover, that is past. I'm talking about the present. This junk collecting has reached the limit. We will never get all of this stuff out of the basement."

"But, Papa!" said Eddie. "I don't want it out. It's my valuable property."

"Valuable property!" exclaimed his father. "Junk! Nothing you ever bring home is worth the room it takes."

"I brought the telegraph pole," murmured Eddie.

"Well, yes, the telegraph pole," said his father.

The following Saturday Rudy and the twins went on a hike with some of the boys in Rudy's class in school. Eddie wanted to go, too, but they said that he was too little. He felt very badly until his mother said that he could go for a drive in the car with herself and his father. They were going out into the country to see if they could find a shop where they could buy a nice tilt-top table.

It was a beautiful day, and as they drove along the roads Eddie saw the cows and horses on the farms. He saw men working in the fields. He read the signs along the road. *Fresh Eggs. Broilers.*

The first time Eddie saw the word "broiler," he said, "What is a broiler?"

"It's a young chicken that is small enough to broil," said his mother.

Eddie could read most of the billboards. He found it exciting to be able to read, to have letters mean something.

They had been driving for about an hour when Mr. Wilson brought the car to a stop in front of a store. There was a large sign hanging outside which Eddie could not read. "What does that sign say, Pop?" asked Eddie.

"It says *Antiques*," said his father.

"Are we going to see Aunt Teek?" asked Eddie. "Does she own the store?"

"Not Aunt Teek," said his father. "Antiques. Antique means old. When you see that sign, it means that the shop sells old things."

"You mean junk?" said Eddie. "Sounds exciting!"

"No, indeed!" said his father. "These things are valuable."

By this time, Mr. and Mrs. Wilson and Eddie had gotten out of the car. They walked up the path to the porch.

"I never saw a store with a porch before," said Eddie.

"Well, you're in the country now," said his mother. "They often have porches."

Eddie looked around the porch. It was full of all kinds of objects. Among them were some huge kettles, some fire screens, and brass and iron andirons. There were long iron forks and tongs for handling the logs in a fireplace. There was an old wooden bench, and a big wooden box with pictures painted on it.

"Gee!" said Eddie. "It sure looks like junk."

The windows of the shop were filled with shelves, and the shelves were covered with glass vases, cups, plates, saltcellars, pitchers, and sugar bowls.

The inside of the store was crammed with furniture —tables, chairs, chests of drawers, and cabinets full of china. The store was big. It seemed to Eddie to go back, and back, and back.

"Jeepers!" thought Eddie. "I'll bet a fellow could find some very valuable property around here."

While his father and mother were busy talking to the owner of the shop, Eddie wandered toward the back of the place. He looked over the shelves; he peered into open boxes and barrels. Finally he went through a doorway into what seemed to be a storeroom. There he came upon a man opening a barrel.

"Hello, son!" said the man. "Can I do something for you?"

"I'm just looking around," said Eddie. "My father and mother are out there." Eddie pointed to the front of the store.

In a moment Eddie's eyes fell upon something that interested him very much indeed. On a shelf stood an old carriage lamp. It was rusty and covered with dust.

"Do you want to sell that lamp?" Eddie asked the man who was opening the barrel.

The man looked up. "I guess we do," he replied.

"How much is it?" asked Eddie.

"Oh, 'bout a quarter," said the man.

Eddie reached into his pocket and pulled out all of his money. He had seventy-five cents. Twenty-five cents was his weekly allowance. His father had given it to him that morning. The other fifty cents he had earned during the week, delivering orders for Mr. Henderson. His regular boy was away.

"Okay!" said Eddie. "I'll take it."

The man took the lamp from the shelf and blew the dust off of it. "Want it wrapped up?" he asked.

Just then Eddie's eye fell upon another interesting object. It had been hidden behind the carriage lamp. "What is that?" asked Eddie, pointing to what looked like a small iron urn with a wheel on each side. It, too, was rusty.

"Oh, that?" asked the man, lifting it down. "That's an old-fashioned coffee grinder."

"Those wheels are super!" said Eddie, his eyes very big. "How much is that?"

"Oh, I guess I can let you have that for fifty cents," said the man.

Eddie looked at the coffee grinder for a few moments. Then he said, "I'll take that, too."

"Want them wrapped?" asked the man.

"Yes, please," replied Eddie, taking a look out to the front of the store. His mother and father were busy looking at some dishes.

"Suppose I put them in this carton," said the man.

"That will be fine," said Eddie.

Eddie watched the man put the coffee grinder into the bottom of the carton. Then he put the lamp on top. When he folded over the flaps, they didn't close because

the end of the lamp was too long. The man tied a piece
of cord over the top to hold the flaps down, but the end
of the lamp still showed. "I guess that will do," he said.

"Oh, sure!" replied Eddie, as he handed over his
seventy-five cents. "That will do."

Eddie decided to go out of the back door with his
package. Once outside, he ran to the car. He thought it
would be best to put the package in the trunk of the car.
His father had left the keys in the car, so Eddie unlocked
the trunk and placed the package on the shelf. Then he
locked the trunk and put the keys in his pocket.

Eddie sauntered back to the front porch. He was examining a broken lock when his father and mother came out.

"Look, Papa," said Eddie. "This is a swell lock."

"It's a piece of junk," said Mr. Wilson. "No more junk is going into our house, Eddie. Put it down."

Eddie put the lock down and walked to the car with his father and mother. "You left the keys in the car, Pop," said Eddie, handing over the bunch of keys.

"Oh, thanks, Eddie," said his father.

They all climbed into the car. Eddie sat between his father and mother.

"Didn't they have any table, Mother?" asked Eddie.

"No, dear," replied Mrs. Wilson. "But they expect one in next week."

For some time they drove in silence. Then suddenly Eddie said, "Well, I had a very enjoyable time."

Mr. and Mrs. Wilson immediately looked down at Eddie. He looked up at them with a sweet smile on his face. Then they looked at each other. Mr. Wilson put on the brakes and stopped the car. He turned around and looked on the back seat of the car and on the floor. There was nothing there.

"What did you say, Eddie?" his father asked.

Eddie looked up and said, "I just said I've had a very enjoyable time."

Mr. Wilson took the keys from the car, opened the door, and stepped out. He walked around to the back of the car, opened the trunk, and there was Eddie's package.

Eddie, standing beside his father, said, "Please, Papa, it isn't junk. It's swell stuff."

"Eddie!" said his father, "when I said, 'No more junk,' I meant it. This isn't going another foot of the way home." To Eddie's amazement, his father placed the package in a ditch beside the road.

As Mr. Wilson leaned over, he saw the end of the carriage lamp sticking out of the top of the carton. He pulled off the cord, and lifted the lamp out of the carton.

"Say!" he cried. "Why, this is a carriage lamp. Say! This is mine. Why, I have been wanting one of these for a long time. I want it to go on the post at the front gate. Why, this is a beautiful carriage lamp. It just needs to be refinished. Well, now! This is mine!"

"But I bought it, Papa," said Eddie. "I paid for it."

"Well, I'll give you a dollar for it, Eddie," said his father. "How is that?"

"Okay!" said Eddie.

In the midst of this discovery, Mrs. Wilson joined Eddie and his father.

"Look, Mother!" Mr. Wilson cried. "Look at this fine carriage lamp. This is mine."

Mrs. Wilson was busy looking into the carton which still lay in the ditch. "Why, look at this old coffee grinder!" she cried. "Oh! What a duckie coffee grinder! Oh, this is mine! These old coffee grinders make the most beautiful lamps you ever saw! Mrs. Porter has one, and it's lovely. With a coat of red paint, this will be perfect."

Mrs. Wilson held the old coffee grinder very lovingly. "Oh! This is mine!" she said.

"But I bought it, Mamma," said Eddie. "I paid for it."

"Oh, well. I'll give you a dollar for it," said his mother. "Is a dollar all right?"

"Ah, Mamma!" said Eddie. "I like that coffee grinder. I like it a lot."

"Well, I'll give you two dollars for it," said his mother. "That's a lot of money, Eddie. Think how rich you will be."

"Okay!" said Eddie.

The three went back to the car. Mr. Wilson went first, carrying his carriage lamp. Then Mrs. Wilson, car-

rying her coffee grinder. Little Eddie brought up the
rear, with three dollars in his small fist.

When they were almost home, Mr. Wilson said, "By
the way, Eddie, how much did you pay for that lamp?"

"A quarter," said Eddie.

"And how much did you pay for the coffee grinder?"
asked his father.

"Fifty cents," Eddie replied.

"Not bad!" said his father, looking at his mother.

"You know, Papa!" said Eddie. "I've been thinking. Do
you know what I'm going to be when I grow up?"

"No," replied Mr. Wilson. "What are you going to be?"

"I'm going to be a junk man," said Eddie. "That's a
good way to get rich."

"How about letting me go into business with you?"
asked his father.

"Okay, Papa!" said Eddie. "Will we have a store?"

"Oh, certainly!" said his father. "And we'll have a big
sign that says, *Wilson and Son—All Kinds of Junk*."

*This author has written other books about
Eddie, including* Eddie and Gardenia *and*
Eddie's Pay Dirt, *both published by William
Morrow and Company.*

Susanna's Auction

From the French

Illustrations by Boutet de Monvel

SUSANNA is no longer a little girl. She is now three years old. That is not so very old, but even at that age a girl may be head-strong and like to have her own way in everything.

And such is the case with Susanna. When she has made up her mind to do a thing she is not willing to give it up. She wishes to do just as she pleases. Susanna is very, very obstinate.

And Susanna has another fault. She will climb up on the furniture. Nobody can tell how many times she has fallen and pulled over the table and chair upon which she was climbing, and broken things.

And this very story is written to tell you the sad things that happened to Susanna through these two faults of hers—her obstinacy and her love of climbing.

One day when she and her mamma were in the parlor together Susanna climbed upon a seat, as usual.

Now if she had been content to sit down upon the seat like a well-behaved little girl and look over the picture book which lay on the table beside her, nobody would have said a word.

But Susanna never looks at a picture book long at a time, no matter how pretty the pictures are. So she soon shut it up and pushed it one side.

Then she got up on her knees upon the seat and began

Susanna's Auction, with illustrations by Boutet de Monvel, is published by The Macmillan Company.

to tip a vase of flowers that stood upon the table first over one side and then the other with both hands.

"Take care, Susanna!" said her mother. "You will break the vase."

But Susanna kept right on tipping the vase and smelling the flowers, without minding at all what her mother said.

"Susanna, do you not hear me?" said her mother, speaking again. "I tell you you will break the vase."

Then Susanna, without turning her head, or even looking at her mother, replied:

"If I break it I can pay for it!" That was the rude and saucy thing that Susanna said; and just at that moment the door opened and in walked papa!

There stood Susanna looking sullenly down at the broken vase.

"What is the matter?" he asked. "Has Susanna been naughty? Has my little daughter been disobedient?"

But Susanna did not answer. She shut her lips tightly, and did not lift her eyes. So mama had to tell the story.

Papa listened. When mama had finished he spoke, and his voice sounded harsh and cold, not a bit like the gentle tones in which he usually spoke to his little daughter.

"Very well," he said, "it is all very simple; Susanna said

if she broke the vase she could pay for it. She has broken it, and now let her pay for it.

"Unless," he added, "she is really sorry for her disobedience, and will ask pardon, and will try to do better in the future."

He stopped and looked at Susanna. But she only shut her lips together tightly, and it was plain that she was not one bit sorry, and that she did not mean to speak.

Then mamma came up, oh, the poor mamma! who was grieved to see her little daughter so naughty, and

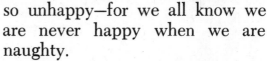

so unhappy—for we all know we are never happy when we are naughty.

"Come, Susanna," she said gently. "Ask pardon of papa and mama."

But Susanna was mute.

"Will you not ask pardon?" she said.

Not a word from Susanna.

"Ah, very well," said papa. "It seems that Susanna prefers to pay for the vase. Then let her go for her money."

Now Susanna kept her money in a pretty little velvet purse that her Uncle Felix had given her on her very last birthday. And in this purse was a gold piece, and some silver coins, all bright and new. She was fond of the purse and the money, too. And when papa said "Let her fetch the money," she could have cried right out loud had she not been so "stuffy."

But though she kept her lips pressed tightly together, when she went to get it, she could not help hugging it and talking to it and kissing it all the way back. But there was something worse than that loss in store for her.

Susanna came back, opened the purse, took out the gold piece and the silver coins, and handed them to mama—in all, two dollars and fifty cents.

"But," said papa, "the vase cost much more than that. The vase is not worth less than twenty dollars! Did you know that, Susanna?"

Susanna did not answer.

"My dear," said papa gravely, turning to mama, "what do you think about it all?"

"I think that Susanna is sorry for what she has done, and that she is all ready to say so, and to go to papa and kiss him. Is it not so, Susanna?"

Susanna dropped her head.

"Come, my little daughter," said mama, "be a good girl; give me your hand, and we will go and ask pardon of papa."

Susanna put both her hands behind her back.

"Susanna!" said mama.

"Let her alone, my dear," said papa. "Since she is determined not to ask pardon, and her two dollars and a half is not enough to pay for the vase, we must sell what things belong to her. Let us see! What has she got?"

"There are her gowns, her pretty hat, her"—Mama was going to say more, but papa interrupted her.

"I beg your pardon," he said, "but a little girl's clothes belong to her parents. They only provide them for her so that she will not have to go without."

Here Susanna made up a face. But papa went on. "She has really nothing of her own except her toys and her dolls. We must sell those. We will sell them at auction," he added.

"But where?" asked mamma.

"Right here, tomorrow," said papa. "We will invite all the cousins, boys and girls, to come and pass tomorrow afternoon with us. Then we shall have plenty of buyers."

The next day at two o'clock they arrived—all the boy and girl cousins, and all the uncles and aunts. There were a great many, for the family was a large one. Some little friends were also invited. The parlor where the auction was to be held was crowded. All the heavy pieces of furniture were taken out, and five rows of chairs were set for the children. The elder people stood behind them, and in the dining room.

And Susanna? What did she say to all the preparation? Not a word! She remained sullen. Once during the night mamma thought she heard a stifled sob or two from the little bed which stood near her own; and she asked Susanna if she were crying.

"No, mamma," said Susanna. "I am wiping my nose."

There was nothing then but to go on with the auction. And this was done.

All Susanna's dolls and toys were brought out and arranged upon the table, and the auction began.

Uncle George was the auctioneer. Now Uncle George is usually the jolliest of uncles. He knows how to play all sorts of games and can tell the most delightful stories. But on this occasion he was grave. He did not even smile. He walked slowly up the steps and in behind the table. He had a small ivory hammer in his hand. He

looked around upon the boys and girls with a sad and gloomy air.

Uncle Julius, who has a loud voice, took his place beside Uncle George to help him. "Gentlemen," he said —an auctioneer never addresses the ladies—"gentlemen, we will open the sale with this doll. It is dressed and has joints; its hair is frizzed and it has a china head and blue enamel eyes. Pass it on, please," and he handed it down to the buyers to examine. There was a murmur of delight among the girls as they passed it from one to another.

"Oh! what a sweet china head," whispered Marie to Helen.

"What am I offered for it?" asked Uncle Julius.

No one answered.

"Such dolls are certainly worth five cents," said Uncle George.

There was a stir among the buyers.

"Why don't you bid?" asked Andrew of his little sister Marie. "Call out three cents."

"Three cents!" said little Marie.

"I beg your pardon!" interrupted Uncle George. "But this is a real sale. I must warn you that I can have no joking. I said that such dolls were worth five cents. At auctions all articles bring more than in the shops. The only way to do is to make a higher bid—say six cents, seven cents, eight cents."

"Eight cents!" shouted Eliza very loud.

"That's right," said Uncle George. "I see that you understand, Eliza. Go on!"

"Ten cents!" shouted Helen, making a bid for Marie.

Eliza stood up, trembling with eagerness, and cried: "Eleven cents!"

Helen, too, sprang up from her chair, and the struggle began.

"Twelve cents!" "Thirteen cents!" "Fourteen!" "Fifteen!"

Then there was a dead silence. Eliza sat down; she had to give up. She had got to the end of her money.

"Sixteen cents! I am offered sixteen cents for this fine china-headed doll. Shall I not have another bid? Shall I not have seventeen cents?" asked Uncle George.

He waited an instant, but no one spoke. Then he brought his ivory hammer down upon the table. "The doll belongs to Miss Helen, that is—I believe—to the little Marie," he said. And it was handed to Marie.

After that the rest of the dolls were sold, and then came toys of all kinds. For Susanna had had many presents from her uncles and aunts as well as from the friends of her papa and mamma. And those kind friends had never suspected that some day their gifts would have to be sold at public auction, just on account of Susanna's obstinacy.

It would take too much space to tell how toy after toy was sold, in order that Susanna's possessions might pay for the broken vase.

But some things must not be passed by.

You remember the struggle between Eliza and little Marie over the fine doll with a china head and blue enamel eyes? Before the sale of the dolls was over they had another.

This time it was a sleeping doll that they both wanted, that is, a doll that shuts its eyes and goes to sleep when laid in the bed. But Marie outbid Eliza a second time and the sleeping doll was knocked off to her.

But when it was handed to her by Uncle Julius she found that it would not go to sleep. It was out of order, and it lay flat with its eyes wide open. Then Marie, being a small girl only three years old, began to cry.

Eugene was also very young, and when he saw his dear little cousin crying he, too, began to cry out of sympathy. And the two made such a disturbance the auction had to stop till Marie was comforted.

When the animals were put up for sale the boys began to bid, and soon a battle was raging between Andrew and Leopold over an elephant with big ears. They bid very fast, one over the other, and the elephant seemed likely to be sold at a high price, when Leopold suddenly thought to remark that his left ear was torn. He said this so loud that Andrew heard him. He was going to outbid Leopold, but when he heard him say that, he stopped an instant to examine the elephant. While he was looking, Uncle Julius, hearing no one bid, knocked it off to the crafty Leopold.

Mention must be made, too, of a lovely sheep, which had real wool. It wore a blue ribbon around its neck, and went on wheels and could bleat. There was much lively bidding for this, and great excitement, as Uncle Julius caused it to bleat after every bid, and Leopold paid the last cent in his purse to secure it.

There was a cow which had a great success and brought a good price. She gave milk and could bellow. A general scrimmage took place over this cow, for everybody wanted her. She was finally knocked off to Helen for forty cents. Leopold, who had farming tastes, was quite wretched because he could not even bid upon her, and resolved to make a private trade with Helen, and exchange his elephant for her.

"But where was Susanna during all this time?" "How did she appear while her auction was going on?" "Was she sorry to see her dolls and cows and sheep and elephants sold?" "Did she not run to papa and ask pardon and beg him to stop it?" I hear these questions from the readers.

Alas, no!

She looked on, at first, with an air of indifference.

She did not seem to care even when Uncle Julius milked her cow to show that it really did give milk. During the battle between Andrew and Leopold over the big-eared elephant, she showed no interest. Soon after that she became sullen and put her chin down into her collar and set the toe of one boot over the other and was "the very picture of obstinacy."

But the story is not yet finished.

Everything was sold. Uncle Eugene had just bought the last—a whole lot of toys for three cents, to give to the poor children in that part of the city —when Susanna's nurse discovered another doll tucked away in a corner of the closet where Susanna's playthings were kept. She brought her out and gave her to Uncle Julius.

It must be owned that she was a very shabby doll. She had, however, seen better days. She had been given to Susanna by her friend Joseph. And Susanna had been so much pleased with her—for she was then a beautiful creature—that she had named her Josephine as a compliment to the giver.

But of late Susanna had been so taken up with her other children that she had allowed poor Josephine to be knocked about, until she had lost first an arm, then

a leg, then an eye, and at last more than half her hair.
Yes, she was a very shabby child—a poor useless invalid.
But, shabby as she was, she must be sold with the rest
of the family.

Uncle Julius held her up that all might see her, and
said, "We will now sell a sick doll, which"—

But his sentence was never finished. Susanna, struck
with shame and sorrow at the thought of having her
sick child sold, threw herself upon Uncle Julius and
tried to seize hold of Josephine, crying out:

"No! no! it is Josephine! I can't have
Josephine sold!"

Then came a great flood of tears.
As her papa and mama hastened to
her, she cried again: "Pardon, papa!
Pardon, mama! It is Josephine! I
can't have Josephine sold. Pardon!
pardon!"

The auctioneer arose from his chair
with dignity. "Do you ask pardon,
Miss?" he said.

"Yes. I want Josephine," was the
answer.

"That is sufficient," said Uncle
George. "The auction is over. Uncle Julius, return Josephine to her mother."

Uncle Julius did so, and Susanna hugged her and
covered her with kisses. And at the same time her papa
and mamma kissed Susanna, who promised to be a good
child in the future.

"And so I suppose they gave back to her all her playthings," somebody says. By no means. You forget that
Uncle George said the sale was a real one. So, of course,
the things were really sold, and could not be taken back.

But to keep Susanna in mind of her promise to be a
good child, her papa and mamma bought a set of bed-

room furniture for Josephine. Still, although her little mother now loves her dearly, and with constancy, Josephine can never regain the leg and arm and eye which she has lost. But Susanna tells her that if she is obedient her hair will grow again.

This story was first written in French about a little French girl. But boys and girls everywhere know just how Suzanna felt. If you liked this story you will also enjoy reading The Most Wonderful Doll in the World *by Phyllis McGinley, published by Lippincott.*

How Little Pear
Went to the Fair

BY ELEANOR FRANCES LATTIMORE

Illustrations by the author

> *Eleanor Lattimore lived in China during her own childhood. From her memories she writes about Little Pear, who was five years old and very curious.*

THE men in the village of Shegu, where Little Pear and his family lived, were mostly farmers. All day they worked in the fields that lay on all sides of the village. Sometimes they would go to market fairs at neighboring villages to sell their grain and vegetables and to buy what they needed from other farmers.

Little Pear's father was a farmer. One day in the summer he came in from the fields very early. "There is a fair today," he said, "in the village of Wuku. I am going there to sell some of my onions and cabbages and to buy some melons and sweet potatoes. I have heard that it is a very large fair, with many things to buy besides vegetables. So I shall bring a present to each of the children when I come home."

Dagu, Ergu, and Little Pear all became very much excited. Dagu loved pretty things to wear. "I should like some silk flowers to put in my hair," she said.

Ergu liked bright-colored things to play with. "I should like a lantern," she said, "shaped like a fish or like a rabbit."

Little Pear said nothing, because what he wanted most of all was to go to the fair himself. While the others were talking he slipped out into the courtyard.

The village of Wuku was three miles away. Little Pear's father was going to walk there, pushing his wheelbarrow full of vegetables. The wheelbarrow stood in the courtyard, all ready and laden with the onions and cabbages. Little Pear walked around the wheelbarrow, looking to see whether there was any space anywhere big enough for a small boy to squeeze into. And yes! there was one. Little Pear crawled in among four cabbages and covered himself up as well as he could with some onions. Then he lay very still.

When Little Pear's father started out in the direction of Wuku it seemed to him that his wheelbarrow was

rather heavy, but he only thought, "What a fine load of vegetables I have!" He never guessed that Little Pear was hidden in the load.

"Where is Little Pear?" asked Ergu, after she and Dagu had watched their father out of sight.

"That naughty boy!" said Dagu. "He is always up to some mischief."

"I hope he hasn't run away," said his mother anxiously. But then she remembered that Little Pear had on his silver good-luck chain. "He has probably just gone to play with Big Head," she said, and went back to her work in the house.

Dagu and Ergu went back to their work too. They sat on the doorstep sewing, while the canary sang and hopped around in his cage above them. They were making shoes—shoes of black cloth, with soles made of layers and layers of white cloth, stitched together very firmly. As they embroidered flowers and butterflies on the toes of their black shoes and stitched the cloth soles, they thought of the fair and hoped that their father would return soon.

Meanwhile their father was jogging along a rough country road with his wheelbarrow, and Little Pear was curled up tight among the cabbages and onions. He was lying very still, for he was afraid that if his father should discover him he would send him home. Little Pear thought, "I shouldn't mind being spanked—so very much; but I *do* want to see the fair!"

Joggetty, joggetty, jog. The wheelbarrow went bumping along the rough road. Little Pear wanted to poke his head out, to see the countryside as they passed. But he thought that he had better keep still. From where he lay he could hear all sorts of strange sounds on all sides of him. There were donkey bells, and the jingling of traveling tinkers. There was the creaking of cart wheels, the grunting of pigs, and every once in a while there was the braying of a donkey. There were many footsteps, and voices—loud and high, and old and young. "There are lots of people going to the fair," thought Little Pear.

Joggetty, joggetty, jog. Then suddenly the wheelbarrow stopped. "Is this the fair?" Little Pear wondered, and he peeped out very cautiously from under the onions with one black apple-seed eye. Yes, they had reached the village of Wuku. It looked just like Little Pear's own village, only it was more crowded than his had been even during the New Year's festival. On every side were the people who had come to buy and sell. There were young men with round smiling faces. There were old men with high wrinkled foreheads and thin gray beards. There were farmers and merchantmen and fruit-growers, and men who sold pigs or sheep, and men who sold birds.

The fair was all along the main street of the village. Fruit and vegetables were arranged in tempting piles along both sides of the street. There were trays of candy, too—the thin flat kind made of sesame seeds stuck together with syrup, and cut in squares; the square black kind that looked like charcoal; and best of all, tang-hulurs.

There were men selling all sorts of things besides food. There were men with bundles that they untied and spread out along the sides of the street. Some of these bundles were filled with porcelain dishes, and some were filled with beads. Some had small square chests in them, with little drawers filled with curious things—small people carved out of wood, and tiny silver fishes that wriggled as though they were alive.

Little Pear saw everything as well as he could from his hiding-place. He was peeping out with both eyes now, but nobody noticed him because everybody was too busy buying and selling. The middle of the street was thronged with people, all jostling each other, and each man calling out in a loud voice the name of the thing he was selling.

"Perhaps I can climb out of this wheelbarrow without being seen," thought Little Pear, but just then there was a sudden disturbance. A man who had brought some pigs to sell was trying to pass a man with a flock of sheep. The sheep and the pigs were all getting mixed up, and the two men were angry and excited. Each one shouted out that it was the other's fault. The sheep bleated, the pigs grunted, and Little Pear, who was watching, suddenly began to laugh.

"What is the matter with your onions?" asked a farmer, who had stopped to buy from Little Pear's father. "Your onions have a voice; they are laughing."

Little Pear's father grew very angry. "Some bad boy has hidden himself under my wheelbarrow," he said. And he looked under the wheelbarrow. There was no one there.

"Look inside," suggested the farmer. So Little Pear's father lifted up the onions—and there was Little Pear!

By this time a crowd of people had gathered around

the wheelbarrow. They all laughed loudly when they saw what was inside. "Did he grow on your farm?" they asked Little Pear's father. "You must have a very remarkable farm!" Then they all laughed again, and they all stared at Little Pear, who sat among the cabbages with his pigtail standing straight up in the air.

Little Pear's father started to be angry, but when he saw that everybody thought it was a joke he laughed too. "This is not for sale," he said, patting Little Pear on the head, "but the rest is."

The men were all in a good humor now. They started to buy the cabbages and onions. Soon everything was sold, and Little Pear's father had an empty wheelbarrow and several strings of money. "Perhaps it is a good thing that you came," he said to Little Pear. "Now I shall buy some sweet potatoes and some melons."

When they returned home that evening Little Pear rode in the wheelbarrow again, but this time he sat on top of the load instead of being hidden. In one hand he held a present for Dagu—some beautiful silk flowers fastened on long pins to put in her hair. In his other hand was the present for Ergu—a lovely green lantern shaped like a rabbit. And as for Little Pear—well! he had had a trip to the fair!

Another book about Little Pear is called Little Pear and His Friends, also published by Harcourt, Brace and Company. A third book is Little Pear and the Rabbits, published by William Morrow and Company.

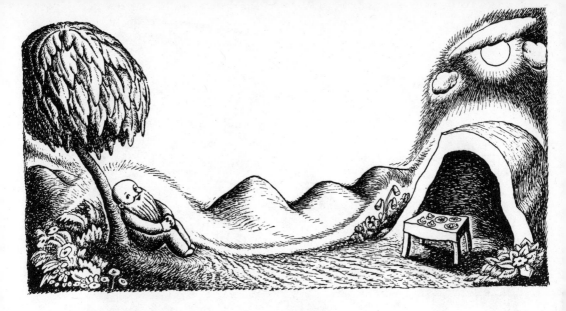

The Funny Thing

BY WANDA GÁG

Illustrations by the author

It was a beautiful day in the mountains. The sun was playing hide-and-seek among the fluffy, floating clouds, and the air was soft and warm.

Bobo, the good little man of the mountains, was waiting for the birds and animals to come. To come for what do you suppose?

To come for food—because at
the door of his mountain
cave, Bobo had many
good things for
them to eat.

He had nut cakes for the fuzzy tailed squirrels.
He had seed puddings for the pretty fluttering birds.

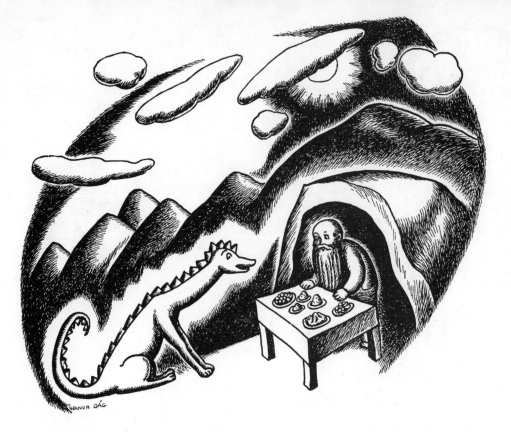

He had cabbage salads for the long-eared rabbits.

He had tiny cheeses—no bigger than cherries—
and these were for the little mice.

Now on this beautiful sunny day, there came a Funny
Thing which Bobo had never seen before. It looked
something like a dog and also a little like a giraffe, and
from the top of its head to the tip of its curled tail, there
was a row of beautiful blue points.

"Good morning," said Bobo. "And what kind of an
animal are you?"

"I'm not an animal," said the Funny Thing. "I'm an
aminal!"

Bobo was about to say that there was no such word
as *aminal*, when the Funny Thing looked around fierce-
ly and cried, "And what have you for a hungry *aminal*
to eat?"

"Oh," said Bobo, "here are some lovely nut cakes."

"I also have some fine seed puddings."

"This cabbage salad is very nice—"

"—and I'm sure you'd like these little cheeses."

But the Funny Thing turned away and said, "I never heard of such silly food! No *aminal* would eat those things. Haven't you any dolls to-day?"

"Dolls!" cried Bobo in surprise.

"Certainly," said the Funny Thing. "And very good they are—dolls."

"To eat?" cried Bobo, opening his eyes very wide at such an idea.

"To eat, of course," said the Funny Thing smacking his lips. "And very good they are—dolls."

"But it is not kind to eat up little children's dolls," said Bobo, "I should think it would make them very unhappy."

"So it does," said the Funny Thing, smiling pleasantly, "but very good they are—dolls."

"And don't the children cry when you take away their dolls?" asked Bobo.

"Don't they though!" said the Funny Thing with a cheerful grin, "but very good they are—dolls."

Tears rolled down Bobo's face as he thought of the Funny Thing going around eating up dear little children's dolls.

"But perhaps you take only naughty children's dolls," he said, brightening up.

"No, I take them specially from good children," said the Funny Thing gleefully, "and *very* good they are—good children's dolls!"

"Oh, what shall I do?" thought Bobo, as he walked back and forth, back and forth. He was trying to think of a plan to make this naughty *aminal* forget to eat dolls.

At last he had an idea!

So he said to the Funny Thing, "What a lovely tail you have!"

The Funny Thing smiled and wriggled his tail with a pleased motion.

"And those pretty black eyebrows," Bobo continued.

The Funny Thing looked down modestly and smiled even more.

"But most wonderful of all is that row of blue points down your back," said Bobo.

The Funny Thing was so pleased at this that he rolled foolishly on the ground and smiled very hard.

Then Bobo, who was really a wise old man, said to the Funny Thing, "I suppose you are so beautiful because you eat a great many jum-jills?"

The Funny Thing had never heard of them.

"Jum-jills?" he asked eagerly. "What is a jum-jill—is it a kind of doll?"

"Oh no," said Bobo. "Jum-jills are funny little cakes which make blue points more beautiful, and little tails grow into big ones."

Now the Funny Thing was very vain and there was nothing he would rather have had than a very long tail and bigger and more beautiful blue points. So he cried, "Oh please, dear kind man, give me many jum-jills!"

"Very well," said Bobo. "Sit down under this tree and wait for me."

The Funny Thing was all smiles and did as he was told, while Bobo went into his cozy little home, which was like a sort of tunnel under the mountain.

First he had to go through his little bedroom. Next he came to his study and finally he reached the kitchen, where he usually made up the food for the birds and animals.

Now he took a big bowl, into which he put:

> seven nut cakes
> five seed puddings
> two cabbage salads
> and fifteen little cheeses.

He mixed them with a spoon and rolled them into little round balls.

These little balls were jum-jills.

He put them all on a plate and carried them out to the Funny Thing, who was still waiting under the tree.

"Here are your jum-jills," said Bobo, as he handed the plate to the Funny Thing.

The Funny Thing ate one and said, "And very good they are—jum-jills."

Then he ate another and said, "And very good they
are—jum-jills."

And so on until he had eaten them all up. "And *very*
good they are—jum-jills," he said with a smack of his
lips, after they were all gone.

Then the Funny Thing went home, but the next day
he came back for more jum-jills. His tail was already a
little longer, his blue points were beginning to grow,
and he looked very happy indeed.

Every day the Funny Thing came back for more
jum-jills. He came for a long, long time and each day
his tail was a little longer. But on the twentieth day his
tail had grown so long that he couldn't move about
much.

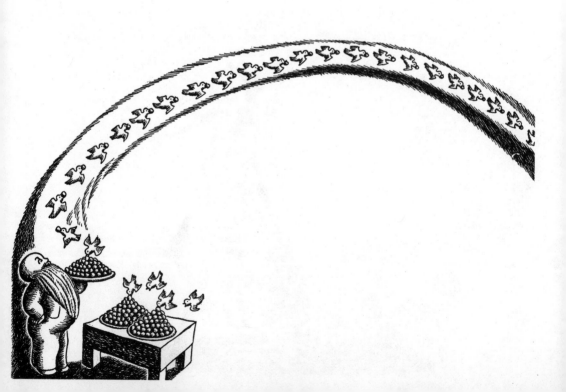

So
he chose
a nice big mountain
and sat on the very top of it.
Every day Bobo sent birds to carry
jum-jills to the Funny Thing, and as
the Funny Thing's tail grew longer and longer,
he curled it contentedly around his mountain.

His one joy in life was his beautiful blue-pointed tail,
and by and by the only words he ever said were:
"And very good they are—jum-jills!"
So of course he ate no more dolls and we have kind
old Bobo to thank for that.

If you have had fun reading The Funny
Thing, *your fun will continue when you read
Wanda Gág's* Millions of Cats, Gone is
Gone, Nothing at All, *and* Snippy and Snap-
py, *all published by Coward-McCann.*

The Little Old Woman Who Used Her Head

BY HOPE NEWELL

Illustrations by the author

The Little Old Woman

ONCE upon a time there was a Little Old Woman. She lived in a little yellow house with a blue door and two blue window boxes. In each of the window boxes there were yellow tulips.

All around her house was a neat blue fence. Inside the fence was the Little Old Woman's soup garden. She called it a soup garden because she raised vegetables in it, to cook in her soup. She raised carrots, potatoes, turnips, garlic, cabbages and onions.

The Little Old Woman was very poor. If she had not been so clever, she probably could not have made both ends meet. But she was a great one for using her head. She always said, "What is the good of having a head if you don't use it?"

So, as you will see, she managed to get along very well.

How She Got a Feather Bed

The Little Old Woman had only one blanket for her bed. It was a nice red flannel blanket, but it was full of holes.

"I must get a new blanket before winter comes," she said. "Or better yet, I might buy me a feather bed. How warm and cozy I would be in a feather bed on cold winter nights!"

But feather beds cost a lot or money, so the Little Old Woman bought a flock of geese instead. As she was driving them home from the market, she said to herself:

"These twelve geese will lay eggs for me all summer. Then when winter comes I will pluck their feathers and make myself a feather bed. What a clever Old Woman I am!"

When the Little Old Woman arrived home, she drove the geese into the yard and closed the gate. Then she ate her supper and went to bed.

The next morning she heard a great noise in the yard. When she opened the door the geese came running to her.

"Honk, honk!" said the big gander, flapping his wings.

"Honk, honk!" said all the other geese, flapping their wings.

Everywhere she went, the twelve geese followed her, saying, "Honk, honk!" and flapping their wings.

"Dear me," said the Little Old Woman, "I do believe they want something to eat. I must buy them some corn."

So she went to the market and bought a bag of corn for the geese.

Every morning when she opened the door, the geese came running to her.

"Honk, honk!" they said, flapping their wings.

Then she remembered to give them some corn.

The geese ate so much corn that pretty soon the Little Old Woman had to buy another bag of corn. After a while, that bag was empty too, and she had to buy another bag of corn.

"These geese eat a lot of corn," she said, "but after all, they are growing bigger and bigger. Their feathers are growing thicker and thicker. They will make me a fine feather bed when winter comes."

By and by the nights began to grow cold. The red flannel blanket was so full of holes that it did not keep the Little Old Woman warm. She shivered all night long.

"Winter will soon be here," she thought. "It is high time I plucked the geese and made my feather bed."

The next morning she went out to pluck the geese.

"How warm and contented they look," said the Little Old Woman. "They will be cold if I pluck their feathers. Maybe if I cut the holes out of the red blanket, it will be warm enough for me."

But when she fetched her scissors and cut the holes out of the red blanket, the holes were still there. In fact, they were bigger than ever.

"What am I to do?" she thought. "If I take their feathers, the geese will be cold. If I do not take their feathers, I will be cold. I suppose I had better use my head."

And here is how the Little Old Woman used her head. First she tied a wet towel around her forehead. Then she sat down with her forefinger against her nose and shut her eyes.

She used her head and used her head and used her
head. She used her head so long that it began to ache,
but finally she knew what to do.

"The red blanket is no good to me," she said. "I will cut
it into twelve pieces and make each of the geese a warm
red coat. Then I can pluck their feathers to make me a
feather bed."

The Little Old Woman set to work and made each of
the geese a little red coat. On each coat she sewed three
shiny brass buttons.

"Now I must pluck the geese and make my feather bed," said the Little Old Woman.

She took a basket and went out to pluck the geese. She plucked the big gander and put his feathers in the basket. She plucked the grey goose and put her feathers into the basket. Then she plucked the other geese and put their feathers into the basket.

When all the geese were plucked, the Little Old Woman put a little red coat on each goose and fastened it with the shiny brass buttons.

"How handsome the geese look," she said. "I was very clever to think of making the little red coats to keep them warm."

Then she carried the basket of feathers into the house and sewed them into a strong ticking to make a feather bed.

When the bed was all finished, the Little Old Woman said to herself:

"I shall sleep very warm this winter. How wise I was to buy a flock of geese to make a feather bed. It all comes of using my head."

How She Saved Her Corn

The Little Old Woman was bothered with rats. They gnawed holes in the bag of corn that she kept for the geese, and carried away the corn. They got in the cupboard and ate her victuals. They made nests in her bureau drawers. There were eight of them in all.

"These rats will eat me out of house and home if I am not careful," said the Little Old Woman. "I will catch them in a trap and drown them."

So the Little Old Woman went to the market and bought a large trap. She set the trap and baited it with bacon. Pretty soon she caught a rat.

"So far, so good," said the Little Old Woman. "Now I will drown this rat and catch another one."

But when the rat looked at her with his bright black eyes, she did not like to drown him.

"Poor thing, he looks hungry," she thought. "I will give him a bit of corn before I drown him."

After the rat had eaten the corn, he frisked about in the trap. Then he curled himself up and sat looking at the Little Old Woman with his bright black eyes.

"There is no hurry about drowning the rat," she said.

"Besides, I shall be very busy with my baking today. I will drown him tomorrow."

The next morning the Little Old Woman said to herself:

"I must drown that rat today so I can set the trap to catch another one."

But when she went up to the trap, the rat sat up on his hind legs and looked at her with his bright black eyes. She did not like to drown him.

"I shall be very busy in my garden today," thought the Little Old Woman. "Perhaps I had better wait until tomorrow to drown the rat."

The next morning the Little Old Woman said to herself:

"Today I must surely drown that rat so I can set the trap and catch the rest of them. There are seven more rats to catch, and they are eating me out of house and home."

But when she went up to the trap, the rat looked at her with his bright black eyes. Then he sat up on his hind legs and sniffed at her fingers.

"I may as well feed him some corn before I drown him," said the Little Old Woman.

When she brought the corn, the rat ate out of her hand.

"This is a very friendly rat," she said to herself. "I cannot bear to drown him. Perhaps if I open the trap and let him loose, he will run away."

The Little Old Woman opened the trap and turned the rat loose. But the rat did not run away. He came close to her and sat up on his hind legs. He sniffed at her fingers and looked at her with his bright black eyes.

"How tame he is," said the Little Old Woman. "I will keep him for a pet. But I will catch the other rats and drown them."

She set the trap again and baited it with bacon. Pretty soon she caught another rat.

"Now I will drown this one and set the trap to catch another," she said.

But when he looked at her with his bright black eyes, she did not like to drown him either. Instead of drowning him, she fed him some corn.

Every morning she gave him corn, and in a few days he was just as tame as the first rat. Meanwhile, the other six rats were getting into the cupboard and eating her victuals. They were making nests in her bureau drawers. And they were gnawing holes in the bag of corn and carrying away the corn.

"Something will have to be done," said the Little Old Woman. "The six rats I have not caught are eating me out of house and home. But whenever I catch a rat, I cannot bear to drown him. It is high time I used my head."

So the Little Old Woman tied a wet towel around her forehead and sat down with her forefinger against her nose and closed her eyes.

She used her head and used her head, and it was not very long before she knew what to do.

"I will catch the rest of the rats, one by one," she said. "When they become tame, I will keep them for pets.

"Every day I will feed them corn so they will not eat my victuals. I will also fix them a nice box to sleep in, so they will not make nests in the bureau drawers."

The Little Old Woman caught the rest of the rats one by one. When they became tame she kept them for pets. At night they slept by the fire in the nice box she had fixed for them. Every morning when she gave them corn, the rats sat up on their hind legs and ate out of her hands.

"Rats make very fine pets," said the Little Old Woman. "How clever I was to tame them. I will have to buy a little extra corn now and again. But it is far better to have eight pet rats than to be eaten out of house and home by wild rats."

How She Kept Her Geese Warm

One cold winter night, the Little Old Woman was out in the barn putting her geese to bed. She gave them some corn and took off their little red coats. Then she brushed each little coat with a whisk-broom and carefully shook out the wrinkles.

As she was folding the coats in a neat pile, she thought:

"My poor geese must be very cold at night. I have my cozy fire and my feather bed. But they have not even a blanket to keep them warm."

After the geese had eaten their corn, they began to go to roost.

"Honk, honk!" said the big gander, and he hopped up on the roost.

"Honk, honk!" said the grey goose, and she hopped up on the roost.

"Honk, honk!" said all the other geese, and they hopped up on the roost.

Then the Little Old Woman closed the barn door and went into the house. When she went to bed, she lay awake worrying about the geese. After a while she said to herself:

"I cannot sleep a wink for thinking how cold the geese must be. I had better bring them in the house where it is warm."

So the Little Old Woman dressed herself and went out to the barn to fetch the geese. She shooed them off the roost and put on their little red coats. She picked up two geese, and tucking one under each arm, she carried them into the house.

Then she went out to the barn and picked up two more geese. She tucked one goose under each arm and carried them into the house.

When the Little Old Woman had brought all the geese into the house, she said to herself:

"Now I must get them ready for bed again."

She took off their little red coats and gave the geese some corn. Then she brushed each little coat with a whisk-broom and carefully shook out all the wrinkles.

As she was folding the coats in a neat pile, she thought:

"It was very clever of me to bring the geese into the house. Now they will be warm, and I shall be able to sleep."

Then the Little Old Woman undressed herself again and went to bed.

After the geese had eaten their corn, they began to roost.

"Honk, honk!" said the gander, and he hopped up on the foot of the Little Old Woman's bed.

"Honk, honk!" said the grey goose, and she hopped up on the foot of the Little Old Woman's bed.

"Honk, honk!" said all the other geese, and they tried to hop up on the foot of the Little Old Woman's bed.

But it was not a very big bed, and there was not enough room for all the geese to roost. They began to fight. They pushed and shoved each other. They hissed and squawked and flapped their wings.

All night long the geese pushed and shoved each other. All night long they hissed and squawked and flapped their wings.

They made so much noise that the Little Old Woman did not sleep a wink.

"This will never do," she said. "When they were in the barn, I did not sleep for thinking how cold they must be. When they are in the house, I cannot sleep because they make so much noise. Perhaps if I use my head, I shall know what to do."

The Little Old Woman tied a wet towel around her forehead. Then she sat down with her forefinger against her nose and shut her eyes.

She used her head and used her head, and after a while she knew what to do.

"I will move the roost into the house," she said. "The geese will have the cozy fire to keep them warm. Then I will move my bed out into the barn. My feather bed will keep me warm, and I will not be worrying about the geese. They will not keep me awake with their noise. I shall sleep very comfortably in the barn."

The Little Old Woman moved the roost into the house, and she moved her bed out into the barn.

When night came again, she brought the geese into

the house. After she had fed them some corn, she took off their little red coats. Then they all hopped up on the roost, and the Little Old Woman went out to the barn to sleep.

Her feather bed kept her as warm as toast. She was not worried about the geese, because she knew that they were warm too. So she slept as sound as a top all night long.

How She Saved Her Last Match

When the Little Old Woman looked in her match box one morning, she saw that she had only one match left.

"Dear me," she sighed. "Tomorrow is market day and I cannot buy any more matches until then. I will not let my fire go out, for I must save this match to light my lamp tonight."

As she was eating her breakfast, she thought:

"Since I must keep the fire going all day, I may as well use it. I will heat the flat irons and do my weekly ironing."

After the Little Old Woman had washed and dried her breakfast dishes, she made ready to do her ironing. She set the irons on the stove to heat and laid the ironing board across the backs of two chairs. She fetched a soap box to stand on so she could reach the ironing board.

When the flat irons were hot, she brought out her basket of clothes and began to iron. After she had ironed a few pieces, she began to worry about the match.

"Suppose the match got broken," she thought. "I could not light my lamp tonight. I had better wrap it in a piece of cotton."

She set down her iron and plucked a piece of cotton out of the red chair cushion. She wrapped the match in the cotton so it would not get broken.

She laid it carefully in the box and went back to her ironing. After she had ironed a few more pieces, she began to worry about the match again.

"Suppose the match got damp," she thought. "I could not light my lamp tonight. I had better put it in a tin can."

The Little Old Woman set down her iron and went to fetch a tin can. She put the match in the tin can and put a cover on it so it would not get damp. She put the can carefully on the mantelpiece and went back to her ironing.

But after she had ironed quite a few pieces, she began to worry about the match again.

"Maybe it is not a good match and will not light when I strike it," she thought. "Then I could not light my lamp tonight."

The more she thought about it, the more worried she was.

"Dear me," she thought, "I know the match will not get broken, for I have wrapped it in cotton. I know it will not get damp, for I have put it in a tin can. But how am I to know whether it will light when I strike it?"

She worried so much about the match that she forgot to mind her ironing. For a long time she did not iron a single piece. She just stood on the soap box wondering if the match would light. Finally she said:

"This is no way to act. If I go on worrying about the match I shall never get my ironing finished. Maybe if I use my head, I shall find out what to do."

So the Little Old Woman tied a wet towel around her head and sat down with her finger against her nose and shut her eyes.

She had hardly used her head any time before she knew what to do.

"How silly I am," chuckled the Little Old Woman. "I should have known what to do without even using my head. I will strike the match this minute and then I'll find out if it will light."

She took the match out of the tin can and unwrapped the cotton from it. Then she struck the match against the mantelpiece.

But it did not light.

She struck it again.

But the match did not light.

She struck it a third time, and the match burst into flame.

As she watched it burn, she said, "This match burns very nicely indeed."

When the match had burned out, the Little Old Woman went back to her ironing.

"Now I will not be worrying about the match," she thought. "I shall be able to mind my ironing."

She ironed and ironed, until by and by the basket was empty. Then she put her ironing board away and set her irons on the back of the stove to cool.

"It's getting dark now," she said to herself. "I had better light my lamp."

She filled the lamp with oil and trimmed the wick so that it would burn brightly.

"But now I have no match to light it with," exclaimed the Little Old Woman. "Dear me, perhaps I should have used my head a little longer after all."

After she had thought about it a while, she said:

"Oh, well, I can light a piece of paper from the fire in the stove, and light the lamp from that."

When she had lighted the lamp with a piece of paper, she looked at the big pile of ironing she had done.

"It is just as well that I did strike the match to see if it would light," she said. "Otherwise, I would have worried all day, and I would never have finished so much ironing. I am a very clever Old Woman after all!"

How She Planted Her Garden

All winter long the Little Old Woman had saved some tulip bulbs from her window boxes and some onion bulbs from her soup garden for her spring planting. She had kept them safe and dry in a big tin box by the fireplace.

One bright sunny morning, she said to herself: "Spring has come, and I must make ready to plant my tulips and onions."

She tied her red checked apron around her waist and laid out her garden tools. Then she opened the big tin box. She emptied the bulbs out on the table and looked at them.

"Let me see," she thought. "The big brown bulbs are one kind, and the little white bulbs are another kind. I must look sharp so I will know which are tulips and which are onions."

So she put on her glasses and looked sharply at the white bulbs. Then she looked sharply at the brown bulbs. But for the life of her, she could not tell which were tulips and which onions.

"Dear me," she sighed, "I should have tied a red string on my finger so I would remember which were which. How am I to know what kind to plant in the window boxes and what kind to plant in the soup garden?"

The Little Old Woman thought and thought. First

she decided that the big brown bulbs were tulips, and the little white bulbs were onions. Then the next minute she was just as sure that the little white bulbs were tulips and the big brown bulbs were onions. But to save her, she could not make up her mind.

"This is a fine mess I have got into," she said. "I shall have to use my head to get myself out of it."

So the Little Old Woman tied a wet towel around her forehead. Then she sat down with her forefinger against her nose and shut her eyes.

She used her head and she used her head, and at last she knew what to do.

"How silly of me to get so mixed up," she chuckled. "After all, soup garden bulbs are bound to turn into onions. And surely window box bulbs will know enough to grow into tulips. It does not matter which way I plant them."

So she planted the little white bulbs in the window boxes, and then she planted the big brown bulbs in the soup garden where they would have more room.

"I must remember to water my window boxes," said the Little Old Woman.

She had a little red sprinkling can to water the window boxes, so she tied a red string on her finger to remind her to water them.

"But I must remember to water the soup garden as well," she thought.

So she bought a little blue sprinkling can for the soup garden. Then she tied a blue string on her finger to remind her to water it.

Every day the Little Old Woman watered the window boxes with the little red sprinkling can. Then she watered the soup garden with the little blue sprinkling can.

After a while she saw some little green shoots growing in the window boxes.

"I shall soon have some pretty tulips to look at," she said.

When she went out to water the soup garden she saw some little green shoots in it too.

"I shall soon have some nice onions for my soup," she said.

Every morning she looked in the window boxes to see if there were any tulip buds. The green shoots grew taller and taller, but she could not find a bud on them.

Then she would go out in the soup garden and pull up a bulb. But although the bulbs grew bigger and bigger, they did not taste like onions at all.

At last the plants in the window boxes were full grown. They were tall and green, but there was not a sign of a tulip bud among them.

"These plants are no good," said the Little Old Woman. "I will pull them up and plant something else."

So she pulled up one of the bulbs. When she looked

at the root, she saw that it was a nice fat onion. She pulled up another plant, and there was another onion.

"This is very strange," she said. "I think I will just have a look at the soup garden plants."

When she looked at the soup garden plants, she could hardly believe her eyes. Every one of them had a lovely yellow tulip blooming on it.

"How pretty they look," said the Little Old Woman. "I was very clever to plant them in the soup garden. I am sure they will be a great treat to the geese and to travelers passing by.

"And how smart I was to plant the onion bulbs in the window boxes. They will be very handy when I need an onion for my soup. What a wise Old Woman I am!"

How She Made Her Apron Longer

The Little Old Woman needed a new apron, but she had no money to buy one.

"If I had a nice piece of calico, I could make myself an apron," she thought. "I will look through my scrap-bag and see what I can find."

So she got out her scrap-bag and put on her spectacles. Then she sat down to look for a piece of calico to make herself an apron.

She opened the bag and began to take out the scraps of calico, one by one.

First she pulled out a piece of blue calico. It was no bigger than a handkerchief.

"This blue calico would make a fine pocket for an apron," she thought. "But what good would an apron pocket be without an apron?"

So she laid it aside and pulled out a piece of red calico. It was quite a long piece, but it was no wider than a necktie.

"This red calico would make me a fine pair of apron strings," said the Little Old Woman. "But what good would a pair of apron strings be without any apron?"

So she laid aside the red calico and pulled out a very long piece of black calico.

"This piece of black calico would make me a fine apron," she thought. "But it is too long. I am sure that it would drag on the ground. And what good would an apron be if it dragged on the ground?"

So she laid aside the black calico and then she pulled out another piece. This time she pulled out a short piece of purple calico.

"I should like a purple calico apron very much," she said to herself. "But it would be too short. It would not cover my skirt. And what good would an apron be if it did not cover my skirt?"

So the Little Old Woman laid aside the purple calico and went on pulling pieces out of her scrap-bag one by one. Some pieces were too long and some were too short. Some pieces were too wide and some were too narrow. But none of them were the right size to make her an apron.

Finally, there was just one piece of calico left. It was a very pretty piece of yellow calico with green polka dots.

"This is a very fine piece of calico indeed," said the Little Old Woman. "It is not too wide and it is not too narrow and it is not too long. To be sure, it is just a trifle short. However, if I scrimp and save and cut it sparingly, I do believe it will make me a very fine apron."

So the Little Old Woman fetched her scissors. She scrimped and saved and cut the piece of yellow and green polka dot calico sparingly. Then she held it up against her and looked in the mirror.

"It is not too wide," she said, "and it is not too narrow.

It is not too long, but it is just a little bit too short. I must figure out a way to make it longer."

After the Little Old Woman had figured and figured, she said to herself:

"I need another piece of yellow and green polka dot calico to make a ruffle. Then I could sew the ruffle on the bottom of the apron to make it longer. But where am I to get another piece of yellow and green calico? I shall have to use my head for that."

So the Little Old Woman tied a wet towel around her forehead. Then she sat down with her forefinger against her nose and shut her eyes.

She used her head and used her head. Pretty soon she knew where to get another piece of yellow and green polka dot calico.

"I will cut a piece off the top of the apron," she said. "Then I will make it into a ruffle and sew it to the bottom of the apron to make it longer. What a wise Old Woman I am!"

So she took her scissors and cut a piece off the top of the apron and made a ruffle out of it. She sewed the ruffle on the bottom of the apron to make it longer.

When the apron was all finished, the Little Old Woman put it on and looked in the mirror.

"Dear me," she said. "The apron is shorter than ever. I never would have believed that a ruffle could make an apron shorter! That is something worth knowing.

"Oh, well, I always say you can learn something new every day, if you only use your head."

How She Finished Her Red Muffler

One warm summer morning the Little Old Woman looked out of the door of her little yellow house. She said to herself:

"It is too hot to work in my soup garden today. I will sit down by the window and knit myself a red muffler."

So she took her yarn and knitting needles out of the bureau drawer and put on her spectacles. Then she sat down by the window and began to knit herself a red muffler.

Pretty soon the Little Old Woman's geese wanted to go swimming in a pond not far from the house. They went to the gate and flapped their wings.

"Honk, honk!" they said.

The Little Old Woman got up and put her yarn and knitting needles away in the drawer and took off her spectacles. She went out and opened the gate so the geese could go to the pond.

When all the geese were out of the yard, the Little Old Woman closed the gate and came back to the house. She took her yarn and knitting needles out of the bureau drawer and put on her spectacles. Then she sat down by the window and went on knitting her red muffler.

HONK!
HONK!
HONK!

She had hardly knitted a dozen stitches before the geese came back from the pond. They stood outside the gate flapping their wings and shaking the water off their backs.

"Honk, honk!" they said.

The Little Old Woman got up again. She put her yarn and knitting needles away in the bureau drawer and took off her spectacles. She went out and opened the gate.

When all the geese were back in the yard, the Little Old Woman closed the gate and came back to the house. She took her yarn and knitting needles out of the drawer and put on her spectacles. Then she sat down by the window and went on knitting her red muffler.

She had hardly knitted a dozen stitches before the geese wanted to go swimming in the pond again. But the Little Old Woman had no sooner let them out of the gate before they wanted to come back in again.

"Dear me," said the Little Old Woman, "I am spending all my time letting the geese in and out of the gate. At this rate, I shall never get my red muffler done. I think I will use my head and find out what to do."

So she tied a wet towel around her head and sat down with her forefinger against her nose and shut her eyes.

She used her head and used her head, and after a while she found out what to do.

"I will saw two holes at the bottom of the gate," said the Little Old Woman. "When the geese want to go to the pond, they can crawl out through one hole. When they come back from the pond after their swim, they can crawl in through the other hole."

So the Little Old Woman fetched her saw and sawed two holes at the bottom of the gate. As she was coming back to the house, she thought:

"Now I will not have to go out to open the gate for the geese. And I shall have my red muffler knitted in no time. What a clever Old Woman I am!"

She took her yarn and knitting needles out of the bureau drawer and put on her spectacles. Then she sat down by the window and went on with her knitting.

Pretty soon the geese wanted to go swimming in the pond. They went to the gate and flapped their wings.

"Honk, honk!" they said.

But the Little Old Woman did not get up. She sat by the window, knitting her red muffler.

The geese flapped their wings again.

"Honk, honk!" they said.

The Little Old Woman paid no attention to them.

After a while, the old gander spied one of the holes in the gate. He crawled through the hole and went to the pond. Soon the grey goose spied the hole in the gate, and she crawled through it and went to the pond. Before long, all the other geese spied the hole in the gate, and they crawled through it and went to the pond.

The Little Old Woman sat by the window knitting her red muffler. She had hardly knitted a dozen stitches before the geese came back from the pond.

"Now they will flap their wings and say, 'Honk, honk!'" said the Little Old Woman. "But I will not get up and open the gate. By and by they will find the other hole and crawl through it."

But the geese did not flap their wings and say, "Honk,

honk!" And instead of looking for the other hole, every one of them crawled back in the same way they had crawled out.

"How silly the geese are!" said the Little Old Woman. "Here I have made two holes and they only use one of them. I might have spared myself all the trouble of making the other hole."

All morning long, the Little Old Woman sat by the window and knitted her red muffler. All morning long, the geese crawled back and forth through the same hole in the gate.

At last the Little Old Woman finished the red muffler. But the geese were still crawling back and forth through the same hole in the gate.

"It was very clever of me to make two holes after all," said the Little Old Woman. "The geese will have that hole worn out in no time. When it is worn out, the other hole will come in very handy. What a clever Old Woman I am!"

How She Did Her Marketing

One day when the Little Old Woman was weeding her soup garden, the pack peddler came along crying his wares.

"Any tacks, laces, nutmeg graters, ribbons, mousetraps or buttons today?" he cried.

The Little Old Woman shook her head.

"No," she said. "I have no money to spare. It is all I can do to make both ends meet."

"Any hairpins, cooking pots, calico, button hooks, needles or spices?" he cried.

But the Little Old Woman shook her head.

"No," she said. "Today is market day, and I must save my money to buy meat and bread for my supper."

"How about a pair of magnifying spectacles?" asked the peddler.

"Magnifying spectacles!" exclaimed the Little Old Woman. "And what may they be?"

"They are a very useful kind of spectacles," the peddler explained. "When you wear them, everything looks twice as large as before."

"But what good are they?" asked the Little Old Woman. "Why should I want things to look twice as big as before?"

"That is easy to answer," the peddler replied. "The larger things are, the more plainly you can see them."

"I never happened to think of that before," said the Little Old Woman. "What you say is very true."

"Why not put the spectacles on, and see for yourself how large things look?" said the peddler.

"Well, I suppose it would do no harm to try them on," she said. "But, mind you, I have no money to buy them."

"Just as you say," said the peddler.

He opened his pack and took out the magnifying spectacles. The Little Old Woman put them on and looked at her soup garden. She could hardly believe her eyes. The cabbages looked twice as big. The tomatoes looked twice as big. Everything in the garden looked twice as big as it had before.

"How my vegetables have grown!" exclaimed the Little

Old Woman. "And how plainly I can see them! These are very fine spectacles indeed."

"They are quite cheap, too," said the peddler. "If you should buy them, I am sure they would come in very handy."

"That is just what I was thinking," the Little Old Woman replied. "I will fetch you some money from my china teapot."

She hurried into the house and took some money from out of her china teapot to pay for the spectacles.

After the peddler had gone, she said to herself:

"I should like to look at the soup garden through these spectacles again. But first I must go to the market and buy some bread and meat for my supper."

As she was getting ready to go to the market, she thought:

"I will take the spectacles with me and wear them while I am doing my marketing. I will be able to see more plainly, and I will get more for my money."

So the Little Old Woman put the magnifying spectacles in her market basket and took them with her. After she reached the market, she put on the spectacles so she could see more plainly. When she went to buy her bread, she said to the baker:

"What fine rolls you have today! They are nearly as large as a loaf of bread. One roll will be all I will need."

She bought one roll and put it in her market basket. Then she went to buy her meat.

"What fine chops you have today," she said to the butcher. "They are nearly as large as a whole roast. One chop will be all I will need."

So she bought one chop and put it in her market basket.

As the Little Old Woman was coming home from market, she said to herself:

"I have never bought so much bread and meat for so little money. These spectacles are very useful indeed."

When she was home again, she set about preparing her supper. She took the roll out of the market basket.

"This roll is too big for one meal," she thought. "I will cut off a piece and save the rest for tomorrow."

After she had cut off a piece of the roll and put the rest away, she took the chop out of her market basket.

"This chop is too big also," she thought. "I will cut off a piece and save the rest for tomorrow."

So she cut off a piece of the chop and put the rest of it away.

When she had prepared her supper, the Little Old Woman took off her magnifying spectacles. She put them away carefully, and then sat down to eat.

She looked at the piece of roll. It was no bigger than a thimble. She looked at the piece of chop. It was no bigger than a thimble either.

"Mercy!" cried the Little Old Woman. "What has happened to my supper? There is not enough left to feed a mouse!"

She began to look for the rest of her supper. She looked at her plate. She looked under her plate. But she did not find it. She looked on the table. She looked under the table. But she did not find the rest of her supper.

After she had looked everywhere, she said:

"This is very strange. Something seems to be wrong, and I must use my head to find out what it is."

So she tied a wet towel around her forehead and sat down with her forefinger against her nose and shut her eyes.

She used her head and used her head. Pretty soon she found out what to do.

"What a silly Old Woman I am!" she said. "How can I find my supper when I cannot see plainly? I must put on my magnifying spectacles."

The Little Old Woman got her magnifying spectacles and put them on. Then she came back to the table. She looked at her plate, and there she saw her supper as plainly as anything.

As she sat down to eat, she said to herself:

"It was very wise of me to put on my magnifying spectacles. Now I see my supper very plainly. And what a fine big supper it is, to be sure! I am afraid I shall not be able to eat half of it."

How She Rested Her Head

All the year round the Little Old Woman used her head to find out what to do.

One evening she said to herself, "How time does fly! It seems only yesterday that I made my geese their little red coats and plucked their feathers to make my feather bed. Now it is fall again.

"I have used my head so much this year that I think I will give it a rest."

So the Little Old Woman sat down in her rocking-chair to rest her head.

"The nights are growing colder," she thought. "I had better sit closer to the fireplace."

She got up and moved her chair closer to the fireplace and sat down again. She folded her arms across her apron and put her feet on her little footstool.

"A fireplace is nice and warm," she said to herself. "I must gather some wood tomorrow so I can make a fire. My fireplace will be even warmer when I build a fire in it. And besides, a fire is so cozy to look at.

"The evenings will be very long now. I shall have plenty of time to sit by my fire and think. I shall think about pleasant things for that will rest my head.

"I shall think how warm my geese are in their little red jackets. I shall think how comfortable my rats are in their little box.

"I shall think how comfortable I am in my feather bed.

"It will be very pleasant to sit by my fire and think how contented and happy we are, and all because I used my head."

The little old woman continues to use her head in Hope Newell's The Little Old Woman Carries On, *and* More About the Little Old Woman Who Used Her Head, *both published by Thomas Nelson & Sons.*

The Story of the Four Little Children Who Went Round the World

BY EDWARD LEAR

Illustrations by the author

ONCE upon a time, a long while ago, there were four little people whose names were Violet, Slingsby, Guy, and Lionel; and they all thought they should like to see the world. So they bought a large boat to sail quite round the world by sea, and then they were to come back on the other side by land. The boat was painted blue with green spots, and the sail was yellow with red stripes; and when they set off, they only took a small Cat to steer and look after the boat, besides an elderly Quangle-Wangle,

From *Nonsense Songs and Stories,* by Edward Lear.

343

who had to cook the dinner and make the tea; for which purposes they took a large kettle.

For the first ten days they sailed on beautifully, and found plenty to eat, as there were lots of fish, and they had only to take them out of the sea with a long spoon, when the Quangle-Wangle instantly cooked them, and the Pussy-Cat was fed with the bones, with which she expressed herself pleased on the whole, so that all the party were very happy.

During the day-time, Violet chiefly occupied herself in putting salt-water into a churn, while her three brothers churned it violently, in the hope that it would turn into butter, which it seldom, if ever, did; and in the evening they all retired into the Tea-kettle, where they all managed to sleep very comfortably, while Pussy and the Quangle-Wangle managed the boat.

After a time they saw some land at a distance; and when they came to it, they found it was an island made of water quite surrounded by earth. Besides that, it was bordered by evanescent isthmuses with a great Gulf-stream running about all over it, so that it was perfectly beautiful, and contained only a single tree, 503 feet high.

When they had landed, they walked about, but found to their great surprise that the island was quite full of veal-cutlets and chocolate-drops, and nothing else. So they all climbed up the single high tree to discover, if possible, if there were any people; but having remained on the top of the tree for a week, and not seeing anybody, they naturally concluded that there were no inhabitants, and accordingly when they came down they loaded the boat with two thousand veal-cutlets and a million of chocolate-drops, and these afforded them sustenance for more than a month, during which time they pursued their voyage with the utmost delight and apathy.

After this they came to a shore where there were no less than sixty-five great red parrots with blue tails, sitting on a rail all of a row, and all fast asleep. And I am sorry to say that the Pussy-Cat and the Quangle-Wangle crept softly and bit off the tail feathers of all the sixty-five parrots, for which Violet reproved them both severely.

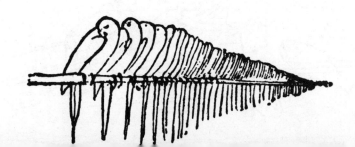

Nothwithstanding which, she proceeded to insert all the feathers, two hundred and sixty in number, in her bonnet, thereby causing it to have a lovely and glittering appearance, highly prepossessing and efficacious.

The next thing that happened to them was in a narrow part of the sea, which was so entirely full of fishes that the boat could go no further; so they remained there about six weeks, till they had eaten nearly all the fishes, which were Soles, and all ready-cooked and covered with shrimp sauce, so that there was no trouble whatever. And as the few fishes who remained uneaten complained of the cold, as well as of the difficulty they had in getting any sleep on account of the extreme noise made by the Arctic Bears and the Tropical Turnspits, which frequented the neighbourhood in great numbers, Violet most amiably knitted a small woollen frock for several of the fishes, and Slingsby administered some

opium drops to them, through which kindness they became quite warm and slept soundly.

Then they came to a country which was wholly covered with immense Orange-trees of a vast size, and quite full of fruit. So they all landed, taking with them the Tea-kettle, intending to gather some of the Oranges and place them in it. But while they were busy about this, a most dreadfully high wind rose, and blew out most of the parrot-tail feathers from Violet's bonnet. That, however, was nothing compared with the calamity of the Oranges falling down on their heads by millions and millions, which thumped and bumped and bumped and thumped them all so seriously that they were obliged to run as hard as they could for their lives, besides that the sound of the Oranges rattling on the Tea-kettle was of the most fearful and amazing nature.

Nevertheless they got safely to the boat, although considerably vexed and hurt; and the Quangle-Wangle's right foot was so knocked about that he had to sit with his head in his slipper for at least a week.

This event made them all for a time rather melancholy, and perhaps they might never have become less so, had not Lionel, with a most praiseworthy devotion and perseverance, continued to stand on one leg and whistle to them in a loud and lively manner, which diverted the whole party so extremely, that they gradually recovered their spirits, and agreed that whenever they should reach home they would subscribe towards a testimony to Lionel, entirely made of Gingerbread and Raspberries, as an earnest token of their sincere and grateful infection.

After sailing on calmly for several more days, they came to another country, where they were much pleased and surprised to see a countless multitude of white Mice with red eyes, all sitting in a great circle, slowly eating Custard Pudding with the most satisfactory and polite demeanour.

And as the four Travellers were rather hungry, being tired of eating nothing but Soles and Oranges for so long a period, they held a council as to the propriety of asking the Mice for some of their pudding in a humble and affecting manner, by which they could hardly be otherwise than gratified. It was agreed therefore that Guy should go and ask the Mice, which he immediately did; and the result was that they gave a Walnut-shell only half full of Custard diluted with water. Now, this displeased Guy, who said, "Out of such a lot of Pudding as you have got, I must say you might have spared a some-

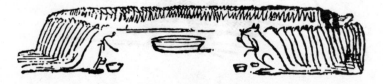

what larger quantity!" But no sooner had he finished speaking than all the Mice turned round at once, and sneezed at him in an appalling and vindictive manner (and it is impossible to imagine a more scroobious and unpleasant sound than that caused by the simultaneous sneezing of many millions of angry Mice), so that Guy rushed back to the boat, having first shied his cap into the middle of the Custard Pudding, by which means he completely spoiled the Mice's dinner.

By-and-by the Four Children came to a country where there were no houses, but only an incredibly innumerable number of large bottles without corks, and of a dazzling and sweetly susceptible blue colour. Each of these blue bottles contained a Blue-Bottle-Fly, and

all these interesting animals live continually together in the most copious and rural harmony, nor perhaps in many parts of the world is such perfect and abject happiness to be found. Violet, and Slingsby, and Guy, and Lionel were greatly struck with this singular and instructive settlement, and having previously asked permission of the Blue-Bottle Flies (which was most courteously granted), the boat was drawn up to the shore, and they proceeded to make tea in front of the bottles; but as they had no tea-leaves, they merely placed some pebbles in the hot water, and the Quangle-Wangle played some tunes over it on an Accordion, by which of course tea was made directly, and of the very best quality.

The Four Children then entered into conversation with the Blue-Bottle-Flies, who discoursed in a placid and genteel manner, though with a slightly buzzing accent, chiefly owing to the fact that they each held a small clothes-brush between their teeth; which naturally occasioned a fizzy extraneous utterance.

"Why," said Violet, "would you kindly inform us, do you reside in bottles? and if in bottles at all, why not rather in green or purple, or indeed in yellow bottles?"

To which questions a very aged Blue-Bottle-Fly answered, "We found the bottles here all ready to live in, that is to say, our great-great-great-great-great-grandfathers did, so we occupied them at once. And when the winter comes on, we turn the bottles upside-down, and consequently rarely feel the cold at all, and you know very well that this could not be the case with bottles of any other colour than blue."

"Of course it could not," said Slingsby; "but if we may take the liberty of inquiring, on what do you chiefly subsist?"

"Mainly on Oyster-patties," said the Blue-Bottle-Fly, "and when these are scarce, on Raspberry Vinegar and Russian leather boiled down to a jelly."

"How delicious!" said Guy. To which Lionel added, "Huzz!" and all the Blue-Bottle-Flies said "Buzz!"

At this time, an elderly Fly said it was the hour for the Evening-song to be sung; and on a signal being given all the Blue-Bottle-Flies began to buzz at once in a sumptuous and sonorous manner, the melodious and mucilaginous sounds echoing all over the waters, and resounding across the tumultuous tops of the transitory

Titmice upon the intervening and verdant mountains, with a serene and sickly suavity only known to the truly virtuous. The Moon was shining slobaciously from the star-bespangled sky, while her light irrigated the smooth and shiny sides and wings and backs of the Blue-Bottle-Flies with a peculiar and trivial splendour, while all nature cheerfully responded to the cerulaean and conspicuous circumstances.

In many long-after years, the four little Travellers looked back to that evening as one of the happiest in all their lives, and it was already past midnight, when—the sail of the boat having been set up by the Quangle-Wangle, the Tea-kettle and Churn placed in their respective positions, and the Pussy-Cat stationed at the helm—the Children each took a last and affectionate farewell of the Blue-Bottle-Flies, who walked down in a body to the water's edge to see the Travellers embark.

As a token of parting respect and esteem, Violet made a curtsey quite down to the ground, and stuck one of her few remaining Parrot-tail feathers into the back hair of

the most pleasing of the Blue-Bottle-Flies, while Slingsby, Guy, and Lionel offered them three small boxes, containing respectively Black Pins, Dried Figs, and Epsom Salts; and thus they left that happy shore for ever.

Overcome by their feelings, the four little Travellers instantly jumped into the Tea-kettle, and fell fast asleep. But all along the shore for many hours there was distinctly heard a sound of severely suppressed sobs, and

a vague multitude of living creatures using their pocket-handkerchiefs in a subdued simultaneous snuffle—lingering sadly along the wallopping waves, as the boat sailed farther and farther away from the Land of the Happy Blue-Bottle-Flies.

Nothing particular occurred for some days after these events, except that as the Travellers were passing a low tract of sand, they perceived an unusual and gratifying spectacle, namely, a large number of Crabs and Crawfish—perhaps six or seven hundred—sitting by the waterside, and endeavouring to disentangle a vast heap of pale pink worsted, which they moistened at intervals with a fluid composed of Lavender-water and White-wine Negus.

"Can we be of any service to you, O crusty Crabbies?" said the Four Children.

"Thank you kindly," said the Crabs, consecutively. "We are trying to make some worsted Mittens, but do not know how."

On which Violet, who was perfectly acquainted with the art of mitten-making, said to the Crabs, "Do your claws unscrew, or are they fixtures?"

"They are all made to unscrew," said the Crabs, and forthwith they deposited a great pile of claws close to the boat, with which Violet uncombed all the pale pink worsted, and then made the loveliest Mittens with it you can imagine. These the Crabs, having resumed and screwed on their claws, placed cheerfully upon their wrists, and walked away rapidly, on their hind legs, warbling songs with a silvery voice and in a minor key.

After this the four little people sailed on again till

they came to a vast and wide plain of astonishing dimensions, on which nothing whatever could be discovered at first; but as the Travellers walked onward, there appeared in the extreme and dim distance a single object, which on a nearer approach, and on an accurately cutaneous inspection, seemed to be somebody in a large white wig sitting on an arm-chair made of Sponge Cakes and Oyster-shells. "It does not quite look like a human being," said Violet doubtfully; nor could they make out what it really was, till the Quangle-Wangle (who had previously been round the world) exclaimed softly in a loud voice, "It is the Co-operative Cauliflower!"

And so in truth it was, and they soon found that what they had taken for an immense wig was in reality the top of the cauliflower, and that he had no feet at all, being able to walk tolerably well with a fluctuating and graceful movement on a single cabbage stalk, an accomplishment which naturally saved him the expense of stockings and shoes.

Presently, while the whole party from the boat was gazing at him with a mingled affection and disgust, he suddenly arose, and a somewhat plumdomphious manner hurried off towards the setting sun—his steps supported by two super-incumbent confidential cucumbers, and a large number of Waterwagtails proceeding in advance of him by three-and-three in a row—till he finally disappeared on the brink of the western sky in a crystal cloud of sudorific sand.

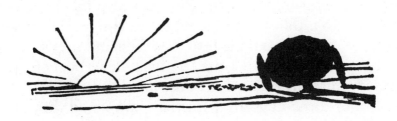

So remarkable a sight of course impressed the Four
Children very deeply; and they returned immediately
to their boat with a strong sense of undeveloped asthma
and a great appetite.

Shortly after this the Travellers were obliged to sail
directly below some high overhanging rocks, from the
top of one of which a particularly odious little boy,
dressed in rose-coloured knickerbockers, and with a
pewter plate upon his head, threw an enormous Pumpkin at the boat, by which it was instantly upset.

But this upsetting was of no consequence, because all
the party knew how to swim very well, and in fact they
preferred swimming about till after the moon rose,
when, the water growing chilly, they sponge-taneously
entered the boat. Meanwhile the Quangle-Wangle
threw back the Pumpkin with an immense force, so that
it hit the rocks where the malicious little boy in rose-
coloured knickerbockers was sitting, when, being quite
full of Lucifer-matches, the Pumpkin exploded surrepti-
tiously into a thousand bits, whereon the rocks instantly
took fire, and the odious little boy became unpleasantly
hotter and hotter and hotter, till his knickerbockers were
turned quite green, and his nose was burned off.

Two or three days after this had happened they came

to another place, where they found nothing at all except some wide and deep pits full of Mulberry Jam. This is the property of the tiny Yellow-nosed Apes who abound in these districts, and who store up the Mulberry Jam for their food in winter, when they mix it with pellucid pale periwinkle soup, and serve it out in Wedgwood China bowls, which grow freely all over that part of the country. Only one of the Yellow-nosed Apes was on the spot, and he was fast asleep; yet the Four Travellers and the Quangle-Wangle and Pussy were so terrified by the violence and sanguinary sound of his snoring, that they merely took a small cupful of the Jam, and returned to re-embark in their boat without delay.

What was their horror on seeing the boat (including the Churn and the Tea-kettle) in the mouth of an enormous Seeze Pyder, an aquatic and ferocious creature

truly dreadful to behold, and happily only met with in these excessive longitudes. In a moment the beautiful boat was bitten into fifty-five-thousand-million-hundred-billion bits; and it instantly became quite clear that Violet, Slingsby, Guy, and Lionel could no longer pre-liminate their voyage by sea.

The Four Travellers were therefore obliged to resolve on pursuing their wanderings by land, and very fortunately there happened to pass by at that moment an elderly Rhinoceros, on which they seized; and all four mounting on his back, the Quangle-Wangle sitting on his horn and holding on by his ears, and the Pussy-Cat swinging at the end of his tail, they set off, having only four small beans and three pounds of mashed potatoes to last through their whole journey.

They were, however, able to catch numbers of the chickens and turkeys and other birds who incessantly alighted on the head of the Rhinoceros for the purpose of gathering the seeds of the rhododendron plants which grew there, and these creatures they cooked in the most translucent and satisfactory manner, by means of a fire

lighted on the end of the Rhinoceros's back. A crowd of Kangaroos and Gigantic Cranes accompanied them, from feelings of curiosity and complacency, so that they were never at a loss for company, and went onward as it were in a sort of profuse and triumphant procession.

Thus, in less than eighteen weeks, they all arrived safely at home, where they were received by their admiring relatives with joy tempered with contempt; and where they finally resolved to carry out the rest of their travelling plans at some more favourable opportunity.

As for the Rhinoceros, in token of their grateful adherence, they had him killed and stuffed directly, and then set him up outside the door of their father's house as a Diaphanous Doorscraper.

If you wish a funny treat, you will want to read Edward Lear's Book of Nonsense, *published by Random House.*

The Good Horse Kristie

BY EMMA L. BROCK

Illustrations by the author

Elmer and Einer wanted a horse more than anything else in the world. They saved and saved until they had enough money to buy an old horse, a safe horse, a good horse named Kristie.

EARLY in the morning before breakfast Elmer and Einer dressed quickly and went out to the barn. As they walked through the doorway, they heard Kristie whinnying.

"She is very fond of us," said Elmer.

"But just wait until she sees her old hat that Axel Peterson gave us last night," said Einer.

"Then she WILL be happy," said Elmer.

"Yes," said Einer, "and she'll go like anything when she has her old hat to wear. Old Axel Peterson said so and he had her for so many years that he must know."

Elmer took the hat down from the nail on which he had hung it the night before. Then he and Einer went into Kristie's stall. Elmer held the hat and Einer held Kristie. Elmer put the hat down on her head and Einer pulled her ears through the holes. Einer tied the strings under her chin. Kristie whinnied loudly and tossed her head.

"Isn't she beautiful!" said Elmer.

"Now she'll go," said Einer. "Let's hurry and eat breakfast."

They ate their whole breakfast in the time they should
have taken to eat half of it.

"Now we're going for a ride," said Elmer.

"Now that she has her old hat again, she will go and
we are riding her to the lake to go swimming."

Elmer and Einer and their father and mother went
out and stood around Good Old Kristie. Their mother
gave her three lumps of sugar. The hired man came too
and sat on the fence.

Old Kristie was looking very gay and ready to step off
at any moment. Her ears stood straight up through the
holes in her hat. Her two eyes looked out brightly from
under the brim. Her braided bangs hung down over her
nose.

"Now she'll go," said Elmer and Einer together.

Elmer brought a box from the barn and put it down
beside her. He and Einer stood on the box and their
father boosted them up on Kristie's back. Elmer sat in
front and held the halter rope in his hands. Einer sat behind and held fast to Elmer's overall straps. Their grins
were wider than ever before.

"Look out," they cried. "Here we go!"

Kristie stepped across the barnyard. She almost
pranced. Elmer and Einer bounced up and down on her
back. Their feet flopped against her ribs. Kristie tripped
as far as the gate and then she stopped.

"Gid-ap!" called Elmer and Einer, slapping their bare
heels against her sides.

But Kristie stood there and quivered from one end to
the other. She looked over her shoulder and quivered
again.

"Well, gid-ap," called Elmer and Einer.

"Gid-ap," called their father and their mother and the
hired man.

"You have your hat on, old girl," called Elmer.

"We want to go swimming," said Einer.

They bounced up and down on her back. Kristie shook all over. Her crooked legs shook under her and her long neck shook. Even her straw hat shook about her ears.

"What can be the matter now?" said Mr. Iverson as he petted Kristie's nose.

"She has plenty of food," said Elmer.

"And a good bed," said Einer.

"And her sugar," said their mother.

"And she's wearing her hat," called the hired man from the fence rail.

Kristie bobbled up and down so that Elmer and Einer could hardly stay on her back. Then she turned and started to run. She galloped across the barnyard at full speed. She stopped suddenly and spread apart her front feet on their two crooked legs. She ducked her head on its long thin neck, way down.

Elmer and Einer yelled loudly and, without stopping a minute, shot over her head and over her straw hat to the ground. Kristie sneezed and tossed her head. She switched her tail back and forth. Elmer picked himself up rubbing his back. Einer picked himself up and rubbed two knees and an elbow.

"Well, I never," said their father and mother and the hired man. "Well, I never!"

Elmer went up to Kristie and straightened her hat. Einer tied the strings more tightly under her chin. Their mother brought her three more lumps of sugar. While Kristie was munching the sugar, Mr. Iverson boosted Elmer up on her back.

"Try it again, yust one of you," he said. "Maybe she doesn't like two."

Kristie finished her sugar lumps carefully. Elmer flopped the halter rope and patted her sides gently with his bare feet.

"Gid-ap, please, Kristie," he said politely.

Kristie did not look happy. She shook herself as hard as she could. Then she leaped forward, stopped suddenly and leaned back on her four crooked legs. In one second Elmer flew from her back and over her head to the ground.

Kristie snorted and shook her head.

"Let me try," said Einer. "Maybe she'll like me better."

His father boosted Einer up on Kristie's back. Einer held perfectly still.

"Gid-ap, please kindly," he said softly.

Kristie was looking crosser than ever. She kicked up her crooked hind legs, bent down her long thin neck and sent Einer flying into the watering trough.

"Well, I never," said Mr. and Mrs. Iverson and the hired man.

"She goes all right," said Elmer.

"Yes, at least, she goes," said Einer, as he wiped the water from his eyes.

"What can be the matter with her?" said their father. "We'll yust have to wait till we go to Town next Saturday night and ask Axel Peterson. She was his horse for a great many years before we bought her from him. He'll know what to do."

Elmer and Einer did not know how they could wait until Saturday. Six days were so long. But each day they fed Old Kristie oats and hay. They took her out in the sun every morning. They gave her a good bed of straw every night. Kristie grew fonder and fonder of them. She would rest her head on their shoulders and sigh.

At last Saturday night came. Right after supper the whole family and the hired man climbed into the little old green car and drove to Town. At the corner drugstore on Main Street they found Old Axel Peterson.

"Hello," he called to Elmer and Einer. "Well, how does she go now?"

"Oh, fine," said Elmer.

"So fast," said Einer.

"But she won't let us stay on her back!" they said together.

"She's plenty cross," said Mr. Iverson.

"You didn't try to ride her?" asked Axel Peterson. "Of course she's cross then. She's not a riding horse yust.

She's a carriage horse only. Did I forget to tell you that?"

"You can't RIDE her?" asked Elmer and Einer.

"Why, no," said Axel. "Of course she won't let you ride her. She'll never let you RIDE her. You hitch her to a carriage, any kind of carriage, and she'll go. Good Old Kristie."

"But we haven't any carriage," said Elmer and Einer, looking very sad indeed. "We haven't any carriage at all."

"Well, I have an old buggy and some harness and I'll give them to you. The buggy's not a golden coach, you know. But I guess it'll do. Hitch her to that and watch her go."

So they went home with Axel Peterson. He fastened the old buggy to the back of their little green car. They pulled it home to their farm and left it standing in the barnyard.

"Now she'll go," said Elmer.

"Yes, now she'll go," said Einer. "Tomorrow we'll drive to the lake and swim."

They grinned and grinned and grinned as they climbed into bed.

The sun had no more than popped above the horizon when Elmer and Einer hopped out of bed and went down to look at the buggy that old Axel had given them the night before. The buggy was old and broken. But it had a seat in the front and four round wheels. Elmer and Einer pushed it back and forth and found that it would roll easily.

"Now watch Kristie go," said Elmer.

"When she's hitched to this buggy, you'll see her go," said Einer.

As soon as breakfast was over, Elmer and Einer put on Kristie's hat and led her out of the barn. Mr. Iverson

came too and looked over the harness. The hired man
came and sat on the fence.

Elmer and Einer helped their father put the harness
on Kristie. In a place or two where the leather straps
were gone, they tied in pieces of rope. Elmer cut a long
willow branch and put it into the whip socket, because
they did not have a real whip.

"There, that is ready," said Mr. Iverson. "Now we'll back her in between the shafts of the buggy."

"Back up, Kristie," called Elmer and Einer.

"Back up," called the hired man.

But Kristie would not back.

"We must pull the buggy up to her," said Mr. Iverson.

He pulled on one side and Elmer and Einer pulled on the other. Just as the buggy was about to reach Kristie, she stepped out of the way. They tried three times and at last Kristie was safely fastened to the buggy.

"Now we'll go," said Elmer and Einer.

They both climbed up on the seat and Elmer took the reins in both hands. Mr. Iverson stood by the farmyard gate, holding it open. Mrs. Iverson brought Kristie four lumps of sugar.

"Here we go," cried Elmer, grinning all across his face.

"Watch us go," said Einer. "Look out!"

Kristie started for the gate, but she was walking sideways. She was looking over her right shoulder and walking sideways. The buggy followed after her.

"Pull on the left rein," called the hired man from the fence rail.

Elmer pulled on the left rein and Einer helped him. But Kristie kept looking over her right shoulder. She looked over her right shoulder no matter what Elmer and Einer did. She walked around the barnyard in circles and the buggy followed after her.

The grins were all gone from the faces of Elmer and Einer.

"We'll never get anywhere this way," said Elmer.

"We'll never go swimming unless we do it in the watering trough," said Einer.

Elmer's and Einer's mouths were turned down so far that the corners were almost lost under their chins.

Kristie kept right on going. She went around in circles in the barnyard, around and around and around. The buggy and Elmer and Einer followed after her.

"Well, I never," said Mr. Iverson, as he caught hold of the reins by Kristie's mouth. "Whoa there," he said, "you'll get dizzy."

Kristie whinnied and leaned up against Mr. Iverson.

"We'll yust have to see Axel Peterson," said Mr. Iverson, "when we go to Town next Saturday. She was his horse a long time before we bought her from him and he will know what is the matter with her now."

"He'll know," said Elmer and Einer, as they climbed down from the buggy.

All that week Elmer and Einer took care of Kristie. Each day they fed her carefully and rubbed her down. She was growing fatter and smoother every day, and every day she grew fonder of them. She whinnied when she heard their voices and she nibbled at their ears and collars. She was very fond of them.

At last it was Saturday night. Right after supper Elmer and Einer and their father and mother and the hired man drove to Town in the little old green car. They found Old Axel Peterson leaning against the drug-store.

"Hello!" he cried to Elmer and Einer. "Well, how does she go with the buggy? Plenty fast yust?"

"Oh, yes," said Elmer.

"Plenty fast," said Einer.

"But she goes in circles," they said together.

"Ya, she does yust that," said their father.

"Goes in circles?" said Axel Peterson, squinting one eye. "Goes in circles, does she?" he said, squinting the other.

"Yes," said Elmer and Einer. "'Round and 'round and 'round."

"Well, well," said Axel Peterson. "You didn't by chance have a whip in the whip socket, did you?"

"Why, yes," said Elmer.

"We made a whip," said Einer.

"Then that's the reason," said Axel. "Of course she

walked in circles. She was looking at the whip, wasn't she? She doesn't like whips, Good Old Kristie doesn't. Of course she was walking in circles."

"So that's it," said Elmer.

"We'll take out the whip," said Einer. "Then she'll go."

"You yust take out the whip and you'll see how she'll go," said Axel.

So Elmer and Einer and the family drove back to their farm. Before they went to bed, Elmer and Einer took the whip out of the whip socket. They broke it up into small pieces so that it did not look like a whip any more.

"Now she'll go straight," said Elmer.

"Now we can go swimming," said Einer. "Just wait until tomorrow."

They grinned and grinned and grinned as they climbed into bed.

Elmer and Einer ate their breakfast so fast that they were through almost as soon as they began. They ran out to the barn and their good horse Kristie. They fed her and rubbed her down. They combed her tail and braided her bangs so that they would not blow in her eyes.

They put on her straw hat and pulled her ears through the holes. They tied the hat strings neatly under her chin.

"Today we are going swimming," said Elmer.

"Just watch us go!"

Their father came and helped them put on the harness. Elmer and Einer led Kristie to the barnyard. Their father wheeled out the buggy. They showed Kristie that there was no whip in the socket to scare her. Then they pulled the buggy up to her and fastened the traces. Everything was ready. Kristie looked happy.

Mrs. Iverson came out of the house with five lumps of sugar. The hired man came out too and sat on the fence. Elmer and Einer climbed up to the seat of the buggy.

"Gid-ap," said Elmer, pulling softly on the reins.

"Gid-ap," said Einer politely.

Mr. Iverson stood by the gate holding his breath. He was waiting to see if Kristie would really go this time. Mrs. Iverson stood beside him and held her breath too. The hired man sat on the fence and held his.

Kristie stretched her long thin neck. She stepped out

with her four crooked legs and walked quickly through the gate.

"Good-by," called Elmer.

"Good-by," called Einer. "We'll be back for dinner."

They were grinning so widely that their fat pink cheeks almost shut their eyes.

"Just look at us go," said Elmer.

"I can hardly believe it is true," said Einer.

Kristie stepped off along the road. She did not stop. She did not prance or buck. She did not walk in circles. She went just as a good horse should, straight along the road toward the lake.

"See how she pulls us along," said Elmer.

"Good Old Kristie," said Einer.

"Old Axel Peterson was right. She's a fine horse," they said together.

The sun shone down and Elmer and Einer drove on toward the lake.

"See how far we have come," said Elmer, looking back at their windmill.

"Oh, yes, she's good," said Einer.

On the left was the road leading to the schoolhouse. When they reached the road, Kristie started to turn into it.

"Oh, no, Kristie," said Elmer, pulling on the right rein.

"Not that way," called Einer, as he pulled too. "We don't want to go to school, Kristie."

But no matter how hard they pulled on the reins, Kristie pulled harder. She bent down her head on its long thin neck and pulled harder. She turned the corner to the left on the schoolhouse road. And the buggy and Elmer and Einer followed after her.

"Well, we can go this way," said Elmer.

"It's a little longer," said Einer, "but if Kristie likes this way better, we can take it."

"We'll turn to the right at the next road," said Elmer.

"It will take us toward the lake again," said Einer.

They drove along the schoolhouse road and past the schoolhouse which was closed for the summer. They reached the next road.

"Turn right here, Kristie," said Elmer.

"Good Old Kristie," said Einer.

But Kristie turned left. No matter how hard they pulled to the right, she pulled harder to the left. She bent down her head on its long thin neck and pulled harder. She turned the corner to the left. The buggy and Elmer and Einer followed after her.

"This is just the wrong direction," said Elmer.

"Yes, we're going away from the lake," said Einer, "farther and farther every minute."

The grins were all gone from their faces. Their mouths were straight and hard.

"It will be a rather long way around to the lake," said Elmer.

"But if Kristie does not mind, I don't suppose we should. She's doing the walking," said Einer.

Kristie stepped gaily along the road. She seemed very happy. The sun was warm, the road was soft, the buggy was not too heavy. They went between fields of wheat and fields of corn, on and on.

"It's a long way to the lake," said Elmer.

"It will be dinnertime before we get there," said Einer.

They came to another crossroad. Kristie turned to the left and hurried along it. And she turned to the left again at the next crossroad and at the next and the next and the next. Every time she came to a road she turned to the left.

"It seems to me," said Elmer, "that I keep seeing the same things over and over. We must be going 'round and 'round."

"And I don't know now which way the lake is," said Einer.

"Nor which way home is either," said Elmer.

"Do you suppose we could stop her?" Einer asked.

"Whoa, there, Kristie," they called out together.

Old Kristie stopped at once. She hung her head down as if she were tired. She stood with her feet far apart as if her legs were shaky.

"Poor Old Kristie," said Elmer, as he climbed down from the buggy.

"You've gone an awful long way getting to the lake," said Einer. "Come on home."

But Old Kristie did not move. She hung her head. She

wobbled on her legs. Then she just lay down in front of the buggy.

"She's so tired," said Elmer. "Poor Kristie!"

"No wonder," said Einer, "after coming all this way to get to the lake."

They sat down beside Kristie and petted her. She whinnied faintly. She was very fond of them. They sat there for a long time. They began to grow hungry.

"It must be nearly dinnertime," said Elmer.

"I think it must be past dinnertime," said Einer.

Their mouths were very sad indeed. Elmer and Einer had to pinch their lips together to keep from crying.

"If we only knew where home is," they said together.

Just then a farmer came along driving a farm wagon.

"Can you please tell us where we live?" said Elmer.

"Our father is Mr. Iverson," said Einer.

"It's two or three miles that way," said the farmer. "Did your horse get tired out?"

"Yes, we've come a long way," said Elmer.

"Ever since breakfast," said Einer.

"I'll help her up and then I'll take you home," said the farmer.

"Oh, thank you!" said Elmer and Einer.

They helped the farmer pull Good Old Kristie to her feet. Then the farmer tied her to the back of his wagon. They went slowly along the road toward the Iversons' farm.

"Well, I never," shouted Mr. Iverson. "Where've you been?"

"Just driving around," said Elmer.

"Kristie always turns left," said Einer. "She just keeps turning left."

"And goes 'round and 'round and 'round," they said together.

"Well, I never," said their father. "What can we do about that? Go ask Axel Peterson, I suppose, next Saturday night. She was his horse many years before we bought her from him. He ought to know."

Kristie was very tired the next day and so were Elmer and Einer. But they fed her and rubbed her down as they always did. Every day that week they fed her and rubbed her down. And every day she grew fonder of them. If they did not tie her up, she followed them about wherever they went. She was very fond of them, indeed.

At last Saturday came. As soon as supper was over and the dishes were washed Mrs. Iverson took off her apron and put on her black hat. The family all climbed into the little old green car and the hired man did too. They drove as fast as they could toward Town. Old Axel Peterson was leaning against the doorpost of the drugstore as usual.

"Well, hello, there!" he called to Elmer and Einer. "Now she goes, doesn't she? She goes fine now, doesn't she?"

"Oh, yes, she goes," said Elmer.

"She certainly goes," said Einer.

"But she always goes to the left," they said together.

"Ya, she always turns left yust," said their father.

"Well, well! Is she doing that trick again?" said Axel. "Is she doing that again?"

"Yes, she is," said Elmer and Einer. "What can we do about it?"

"Well, this is what you do about it," said Axel. "I should have told you before. It's easy."

"What do you do?" asked Elmer and Einer. "Because we'd like to go swimming."

"This is the way. It's easy. When she turns to the left, let her turn. You can't stop her. Then get out of the buggy. Take hold of the reins by the bit and carefully turn her around until she's heading toward the road she turned off from. See?"

"Then what?" said Elmer and Einer.

"Then climb back into the buggy and drive ahead. When she comes to the road she turned off from, she'll just turn left again. AND she'll be going the way you want her to yust. See?"

"Why, of course!" said Elmer. "That's easy."

"Why, yes, that's easy," said Einer.

They were grinning again. They grinned all the way home and they were grinning still when they climbed into bed.

"Tomorrow we'll just go swimming," they said. "Nothing can happen now."

Early in the morning before it was time for the sun to rise, Elmer and Einer ran down to Kristie's stall. They fed her and rubbed her down. Elmer combed her tail. Einer braided her bangs and tied bows at the end.

"Today we're going swimming," both boys said. Each of their grins was as wide as the other.

"I'll bring your hat, Kristie," said Elmer.

But the hat was not hanging on the nail where it belonged. It was not in the stall. It was nowhere to be seen.

"What could have happened to it?" asked Elmer.

"Did we forget to hang it up?" said Einer.

"We must find it right away," they both said. Their eyes were large and anxious and their mouths as small as small could be.

They looked in the well house and in the corncrib.
They looked in the silo. Then they looked in the pig yard
and there it was. The pigs were eating it up as fast as
they could. There was only a small piece of the hat left,
not nearly enough to make Kristie go.

Elmer and Einer walked back to the barn and
dropped down on the bench by the door.

"What can we do now?" they said. "What can we do now?"

"She won't go without it," said Elmer.

"We can't go swimming," said Einer. "We'll never get to the lake till it's frozen over for skating."

Kristie came to the door and whinnied.

"She's wondering what's the matter," said Elmer.

"We'd better not tell her," said Einer. "It would make her feel too bad."

No one ate breakfast that morning. Mr. and Mrs. Iverson came out to watch the pigs chew the hat. The hired man sat on the fence and watched too. Soon there was not a straw of the old hat left. Kristie's hat was gone. Elmer and Einer shut their lips tight to keep from crying.

Then Mr. Iverson took off his own straw hat. He pulled his knife from his pocket and opened a blade. He cut a long hole on each side of the hat. It was plain to be seen it was for a horse's head.

Elmer and Einer led Kristie from the barn. Mr. Iverson put his hat on her head and pulled her ears through the holes. But Kristie did not like the hat at all. It pricked her ears and tickled her neck. The brim was too wide. She began to dance up and down.

"That will not do," said Mr. Iverson.

Elmer and Einer ran into the house for their hats. They cut large long holes in each side for Kristie's ears, very large holes, but the hats were too small. Both Elmer's and Einer's hats were too small. They would not even go over her ears. Kristie shook herself from side to side.

"Neither one of those will do," said Elmer and Einer, and they both sniffed to keep back the tears.

"Try mine," said the hired man, "only don't cut the holes first."

Mr. Iverson held Kristie's ears together and Elmer

and Einer pulled the hat down over them. But Kristie did not like that hat at all. She snorted and tossed her head. The hat went flying through the air, with the hired man running after it.

"What can we do?" cried Elmer and Einer. "What CAN we do? She's so particular about her hats. It must be just right or she'll never go again."

Then they looked at Mrs. Iverson. Their father looked at Mrs. Iverson too, and so did the hired man. Even Kristie seemed to be looking at Mrs. Iverson.

Mrs. Iverson folded her hands in her apron and did not look at any one. Mr. Iverson pulled his hat down on his own head. Bits of hair stuck out through the holes.

"I suppose there is no other old hat in the house?" he asked.

"No-o-o," said Mrs. Iverson. "No OLD hat."

"Then we can't go swimming," said Elmer.

"No," said Einer. "We can't go anywhere at all, even if we do have a horse."

Kristie whinnied and teetered on her four crooked legs.

Mrs. Iverson walked slowly, very slowly, toward the house. Elmer and Einer rubbed their sleeves across their eyes.

"Well," said Mr. Iverson.

"Well," said the hired man.

Then back from the house came Mrs. Iverson. She was carrying her black hat in one hand and she was brushing off the dust with the other. It was the black hat she wore to Town on Saturday nights. It was a good

soft straw and it was a fine round size. The red rose was nodding over the front.

"Kristie can have this if she wants it," she said. "I can borrow it from her when we go to Town on Saturday."

Mr. Iverson cut two neat holes in the black hat. He tried not to make them too large. Mrs. Iverson pinned on two pieces of ribbon for ties. Then Elmer put the hat on Kristie's head and pulled her ears carefully through the holes. Einer tied the ribbon bow under her chin.

"This is a beautiful hat for you, Kristie," said Elmer and Einer.

Then they stood still and held their breath. Mr. Iverson held his breath too and Mrs. Iverson held hers. And the hired man held his.

Good Old Kristie whinnied and nodded her head. The red rose bobbed over the brim.

"She likes it," said Elmer.

"Oh, she likes it," cried Einer. "Let's go swimming right away."

Mr. Iverson helped them harness Kristie to the buggy. Mrs. Iverson brought her six lumps of sugar. The hired man stopped on his way to the fence to pat her nose.

"Good Old Kristie," everyone said.

Kristie whinnied. She was very fond of everybody. Elmer and Einer climbed up on the buggy seat.

"Gid-ap," they said.

Out through the gateway stepped Kristie. She looked very fat and happy. The black hat shaded her eyes and the red rose bobbled over her nose. Along the road toward the lake she walked. When she turned left at the schoolhouse road, Elmer got down and turned her around just as Axel Peterson had told them to. Then he climbed back into the buggy.

"Gid-ap," said Elmer and Einer.

Kristie stepped forward and turned the corner to the left.

"Isn't it easy?" said Elmer, when they were on the right road again. "Isn't it easy?"

At the next crossroad Einer climbed down and turned her around.

"Isn't it easy?" he said.

Elmer and Einer were grinning and grinning. They grinned all the way to the lake. And when at last they were in swimming, they grinned so widely that they almost gulped the lake right down. If they just did things the way that Kristie wanted them done, wasn't it easy? They could go swimming every day! She was a fine old horse, the very best horse in the world!

"Good Old Kristie!"

There are more Kristie stories in the books Kristie's Buttercup and Kristie Goes to the Fair, both published by Alfred A. Knopf, Inc.

Jonathan's Lucky Money

BY MIRIAM E. MASON

Illustrations by George and Doris Hauman

> Back in pioneer days a boy rarely had more than a penny to spend at a time. But this time Jonathan had two bits (twenty-five cents) and a penny.

J ONATHAN was out on the hillside hunting for wild strawberries when he heard the sound which he had been wanting to hear for several days.

It was the sound of the peddler's horn.

Jonathan looked down the road, and he could see the peddler's little cart coming along the road. Two dusty little black mules were drawing the cart, and a dusty little black dog was trotting along behind the cart.

The peddler was sitting high on the seat of his cart. He was a little man and he smoked a little black pipe. His name was Ty Napp. Everything about the peddler was little except his big loud voice and the big fat satchels and bags and boxes which he carried in his cart.

Jonathan left the strawberries and went hurrying to the house.

"The peddler is coming! The peddler is coming!" he called all over the house.

He knew his mother and sisters would be glad to see Ty Napp, the peddler.

In those days the pioneer peddler was an important person. He was just like a traveling department store. He had nearly everything which a pioneer family could want, in his bags and satchels and boxes.

Three or four times a year the peddler stopped at each house, and it was always a great day when he came.

Jonathan's sisters and mother came running from here and there all over the house.

"Do you suppose he will have some of that pink soap that smells like roses?" wondered Lucinda. "I do want a cake of that soap."

"I hope he will have some pretty buttons to go on my new dress," said Priscilla.

Mrs. Brown was hoping he would have a new iron pot to take the place of one which had fallen into the river when they were moving.

Everybody in the Brown family had some special thing to want from the peddler.

Jonathan did not say very much, but he had many thoughts. Jonathan had real money to spend this time. He had his twenty-five-cent piece which the steamboat captain had given him. That was the most money Jonathan had ever had in all his life at one time.

Ty Napp came up to the big gray stone house and his mules stood still. The little dog sat down behind the cart and hung out his tongue. Ty Napp came to the door with a smile on his face. He knew he would sell many things to the Brown family.

He brought in his satchels, two at a time, and opened them for the family to see. Everybody crowded around looking at the combs, the ribbons, the buttons, the sweet-

smelling soap, the marbles, the cinnamon candies, and
the other treasures in the peddler's satchels.

"What are you going to buy with your penny, Jonathan?" asked Emmazetta.

Jonathan smiled in a wise way. Usually he had only
one penny to spend. His sisters did not know that he
had so much money.

It took the Brown family a long time to pick out everything they wanted from Ty Napp's treasures. Jonathan
looked at everything, trying to decide what he wanted
most of all.

"Why are you so particular?" asked his sister America Jane. "There are not so many things which you can get with a penny."

Jonathan only gave her a wise look and kept on hunting and hunting among the peddler's treasures.

At last Jonathan saw what he wanted most of all.

It was a bottle of medicine called Indian Tonic. It was in a big square bottle, and there was an interesting picture on the bottle. It showed how a man looked before taking the medicine, and how he looked after taking it.

The man in the picture looked much better and bigger after taking the medicine than he looked before taking it. He was almost three times as big and he was holding a big ox in his arms just as Jonathan would hold a kitten.

"Is that medicine good for everybody?" asked Jonathan, and Ty Napp answered in his big, roaring voice, "It is good for man and beast!"

Little Jonathan wondered, "Does it really make people so big and strong?"

And again Ty Napp answered in his loud voice, "You can see by the picture. Just look at that picture and you will see what wonderful medicine Indian Tonic is."

Jonathan asked the price of the bottle, and the peddler told him it was four bits.

"Four bits and worth every bit of a dollar!" roared the little peddler.

Four bits is two twenty-five-cent pieces.

Jonathan sighed.

"That is lots of money!"

His sisters laughed at him.

"You are not sick," said Emmazetta. "Why are you interested in medicine? Some good brown soap for your hands and face would be better."

The peddler stayed for dinner, and after dinner Jonathan whispered to him.

"I have a twenty-five-cent piece and a penny. Do you have a smaller bottle of Indian Tonic?"

Ty Napp did not have a smaller bottle of the Indian Tonic. But he was a kindhearted man.

"There is a special price on that big bottle this afternoon," he told Jonathan. "For this afternoon only, that big bottle is two bits and a penny."

When nobody was looking, Jonathan gave the peddler his twenty-five-cent piece and his penny, and Ty Napp gave him the big bottle of Indian Tonic.

"I expect you will be the biggest one in the family when I come back this way," he said, winking at little Jonathan.

Jonathan took the medicine out and put it in the barn where his sisters would not see it.

"Tomorrow I will begin taking the tonic," he planned.

He thought how surprised all his family would be when he suddenly grew so big. He wondered what his sisters would say when he came carrying one of the oxen up to the house.

But he had forgotten that good medicine sometimes has a very bad taste. Every day he went out to take some of the tonic, and every day it smelled and tasted just the same. It was very, very bad.

Every day he said, "Tomorrow I will begin taking the tonic."

Day after day went by. Jonathan's family began getting ready to go to the big camp meeting which would be held up the river, in Maple Grove.

The camp meeting was really a church meeting, but it seemed like a picnic. All the people came to Maple Grove and stayed for two or three days. They brought food and blankets and camped in the grove.

Three times a day the preacher gave long, loud sermons, and when the preacher was not preaching the people sang songs. In between times they ate and visited.

Everybody had a good time and enjoyed the camp meeting each year.

The night before camp meeting the preacher came to Jonathan's house, riding his old white horse, Methuselah. The old horse seemed more slow and tired than usual. Now and then he sneezed or coughed.

"I am afraid Methuselah is not well," said the preacher, looking worried. "He seems to have a cold in his head."

"Maybe he will be better after a good night's sleep," said Jonathan's mother.

Methuselah did not get better in the night. When morning came and it was time to start to the camp meeting, he did not want to go. He stood in the barn with his head hanging down. He looked very sad.

"Something must be done for Methuselah," said the preacher. "I cannot ride him to the camp meeting when he is so sick. I could not preach a good sermon if I left him."

"I do wish we had bought a bottle of horse medicine from Ty Napp when he was here," said Jonathan's father.

They rubbed liniment on old Methuselah, and offered him hot cider and catnip tea to drink. But Methuselah only shook his head and looked sadder and sicker than ever.

"If Methuselah does not get better, there can be no camp meeting," said the preacher.

Suddenly Jonathan remembered his bottle of Indian Tonic. He remembered the things that Ty Napp had told him about the medicine.

He got the big brown bottle from its hiding place in old Jennie's stall, and gave it to his big brothers.

"Try some of this for Methuselah," he said.

The big brothers were so glad to see the medicine that they did not ask Jonathan where he got it. They opened old Methuselah's mouth and poured the medicine down his throat.

"Poor old Methuselah," thought Jonathan, who remembered the taste and smell of the Indian Tonic.

Methuselah did not want to take the tonic. He shook his head and tried to spit it out. But Jonathan's big brothers held his head and poured lots of the medicine down his throat.

A change came over Methuselah. He stopped looking sad. His eyes began to sparkle in a happy way. He tossed his head and snorted.

"Methuselah thinks he is a colt again!" said Jeremiah, surprised.

Methuselah pawed at the ground with his foot. He seemed in a hurry to go. The big brothers led him out of the barn to the front of the house, where the preacher was waiting. He pranced and danced.

The preacher looked surprised.

"What has come over Methuselah?" he asked. "He has not acted so lively since he was a colt."

Jeremiah told about the medicine, and the preacher said that it must be very good medicine.

"I will take it with me to the camp meeting," he said. "Methuselah may need some more of it soon."

"Do you think Methuselah looks any bigger than he did?" Jonathan asked the preacher.

"Methuselah stopped growing many years ago," said the preacher. He smiled kindly at Jonathan. "But he certainly looks very much stronger. I shall never forget what your brothers have done for Methuselah!"

All the Brown family and the preacher went to the camp meeting. The preacher rode ahead because Methuselah was feeling so young and gay and wanted to go so fast.

Several of the old ladies at the camp meeting noticed how frisky and cheerful the preacher's horse was acting. He did not seem like an old, dignified preacher's horse.

He seemed like a young and rather silly colt. The old ladies talked about this.

"Have you seen the preacher's horse?" they whispered back and forth. "He acts in a very high-stepping way. I think a preacher's horse should be more quiet and respectable."

But most of the people did not mind if the preacher's horse was gay. It was nice weather and the camp meeting was a great success. Everybody talked about what a wonderful time they had had.

"It was the finest camp meeting yet," they said.

Jonathan felt proud and happy to hear these words.

"It is a good thing I had that Indian Tonic," he said to himself.

There is a lot more fun in this book and others by the same author, The Major and his Camels and Susan, the Pioneer Cow, published by The Macmillan Company.

INDEX of Authors and Titles

Titles of stories are set in *italic* type; titles of poems in roman type.

ACKNOWLEDGMENTS

The publishers wish to express their appreciation to the following publishers, agents, authors, and artists who have granted permission to use material appearing in this book. Any errors or omissions are unintentional and will be corrected in future printings if notice is sent to The Crowell-Collier Publishing Company.

APPLETON-CENTURY-CROFTS, INC. "The Little Elfman," by John Kendrick Bangs, from *St. Nicholas Book of Verse*, copyright 1923 by The Century Company; reprinted by permission of the publishers, Appleton-Century-Crofts, Inc.

ROWENA BASTIN BENNETT "End of Summer Poem," by Rowena Bastin Bennett, copyright 1949 by The Curtis Publishing Company; reprinted by special permission from *Jack and Jill*.

POLLY CHASE BOYDEN "Mud," by Polly Chase Boyden, from *Child Life Magazine*, copyright 1930 by Rand McNally & Co.; reprinted by permission of the author.

COWARD-MCCANN, INC. *The A B C Bunny*, written and illustrated by Wanda Gág, copyright 1933 by Coward-McCann; *The Funny Thing*, written and illustrated by Wanda Gág, copyright 1929 by Coward-McCann; *The Five Chinese Brothers*, by Claire Huchet Biship, illustrated by Kurt Wiese, copyright 1938 by Coward-McCann; reprinted by permission of Coward-McCann, Inc., publishers.

CURTIS BROWN, LTD. For permission to reprint in Canada "The Goblin" and "The Chickens," from *Picture Rhymes from Foreign Lands*, by Rose Fyleman; "F Is the Fighting Firetruck" from *All Around the Town*, by Phyllis McGinley.

J.M. DENT & SONS, LTD. "Red Riding Hood," from *Grimm's Tales*, by the Brothers Grimm, translated by Marion Edwardes. Reprinted in Canada by permission of J.M. Dent & Sons, Ltd., publishers.

DOUBLEDAY & COMPANY, INC. *Angus and the Cat*, written and illustrated by Majorie Flack, copyright 1931 by Majorie Flack Larson; "The Animal Store," "The Ice Cream Man," "The Visitor," and the illustration for "The Visitor," from *Taxis and Toadstools*, written and illustrated by Rachel Field, copyright 1926 by Doubleday & Company, Inc.; "The Tree Toad" and "Could It Have Been a Shadow?" from *Goose Grass Rhymes* by Monica Shannon, copyright 1930 by Doubleday & Company, Inc.; "The Dentist" and "My Policeman," from *The Fairy Green*, by Rose Fyleman, copyright 1923 by George H. Doran; "Mice," from *Fifty-One New Nursery Rhymes*, by Rose Fyleman, copyright 1932 by Doubleday & Company, Inc.; "A Fairy Went A-Marketing" and "Have You Watched the Fairies?" from *Fairies and Chimneys*, by Rose Fyleman, copyright 1920 by George H. Doran; *Kiki Dances*, written and illustrated by Charlotte Steiner, copyright 1949 by Charlotte Steiner; excerpt from *The Poppy Seed Cakes*, by Margery Clark, illustrated by Maud and Miska Petersham, copyright 1954 by Doubleday & Company, Inc.; *Rosa-Too-Little*, written and illustrated by Sue Felt, copyright 1950 by Sue Felt Kerr; *The Velveteen Rabbit*, by Margery Williams, illustrated by William Nicholson; illustrations by Marguerite de Angeli for "Diddle, diddle, dumpling," "Ding, dong, bell," "Georgie, Porgie, pudding and pie," "Humpty Dumpty," "I Love Little Pussy," "Little Boy Blue," "Little Miss Muffet," "Old Mother Hubbard," "Peter, Peter pumpkin eater," "The North Wind doth blow," "September Dusk," "There was a crooked man," and "Three little kittens," from *Book of Nursery and Mother Goose Rhymes*; reprinted by permission of Doubleday & Company, Inc.

E.P. DUTTON & CO., INC. "The Backwards Boy," by Leslie Thompson, from *Another Here and Now Story Book*, edited by Lucy Sprague Mitchell, copyright 1937 by E.P. Dutton & Co., Inc.; "Bridges," from *Stories to Begin On*, by Rhoda Bacmeister, copyright 1940 by E.P. Dutton & Co., Inc.; "Brownie," "Hoppity," and "Vespers," from *When We Were Very Young*, by A.A. Milne, copyright 1924 by E.P. Dutton & Co., Inc., copyright 1952 by A.A. Milne; "The End," from *Now We Are Six*, by A.A. Milne, copyright 1927 by E.P. Dutton & Co., Inc., copyright 1955 by A.A. Milne, both illustrated by E.H. Sheperd; *Peter Churchmouse*, written and illustrated by Margot Austin, copyright 1941 by E. P. Dutton & Co., Inc.; "Red Riding Hood," from *Grimm's Tales*, translated by Marian Edwardes, Edgar Taylor, and A.A. Dent, *Children's Illustrated Classics*; reprinted by permission of E.P. Dutton & Co., Inc.

FOLLETT PUBLISHING COMPANY "Motor Cars," from *Around a Toadstool Table*, by Rowena Bastin Bennett, copyright 1930; reprinted by permission of Follett Publishing Company, Chicago.

GROSSET & DUNLAP, INC. Illustrations by Dagmar Wilson for "Red Riding Hood" from *Berlitz French for Children*. Permission of Grosset & Dunlap, Inc.

HARCOURT, BRACE & WORLD, INC. "The Ordinary Dog" and "The Extraordinary Dog," from *Magpie Lane*, by Nancy Byrd Turner, copyright 1927 by Harcourt, Brace & World, Inc., renewed 1955 by Nancy Byrd Turner; "This Happy Day," from *The Little Hill*, by Harry Behn, copyright 1949 by Harry Behn; "How Little Pear Went to the Fair," from *"Little Pear*, written and illustrated by Eleanor Frances Lattimore, copyright 1931 by Harcourt, Brace & World, Inc.; used by permission of Harcourt, Brace & World, Inc.

HARPER & BROTHERS "My Zipper Suit" and "What Is It?" from *A Pocketful of Rhymes*, by Marie Louise Allen, copyright 1939 by Harper & Brothers; "Trains," from *I Go A-Traveling*, by James S. Tippett, copyright 1929 by Harper & Brothers; reprinted by permission of Harper & Brothers.

WILLIAM HEINEMANN, LTD. "The Hairy Dog," from *Pillicock Hill*, by Herbert Asquith, published by The Macmillan Company; reprinted in Canada by permission of William Heinemann, Ltd.

DAVID HIGHAM ASSOCIATES, LTD. "City Streets and Country Roads," from *Joan's Door*, published by William Collins Sons & Company, Ltd., "Boys' Names," "Girls' Names," and "A Kitten," from *Silver-Sand and Snow*, published by Michael Joseph, Ltd., all by Eleanor Farjeon; reprinted in Canada by permission of David Higham Associates, Ltd.

HOLT, RINEHART & WINSTON, INC. "Fog," from *Chicago Poems*, by Carl Sandburg, copyright 1916 by Holt, Rinehart & Winston, Inc., copyright 1944 by Carl Sandburg; illustration by Willy Pogany for "Mud," from *My Poetry Book*, new revised edition, selected by Grace Thompson Huffard, Laura Mae Carlisle and Helen Ferris, copyright 1934, 1956 by Holt, Rinehart & Winston, Inc.; reprinted by permission of Holt, Rinehart & Winston, Inc.

HOUGHTON MIFFLIN COMPANY "Dandelions," "June Morning," "September Dusk," and "White Season," from *Pool in the Meadow*," by Frances Frost, copyright 1933, 1961 by Frances Frost; "Taking Off" (author and copyright owner unknown); reprinted by permission of and arrangement with Houghton Mifflin Company, the authorized publishers.

THE JOHN DAY COMPANY, INC. "Stop-Go," reprinted from *I Like Automobiles*, copyright 1931 by Dorothy Walter Baruch; "Barber's Clippers," from *I Like Machinery*, copyright 1933 by Dorothy Walter Baruch, both written by Dorothy Walter Baruch; by permission of the John Day Company, Inc., publisher.

ALFRED A. KNOPF, INC. "City," "Cycle," and "Snail," reprinted from *Fields of Wonder*, by Langston Hughes, copyright 1943 by Curtis Publishing Company, 1926, 1931, 1943, 1945, 1947 by Langston Hughes; excerpt from *Evie and the Wonderful Kangaroo*, by Irmengarde Eberle, illustrated by Louis Slobodkin, copyright 1955 by Irmengarde Eberle Koehler; "The Frog" and "The Yak," reprinted from *The Bad Child's Book of Beasts* by Hilaire Belloc; "The Good Horse Kristie" from *Here Comes Kristie*, written and illustrated by Emma Brock, copyright 1942 by Alfred A. Knopf, Inc.; by permission of Alfred A. Knopf, Inc.

LOIS LENSKI "People," from *Skipping Village*, by Lois Lenski, published by Stokes-Lippincott, copyright 1927 by the author and used by her permission.

J. B. LIPPINCOTT COMPANY "Boys' Names," "Girls' Names," "City Streets and Country Roads," and "A Kitten," from *Poems for Children*, by Eleanor Farjeon, copyright 1926, 1954 by Eleanor Farjeon; "The Chickens" and "The Goblin," from *Picture Rhymes from Foreign Lands*, by Rose Fyleman, copyright 1935 by Rose Fyleman; "Butterfly," "Chickadee," and "Fairies," from *Poems by a Little Girl*, by Hilda Conkling, copyright 1920, 1947 by Hilda Conkling; "F Is the Fighting Firetruck," from *All Around the Town*, by Phyllis McGinley, copyright 1948 by Phyllis McGinley; "Animal Crackers," from *Song for a Little House*, by Christopher Morley, copyright 1917, 1946 by Christopher Morley; "I Keep Three Wishes Ready," from *All Through the Year*, copyright 1932, 1959 by Annette Wynne; "Indian Children," from *For Days and Days*, copyright 1919, 1947 by Annette Wynne; published by J. B. Lippincott Company.

LITTLE, BROWN & CO. "The Postman," from *Tirra Lirra*, by Laura E. Richards, copyright 1932 by Laura E. Richards; by permission of Little, Brown & Co.

FRANCIS E. LITZ "Sleep," from *The Best Poems of Father Tabb*, by John Bannister Tabb, published by Newman Press; reprinted by permission of Francis E. Litz.

LONGMANS, GREEN & CO., LTD. "Children, Children, Don't Forget," from *The Book of Fairy Poetry*, by Dora Owen; reprinted by permission of Longmans, Green & Co., Ltd., publishers.

MACMILLAN & CO., LTD. "Mr. and Mrs. Vinegar," from *English Fairy Tales*, by Flora Annie Steele, illustrated by Arthur Rackham, copyright 1918 by the Macmillan Company; reprinted in Canada by permission of Macmillan & Co., Ltd.

THE MACMILLAN COMPANY "Mr. and Mrs. Vinegar," from *English Fairy Tales* by Flora Annie Steele, illustrated by Arthur Rackman, copyright 1918 by The Macmillan Company; "The Hairy Dog," from *Pillicock Hill*, by Herbert Asquith; "A Swing Song," by William Allingham; "The Moon's the North Wind's Cooky," from *The Collected Poems of Vachel Lindsay*, by Vachel Lindsay, copyright 1914 by The Macmillan Company, renewed 1942 by Elizabeth C. Lindsay; "Night," from *Stars Tonight*, by Sara Teasdale, copyright 1930 by Sara Teasdale Filsinger, renewed 1958 by the Guaranty Trust Company of New York, Executor; "The Sea Gull Curves His Wings," from *Summer Green* by Elizabeth Coatsworth, copyright 1947 by The Macmillan Company; *The Box With Red Wheels*, copyright 1949 by The Macmillan Company, and *The Circus Baby*, copyright 1950 by The Macmillan Company, both written and illustrated by Maud and Miska Petersham; *Billy and Blaze*, written and illustrated by Clarence William Anderson, copyright 1936 by The Macmillan Company; *Scaredy Cat*, written and illustrated by Phyllis Krasilowsky, copyright 1959 by The Macmillan Company; *The Wide Awake Owl*, written and illustrated by Louis Slobodkin, copyright 1958 by Louis Slobodkin; *Susanna's Auction*, translated from the French, illustrated by Louis Boutet de Monvel; "Jonathan's Lucky Money," from *Little Jonathan*, by Miriam E. Mason, illustrated by George and Doris Hauman, copyright 1944 by The Macmillan Company; used by permission of The Macmillan Company.